PRAISE FOR

THE MISSING FIVE

THIS WAS A THRILLING READ by Gwen Pegram, and after careful consideration, I decided to give it 5/5 stars. This is a well-written, carefully plotted novel that mystified me. I simply couldn't put it down. Pegram takes a plot and makes it seem so realistic and life like that it gives you shivers. Fantastic job, Gwen! I look forward to reading more of your work.

—*Bibliophile Book Reviews*

The Missing Five

GWEN PEGRAM

Gwen Pegram
gwenpegrampublishing@gmail.com
Alexandria, VA 22312

A Jackie Trumpleton Novel

THE MISSING FIVE

Paperback ISBN: 978-0-9911285-0-1

ePub download ISBN: 978-0-9911285-1-8

Dare to live the life you have dreamed for yourself.
Go forward and make your dreams come true.

~ Ralph Waldo Emerson

CHAPTER 1

MISSING

All the man knew was that he felt good, damn good, before falling unconscious.

When he awakened, he didn't know how long he had been out. Things were jumbled in his mind and he couldn't organize his thoughts properly. He didn't know where he was but the feeling coursing through his body was pleasurable. It was a recognizable sensation but he couldn't pin it down—couldn't put his finger on it. He blacked out again before he could make sense of it all.

A few hours later, he was aroused by a chill and struggled to open his eyes. A whirling sound and moving ball circled above his head. He had a strange feeling he was being hypnotized. *Where am I?*

A memory started materializing. He remembered a horrible argument he had with his wife that morning. *But, was that yesterday or last week or last month?* He couldn't exactly recollect. He started shivering again, but not from a chill in the air. This was something else.

I wonder if I should be afraid.

His cloudy vision dissipated and he realized that what he heard was a ceiling fan and what he saw was a hanging ornament, a ball at the end of a chain.

No, I'm not being hypnotized.

He looked around the tastefully decorated and furnished room and took it all in. A soy-based candle was burning on one of the end tables. The scent of exotic woods and figs permeated the air and relaxed him. The room was a decent size too, much larger than both the bedrooms combined in his condo, and it was painted a Khaki color with chocolate trim. This was definitely a bachelor's bedroom. Not that frilly, womanly stuff he endured all his life being surrounded by nothing but females—his grandmother, mother, aunts, and three sisters—with no man in sight. Not a father, an uncle, a brother—nothing with a penis.

A brown colored, abstract comforter covering six-hundred thread Egyptian sheets draped the king-size bed. The headboard and footboard were covered with beautiful, cowhide leather. Handsome accessories decorated the walls: African masks were cascaded on two walls and another wall displayed Joseph Holston's collection: "Journey along the Underground Railroad."

What really surprised him was his attire. He had never seen these clothes before. Matter-of-fact, he hadn't worn PJs since he was twelve. He adamantly refused once he turned thirteen. Teenagers don't wear pajamas, he had sighed loudly, rolling his eyes at his mom.

He felt like a king.

As a grownup, he wanted a pair of well-designed, satin pajamas but could not afford them. And now, somehow, he had a pair on that was classically masculine. The top sported a single pocket, cuffless sleeves, and mother of pearl buttons that handsomely complemented the satin finished sleep pants, which was styled with pockets and contrast piping. A silk drawstring was cinched at his waist, not tied in a bow, but hanging loosely to straddle the one-button fly. These pajamas had understated taste and felt luxurious against his skin.

Still mesmerized and trying to keep at bay the question continuously popping to the forefront—*why am I here?*—he went to the bathroom, which was almost the same size as the bedroom. Before his eyes was the largest Jacuzzi tub he had ever seen, up close anyway. Adjacent to the tub was a two, or it could have been a three-person shower stall. There was a rainfall showerhead above and several smaller showerheads sprouting out throughout the entire stall. From the reflection in the mirror, he could see a double walk-in closet with at least ten more beautifully styled pajamas and matching robes arranged on wood hangers. He turned quickly to see if his eyes had deceived him. They had not. On the floor, there were different slippers aligned. Not the Adidas flip flops he wore, but Australian Ascot slippers, Mason Sheepskin moccasins, and L.B. Evans Finn driving moccasins.

He continued to scope out the bathroom. On the granite countertop, adjacent to a vessel sink, was a display of assorted bottles of what he could only assume were expensive colognes because he had never seen or heard of the names on the bottles. He picked up a bottle of Ambre Topkapi. He sprayed the air and was exposed to a pleasant fragrant. There were two bottles by somebody name Clive Christian: one was "C" and the other was "1872." He sprayed one in each hand. He sniffed "C" and it reminded him of a woman's smell—a bouquet of freshly cut flowers. "1872" had a nice citrus scent. He pulled the top off of "Men's Kilian Straight to Heaven" and inhaled it. "Wow!" he said, and spritzed some on the back of his hand and smacked it on each side of his chin. It had an aroma of cedar, nutmeg, and rosewood. These colognes were definitely not what he was used to spraying or slapping on—Calvin Klein, Halston, Givenchy, and Hugo Boss.

He made a three hundred sixty degree turn. He took it all in. *This place is truly magnificent.*

Out of nowhere a thought surfaced about the good feeling he had experienced. *It was a wet dream.* But, for some peculiar reason, he didn't believe it was a dream at all that caused the sensation. It seemed too real, felt too real. And he thought he had glimpsed a vision leaning over him, below his navel and between his legs. But it made no sense because the vision was only an elaborate mask. He shook his head as if to clear this thought.

Then, the questions finally forced through the murkiness.

Where am I? What is this place? How did I get here?
Ian Ferguson had no clue.

CHAPTER 2

THE ASSOCIATES A.K.A. THE GIRLS

A year earlier, across the Atlantic Ocean, five women met as planned, at Perivolas Beach Resort in Santorini, Greece. This was the ideal place to start their long-awaited vacation. The brochure described the picturesque location as "A dream place for the soul" and this was exactly what Jackie Trumpleton and her four associates—Bernadette Petersen, Laura Kennedy, Ruby Tapscott, and Nadine Douglas—needed.

Prior to 9-11, they had vacationed together annually, usually domestically. Their vacation of choice was a two-week stint at a luxurious spa for round-the-clock pampering, rejuvenation, and cosmetic nips or tucks to get rid of excess fat that found a way to attach itself to areas of the tummy, thighs, buttocks, or arms, or flab anywhere else that snuck on during the year. None of the women ever discussed or let slip whether having any of these procedures was fact or fiction.

Each minded her own business and never meddled or intruded on one another's personal space. Everyone understood the two rules of their informal group. The first was modus operandi. If you didn't want to hear the harsh truth, because that's the only feedback that would be given, then don't ask the question. The second rule was Omertà, and an extremely important one, because their vacations were geared to getting their freak on, shedding inhibitions, and sharing clandestine issues.

After 9-11, Jackie proposed they vacation only in even years to pay respect and remembrance to the lives lost on September 11, 2001. "The additional savings would allow us to have more extravagant vacations and we could include an additional week," she said.

The girls concurred.

They had been vacationing together since 1993 with no mishaps. Then, the first time they ventured out of the country, a trip to New Zealand, the unthinkable happened back home. Terrorists hijacked four passenger airliners and flew them into the north and south towers of the World Trade Center in New York City, the Pentagon in Arlington, and a field in Pennsylvania. On that ill-fated morning, almost three thousand innocent people lost their lives.

The girls could recall exactly where they were and what they were doing when the news broke: cruising through the breathtaking Sounds of Fiordland National Park—Dusky, Thompson, Doubtful, and Milford. They heard what they thought could only be rumors buzzing throughout the ship. When the captain confirmed the horrific news over the loudspeaker, the women were traumatized, shaken to the core. It was a harrowing and mind-numbing experience to be in a foreign country at a time when U.S. citizens' sense of security had been shattered.

"Paying tribute to 9-11 by not vacationing in odd years is the least we can do," Jackie said.

* * *

Their vacations always began the same way in order to break the ice.

They started with the dreams and goals each wanted to accomplish during her lifetime. Since they didn't speak to one another between vacations, this practice was a way to reconnect. The list included a variety of desires and aspirations.

One dream that kept surfacing, toyed with, and discussed lightheartedly, especially by Jackie, was the idea to purchase a vacation home together for their golden years. "Girls, I am serious," she said. "Let us really contemplate retiring early and then we can be on holiday every day."

The remainder of the vacation was spent reminiscing and telling soul-wrenching stories that had happened to them. Since they met only every other year, they had a stockpile of tales to pull from and every vacation storytelling episode was different from the previous one.

Their daily lives were monotonous and these vacations were also an opportunity to experience new sexual adventures in different countries around the world. These sexual escapades occurred away from their hotel and were not a topic of conversation. They had a pact. Everything that happened or was spoken during their vacations stayed mum for an eternity and never left the confines of the hotel room. What was said together, stayed together with each other—not as an individual topic of discussion.

As usual, all of them were able to get together. They made it a point to always arrive at the chosen vacation spot around the same time no matter what part of the country they flew in from. When they first saw each other, whether they were at the airport, standing curbside hailing a cab, or in the lobby of the hotel preparing to check in, they dropped everything—luggage, purses, even cell phone if one was on a call—and did their "ring around the roses" dance. They had made up their own words nineteen years earlier to the tune of the nursery rhyme.

> "We sing our song of freedom.
> We got away from boredom.
> Gracias, Gracias.
> We all do the hug."

And the five women would huddle, close in together, and do a group hug.

People stared at them with either amusement or get-out-of-my-way looks.

This ritual was the brainchild of Jackie's. Since the women enjoyed each other's company and had known each other for twenty-some odd years, it seemed natural to vacation together. What was unnatural, Jackie thought, was that the other women considered them all girlfriends. Jackie didn't view their relationship that way. To her, they were associates or the girls. She reconciled years ago what sort of woman she had become, and was content with who she was; and she was not the type of woman who had girlfriends. If asked to describe herself in one word, she would answer, "loner."

Jackie told each woman when she met them why she preferred male friends. "Men do not gossip, whine, or cry, and are not mentally needy. Men do not need another man's acceptance or approval to know who they are. Men live and breathe for one thing and one thing only. Sex. Period. It is as simple as that and I appreciate that diehard trait in a man," she said.

The associates proved to be like men and that is why they jelled and got along. They were all strong-minded, accomplished, and carefree women who arrived at different times in Jackie's life.

She and Bernadette attended elementary school together where they initially bonded until Bernadette's family moved away unexpectedly and they lost touch. Unbeknownst to either, they found out quite by accident when they bumped into each other at the water fountain that they were employed by the same burgeoning dot com company in Silicon Valley. The relationship was rekindled.

Laura was a marcher Jackie met at the National Organization for Women's Convention in Philadelphia. It was during a time period when they, along with other women, were up in arms and prepared to do battle for women's rights and equal partnership with men.

Jackie met Ruby while travelling on an eleven-day cruise throughout southern Europe. It was both of their first cruise and they found out that they were the only single tourists on the two-thousand passenger list.

While Jackie was sitting alone at a bar in a Chicago hotel enjoying a glass of Pinot Grigio, Nadine walked up and ordered the same drink. When she went to pay, she started digging around in her pocketbook but couldn't find her wallet. She looked embarrassed and apologized to the bartender, and turned to leave. Jackie told the bartender to put the drink on her tab. She ended up ordering a bottle of wine and they talked about everything and anything well into the night, and then exchanged phone numbers.

All of them, Jackie included, were as diverse in their chosen professions and character, as their style and outlook on life. Their stations in life varied significantly and that contrast is what united them. They each brought something unique and significant to the group.

* * *

Nadine broke the silence. "This *is* a dream place for the soul," she said. "The brochure didn't do this resort justice."

Jackie, Bernadette, Laura, Ruby, and Nadine were sprawled out on the spacious veranda in beach attire, each with a different bottle of champagne in her hand. They consumed specific sparkling wines so five different cases were on hand, stored in the refrigerator, leaving no room for food. Five additional cases were on standby in the hotel's wine cellar just in case more was needed to cover the entire stay of their three-week vacation. On ice were Moët, Gosset, Henriot, G.H. Mumm, and Diebolt-Vallois.

No flutes for them.

Each could easily down a bottle of the bubbly by herself in one night or day, especially if the drinking started early. So once the corks were popped, they toasted each other with their own individual bottle and began their long-awaited storytelling.

Before they began, Jackie asked, "Who checked anything off her bucket list?"

Ruby raised her hand. "I did," she said excitedly and ran to her room. When she returned, she was holding a large, leather-bound diploma cover. "Ta-dah!" she said, and opened it to show off her Doctor of Philosophy degree from Brown University.

The girls were in awe. After a round of applause and another clinking of the bottles, Jackie asked, "who else?"

The other three said, "Not me," in turn.

Jackie said, "I am real close to accomplishing a long-held dream, but I am not ready to share it yet. I will soon."

She would let the four associates precede her in storytelling because she knew her tale would top theirs; hers was a doozy.

They got comfortable—kicked off their sandals and turned off their cell phones—to hear the tale each girl would share. A tale could go on for a full day or two. And, no matter how long each story lasted, the women respected each other's right to take as long as necessary to convey her story and no one dared interrupt the procession. The only time the women talked during these cathartic gabfests was when the baton passed to the next storyteller.

CHAPTER 3

BERNADETTE STARTS
THE STORYTELLING

Jackie's oldest associate, Bernadette, worked as an executive assistant for a CEO at a well-known international marketing conglomerate in Manhattan, New York, for the same boss, Matthew Caine, for twenty-three years.

"Even though I'm African American," Bernadette said, "and my boss is white, it hasn't stopped the rumor mill from buzzing about our so-called relationship. You wouldn't believe the vulgarities professionals verbalize. It's unreal. 'She *must* be fucking him,' the gossip goes, because *who* in their right mind would work for that mean, ugly son-of-a-bitch."

Bernadette knocked back her champagne and shook her head, which made her newly permed, super straight hairdo done the day before, whip from side-to-side with every movement. "It's sad," she said, "because this rumor is the acceptable theory. The grapevine has it that I'm making a handsome, unheard of six-figure salary just to be a secretary."

Through her not quite inebriated state, she noticed the looks the girls gave one another—one of disbelief. But it didn't cause her pause and she continued on as if she hadn't noticed.

"Secretary, my ass! Executive assistant, thank you very much. And, I'll castigate anyone who dares to call me a secretary to my face," she said, with one hand on her hip and the other hand pointing a finger wildly at them.

As far as Bernadette was concerned, comparing her to a secretary was downright degrading, more deplorable than having a sexual relationship with her married boss. Bernadette could give a hoot about what the gossipers believed because she and Matthew were not, never had, and never would have a sexual relationship of any kind.

"Well," she revealed to the girls, "I wouldn't mind giving Matthew a lap dance for his birthday though or some special occasion maybe. Girly girls, I caught a glimpse of his down under, and good god almighty, it's a nice size package for a white man. I swear it is. It would be like riding a mechanical bull. The pleasure would be all mine."

They burst out laughing.

Bernadette communicated how she and Matthew's working relationship was one of superficial respect. He was a workaholic and she was the first assistant, the only assistant out of a Baker's dozen that he hadn't fired. He informed his superiors who confronted him about Bernadette's exorbitant salary that she had the talent, fortitude, and skill set to keep him on top of his game.

"Let him tell it," Bernadette said, "I was capable of running the damn company."

This was said only in private and for her benefit.

Bernadette continued. "One evening I was working late and overheard a discussion Matthew was having with the Chairman of the Board. Matthew's office door was ajar, which is usually closed when top brass is visiting, so he must have thought I had left for the day, although I hadn't said good night, which I always do. I had stepped out to pick them up some dinner for their late meeting. When I returned, they were conversing about me. You know I was all ears with my nosy self. My boss was saying that he was dumbfounded that a colored gal with no college degree, only a high school education, was as bright and competent as me."

She heard the girls gasp but Bernadette didn't break her flow.

"The chairman reminded him that he fought vigorously to pay me the big bucks. But, Matthew dismissed it."

Bernadette impersonated her boss. "Bernadette is more intelligent than my daughter who graduated from Wellesley. The wife and I made untold sacrifices, paid over a hundred thousand dollars for tuition, and she drops out before her last semester begins to move to some god-awful, third world country to be an international development worker. The girl never had any common sense."

Bernadette chugged the Henriot.

The girls looked worried.

"I tiptoed out of the office before they realized I was still there," Bernadette said. "I didn't want Matthew to know that I had overheard this despicable dialogue and got a bird's eye view of this side of him. I knew we would both be embarrassed. Girls, they must have been shocked when they exited his office to run across the street to pick up sandwiches like they always do. I wish I could've been a fly on the wall when they glimpsed the food setup from P.F. Chang laid out neatly in the executive board room. I'm willing to bet a paycheck that Matthew choked and excused himself to run to the men's room."

She envisioned him upchucking on the chairman's custom-made crocodile shoes.

The girls could see she was distraught over this incident but they didn't interrupt; they didn't utter a word.

"I never forgot that exchange and how it made me feel," Bernadette said. "But you know what, I can only blame myself. I committed the cardinal sin. *Never* forget you're black."

The girls nodded.

"Every black person knows this rule," she said. "No matter how smart you are, how good you are at your job, don't get so uppity, so complacent that you forget. You can *never* forget. Because the moment you do, and inevitably it happens, the white man will say something, or do something, to remind you who he thinks you are, in order to bring you back to Negroland."

Bernadette paused, remembering the incident as if it happened yesterday.

The girls waited in anticipation to find out what happened the following day.

"Matthew and I never discussed that evening's incident. But, when I arrived at work the following morning early as usual, an envelope was on my desk with only my first name inscribed in his handwriting. I picked it up and walked into his office and said pleasantly, 'I'm going to get coffee; would you like a cup?' He looked at the unopened envelope in my hand and said 'yes thank you, if it would not be too much trouble.' Girls, he was shame-faced and I enjoyed making him cringe. I went to Star-bucks and opened the envelope to see a salary adjustment form signed by him and approved by the chairman. My salary had been increased by twenty thousand dollars!"

The girls screamed.

"I guess a thousand dollars for every year I worked for his sorry butt. I knew it was his way of apologizing but I wasn't letting him off the hook that easily. He hurt my feelings. He owed me a verbal apology."

She paused. "Still today, I hear his words ringing in my ears. But it's okay. Since I'm a colored gal, he's paying for that derogatory insult in my salary and bonuses. And guess what?"

"What?" Nadine said.

"Ask me if I brought him back a cup of coffee."

The five colored gals burst out laughing again.

They knew she didn't.

Jackie gave voice to why Bernadette hadn't. "Because he would have been a scalded mother ..."

"Shut your mouth," Laura interjected.

Jackie completed the sentence, "if you had brought him back that cup of coffee."

Ruby waited for the hysterics to die down. "You may be Matthew's colored gal, but at least you are a six-figure colored gal."

There was another fit of laughter and nodding.

Laura interrupted. "Girls, I'm beat; I'm still on Eastern Daylight Saving Time. Why don't we take a nap and then later go to either the black sand beach or the red beach. Tomorrow, I'll proceed with my story."

"Sounds like a plan," Jackie said.

CHAPTER 4

LAURA TAKES THE BATON

Laura worked as a property manager at one of Atlanta's luxury condominiums. She rose up through the ranks at a snail's pace. It was a difficult climb too.

She started out as a part-time volunteer at a garden-style apartment complex in Valdosta, Georgia, when she was sixteen. And it took sixteen years for her just to make it to an assistant property manager.

"It didn't matter how many certifications I had acquired," Laura said—"a Master Property Manager, a Certified Property Manager, and an Accredited Residential Manager—the game plan never changed. There was always an excuse or a reason why *now* was *never* the right time for me to be promoted."

She threw her hands in the air. "One more imaginary certification was always required from the 'man' before I could be promoted to property manager. I swear I wanted to strangle somebody."

Laura constantly relocated in order to advance her career. The negativity surrounding job hopping was of no concern to her. *What would be the consequences? I'm not being promoted by being loyal to the job.*

She looked at Bernadette. "I don't know how you do it—stay with one employer for years on end."

"Leverage, girlfriend, leverage," Bernadette said.

No matter what condo or homeowner association Laura worked for, it seemed the manager in charge was nowhere near quitting or ever planning on retiring; nor did they have any of the certifications that were a requirement for her.

After ten years as an assistant property manager, she religiously searched and submitted resumes online via monster dot com, career builder dot com, and simply hired dot com. Sometimes she got lucky enough to get an interview, but more times than she cared to think about, she didn't.

"I would take the crappiest job if I thought it would lead to advancement," she said.

Laura recalled one job she had as an assistant property manager in High Point, North Carolina. "One day I had to snake a filthy toilet in the men's restroom because shit, yes a pile of shit, had overflowed and started seeping into the adjacent lobby. On that particular day, the chief building engineer and both maintenance men called in sick. 'Ain't that some triple bull?' How appropriate, I thought."

Laura looked to the girls for acquiescence and on cue they complied by nodding their heads.

"The property manager gave me the, 'Well, I'm not going to clean it up look,' so I found some long, yellow rubber gloves, a mop and bucket, and began to cleanup what was the shittiest, excuse the pun, most arduous mess

I'd ever encountered. Right then and there I knew I had to get out of that hell hole."

The girls pinched their noses and screwed up their faces.

Laura's next job was at an association in Cleveland, Ohio, that had an upward mobility program designed to give assistant property managers the opportunity to advance to more challenging, higher-paying positions. Laura thought this would be a great career move for her. But, once again, she was overlooked for a promotion. Compared to the property manager who was retiring at the end of the month, Laura was a go-getter, worked longer hours, and was a hoot, let the younger residents tell it. Everyone loved her sense of humor, except the powers that be. So, when the property manager retired, a younger white woman who was in the program with her was promoted.

"I deserved that promotion, gave all I had and then some," she said. "I detest playing the race card but there is no other explanation for why I kept getting passed over."

Laura relocated again and took the same title position—assistant property manager—at the Condos of Philadelphia. Nine months and a week after she started, Elwood, the property manager, dropped dead. He had a massive heart attack and was found slumped over his desk with an empty Big Mac wrapper still in his hand.

Laura thought her time had finally arrived. In the wake of Elwood's death, Laura celebrated the promotion she knew was coming.

It turned out totally different from what Laura had imagined the night before. The association brought in another white man from a sister facility. The general manager introduced her to the dead property manager's replacement and told her in no uncertain terms that she needed to show the newly hired property manager the ropes, and get him up to speed and acclimated as soon as possible.

Even though Laura shouldn't have been surprised, she was.

"The GM was grinning like a Cheshire cat," she said, "and he grabbed the newbie by the shoulders as if it was his son. Probably was an illegitimate son that popped on the scene unexpectedly." Laura was being sarcastic.

She mimicked the GM's words and continued the satire. "Kevin just graduated from UCLA with a degree in business management. He graduated magna cum laude. That means ..., 'and I cut him off,' I know what it means I said indignantly, that he didn't graduate summa cum laude."

The girls erupted in a fit of hysteria.

"And before I could go berserk and tell both of them to kiss my black ass and go straight to hell without passing go, which of course, would have ended my ...," she made air quotes, "'prospering career,' the phone on my desk rang. Girls, I regained my composure like a Porsche, zero to sixty in four point five seconds."

Laura paused, waiting for her breathing to return to normal.

"Now, I went overboard with the greeting but I had to because talking kept me sane and on an even keel; not to mention thwarting me from jumping over the desk and pummeling that jackass of a general manager with my phone."

The girls nodded, understanding completely. They all had, at least one time in their careers, sometimes unconsciously, sometimes not, considered assault and battery against their bosses.

The human resources director at the Atlanta Condominiums was on the other end of the line.

Laura turned her back to the GM and his flunky as the HR director offered her the position of property manager that she had interviewed for several months back. Since she had not heard anything, she had forgotten all about the job; she assumed another "less" qualified candidate had been selected.

"Y'all, I wanted to scream 'when can I start?' It took every ounce of restraint I could muster not to blurt out those four words. All I said was, 'yes, I can start in a month.' Girls, I could not believe my luck," Laura said. "I would have started the same day if that had been possible. Oh my god, revenge is sweet."

She swiveled a full circle in her chair and yelled woohoo. She looked the GM square in his eyes with a smirk on her face. She swiveled back around to confront her computer and typed her resignation in two words—I quit—in all caps, with three exclamation marks. No date, no salutation. She hit the print key and before she could remove the sheet of paper from the printer, the GM snatched it.

"I guess he assumed I was going to give a month's notice in order to train the newbie. Not in this lifetime," she said.

The GM scanned Laura's resignation and screamed, "This is effective today! You can't do that."

"I snatched the resignation out of his hand, scribbled my signature, and exited stage right."

"Like Snagglepuss," she heard one of the girls whisper.

Laura covered her mouth and snickered. "I wanted to say, 'yes I can cracker,' but held my tongue in check. I knew the best revenge was moving on and being happy."

"And *that* is what it is all about," Jackie said.

"Finally, I got the just due I earned," Laura said. She turned toward Ruby. "It's your turn."

"Wait a minute," Ruby said, pulling herself up from a lounging position, "let me get another bottle of champagne."

CHAPTER 5

RUBY'S TURN

Of the five associates, Ruby was hands down the most gorgeous of them all. In fact, the girls agreed that she was more beautiful than any woman they had ever seen. Beyoncé was selected the "World's Most Beautiful Woman," and she is beautiful no doubt about that, but she had nothing on Ruby.

Jackie pondered *People Magazine's* revelation. They really should search for beauty from all around the globe and not just in their industry's backyard, she thought.

Ruby was a drop-dead knockout in a prude's body. She didn't realize how striking she was so her beauty held her hostage. Her good looks were natural—no makeup at all. Her complexion was called blue-black in the day; it was black-black, but not really black. Her skin was flawless, porcelain like. There wasn't a pimple, a pore, a black head, or blemish to be found. It was silky smooth like melted tar that had been constantly stirred on a hundred degree, stifling summer day.

Ruby was six feet tall with hair so full, thick, and wiry, a machete-like instrument was needed to bushwhack through it just to tame it. She wore it proudly like a lion's mane, even though it was helter skelter all over the place. She was as thin as Olive Oyl so people who came into contact with her mistakenly assumed she was a victim of anorexia. But, unlike Popeye's girlfriend, Ruby had a shape that stopped old men and young boys alike dead in their tracks. Small perky boobs that didn't bounce around when she swayed and a plump, symmetrical backside that begged to be grabbed or spanked, and one that men had erotic dreams about.

She walked with grace, holding her back straight as a pencil and head held high. What neighbors and relatives didn't know was that her hunchback mother, who suffered osteoporosis that commenced at an early age, preached, punished, and prayed with Ruby daily, "If you don't learn to walk upright, straight, you will also contract this horrible disease." Her mother believed wholeheartedly that the cause of her disease was directly related to slouching while walking and sitting incorrectly. She didn't know differently, so her erroneous belief continued unabated.

Ruby hid her sexy body under clothes that looked as if they had been handed down from her grandmother, maybe even from her great-grandmother. Ruby spent every weekend combing through thrift stores from sun up until sundown, driving within a fifty-mile radius looking for flea markets to find those awful-looking, loose-fitting vintage clothes. It tickled her immensely to stumble upon what she perceived as "good finds for pennies on the dollar."

Ruby was holding her bottle of Gosset and out of the blue she asked, "Do you all want to know why I dress the way I do?" stupefying the girls.

Nadine started coughing uncontrollably. Her champagne went down the wrong way.

Laura realized Nadine was choking and jumped up, and proceeded to perform the Heimlich maneuver on her.

Nadine pushed her away, tears rolling down her face. "I'm okay now. It took you long enough to react. I could have died." She looked at Ruby. "Forgive me, my dear," she said, once she got herself together. "Continue on," she waved her hand.

Ruby gave Nadine a shrewd look.

"I know you all are not crude to ask, but you must have speculated all these years about my choice of clothes."

They were speechless. Their silence was the confirmation that Ruby had supplied to herself.

Not one of the girls dared to be the first to acknowledge the question. Yes, they shared secrets. Yes, they listened to each other. But no, they would not break the code by prying to satisfy their own curiosity.

"It's okay," Ruby said.

Still they didn't respond. It was as if they knew that if the rule was broken now, it would be broken forever.

Since there were no takers, Ruby forged ahead. "This is the first time I've brought this skeleton out of the closet. These clothes are my personal reminder, a validation of sorts, that I'm a slut."

The girls looked befuddled by her statement. They definitely didn't view Ruby as nobody's slut, especially dressed in those hand-me-downs.

"I wear these clothes to hide who I am, what I am," she looked down at the floor.

The girls were perplexed.

"I made a deliberate choice to cloak my body, especially from the eyes of prying men. Only when I'm around you all on vacation can I quell the guilt." She paused and took a deep breath, inhaling through her nose deeply, allowing air to fill her lungs to capacity, and exhaling through her mouth noisily, before continuing on.

"I was sexually manipulated"—she couldn't say the word abused because it wasn't entirely true—"when I was thirteen by an older male cousin from the neighborhood and I never told anyone."

The girls moved closer to Ruby to show solidarity but she stood up and turned away.

"But..." she temporarily halted and started again. "But, it was not because I was ashamed of what happened to me. It was not because I thought people in authority wouldn't believe me. I didn't tell anyone because I enjoyed the feeling and I couldn't comprehend why. I could hardly wait for the times when cuz and I played doctor and nurse again—that's what he called it—in anticipation of experiencing that feeling one more time. These episodes only happened when my mother went to work at her night job so I knew it was wrong but I didn't want to stop him from coming over."

Ruby walked to the far side of the veranda and looked out at the sea. She walked back and sat down. "My cousin would arrive around nine thirty and the game would begin. This went on for almost a year. Then, one night when he came over, it was just after I turned fourteen, I showed him my bloodstained underwear as I was taking them off. I was frightened that I'd somehow hurt myself. Boy, I'll never forget his reaction if I live to be a hundred. Everything happened in a swoosh. He jumped up and had his pants on in a flash. I'm shocked his dick wasn't caught in the zipper. He left my house barefoot and without his drawers."

Ruby heard a stifled giggle and looked at Nadine out of the corner of her eye.

"Those encounters ceased as abruptly as they had begun. He never visited my house unaccompanied again. I only saw him on holidays at family gatherings and he shunned me like a bubonic plague. Once the monthly cramping and nauseousness of having periods began, something I learned about from the older girls at school, I forgot all about our rendezvous until I turned eighteen."

Ruby turned to look at the girls. Their faces were filled with compassion. "I learned, quite by accident, that those feelings were orgasms," she said. "I was watching an X-rated movie when I noticed the man was performing the same acts on his partner that my cousin had done to me. The memories came flooding back and I cried. No, I whooped and hollered for a week. I had blocked those events from my memory. When the woman in the film gasped in ecstasy, I saw my reflection, my slutty behavior.

I was horrified about the sexual things I allowed my cousin to do. I gave him my virginity. That was the first time I realized why he discontinued our little game—he was scared I'd get pregnant. I'm a slut in wolves clothing and this is the punishment I've handed myself."

The girls, one after the other, told Ruby how sorry they were this happened to her and she should understand it wasn't her fault, but her cousin's. He was older and knew better.

Ruby looked each woman in the face in succession and then down at her lap. "I kept his underwear," she announced.

"You did what?" Jackie asked.

"Like Monica Lewinsky!" Laura said, not believing she heard Ruby correctly.

"Yes, I kept his drawers," Ruby said.

"Please tell us you washed them," Nadine giggled.

"Well, it's not like you still have them after all these years," Bernadette said.

They're in a shoebox hidden in my mother's attic back home. Ruby did not look up from her lap.

The girls stared at one another and then back at Ruby in disbelief.

"That's my cue to open another bottle," Nadine said, shaking her head.

Jackie stood up. *That is nothing. Wait until you all hear my wild-ass misdeeds. I skipped doing prison time by the skin of my teeth. It is pure luck that I have met any of you.*

"It has been a long day," Jackie said. "We should head over to Thirassia. We could take a water taxi, do a little shopping, and try some of those tomato-keftedes at one of the family-run fish taverns. I read one should not visit the Cyclades without trying them."

"We better wear cross-country then so we can climb those two hundred steps to Manolas," Bernadette said.

"And Ruby, I have a sexy sarong you can borrow," Nadine said. "You have to start showing off that sexy-ass body of yours that we're jealous of."

CHAPTER 6

NADINE IS NEXT

The storytelling continued on the fifth day of their vacation after lunch.

Nadine was Jackie's newest associate. When they met, it was the first time Nadine dared to step foot in a bar in twenty years. The last time she went to a nightclub, it was at Perv's House on the South Side of Chicago.

"I was having a fantastic time," Nadine started, "and was excited when a decent looking dude walked up and offered to buy me a drink. The banter was good, the soul music was jamming, and I was rocking in my chair. I felt on top of the world until he said without warning, with no provocation whatsoever, 'wow, you have a honker on you.'"

The girls' eyes zoomed in on her nose. There was no hook, no bump, no nothing. Her nose was small and in harmony with her face. They looked at each other and shrugged their shoulders. They couldn't comprehend the insult and they didn't interrupt her narrative to ask.

Nadine's horrible childhood memories came flooding back and crashed through the mental levees she had carefully built over the years to protect herself from this returning onslaught. Yet, it happened again. She dropped the drink, saw the shattering of glass, felt the splashing of liquid, and heard the yelling of a man. "Damn bitch!" he said. She wasn't sure who screamed the expletive, whether it was the man who insulted her or a man who got drenched, nor did she care as she ran humiliated out of the nightclub. "If I had known then, what I know today, I would have smashed that glass of Long Island Iced Tea over his head. After I got home, I was glad I ordered the most expensive drink in the bar." *That's probably why he made the comment,* she realized for the first time in twenty plus years.

"I was always the last man standing, well last woman, because of my looks."

Years worth of pictures reeled through her mind's View-Master depicting her and friends club-hopping every Saturday night. Only her girlfriends got the chance to dance and exchange numbers with suitors.

"I could boogie too," she said dejectedly. "I only got to dance when everyone at the table jumped up and danced together."

The girls looked confused. This story wasn't correlating with the beautiful woman sitting before them.

Nadine saw their baffled looks and altered the story she had been prepared to tell. After Ruby's disclosure, she decided that she too would expose a vulnerable side and slaughter the monkey on her back. She revealed a tormented childhood and said her story could be described succinctly as *The Ugly Duckling.*

"Growing up, I wore so many labels given to me un-ceremoniously, first by my parents who should have protected me, and second, by schoolmates who taunted and bullied me. I was called the ugly one, the big-boob, the albino, the one with big lips, the cry baby, the tattle-tale, the fishy girl, the big nose one. Name it and that was my identity. I knew I was the smart one but no one noticed or complimented me on that characteristic. It took a really long time—through my teens, twenties, and thirties—to metamorphose into the woman you see here today. I didn't love myself and travelling that long, yellow brick road was a disaster."

Nadine was the youngest of six adopted children. Being adopted was news to her and a revelation disclosed when she turned sixteen. For years, she puzzled over whether her siblings had different fathers because none of the kids resembled one another, and they looked nothing like their parents. And from the gossip of everyone in the neighborhood, she was the ugliest of the bunch.

When Nadine left home, she never looked back. She worked both full and part-time jobs and lived like a miser for years in order to save money for the many cosmetic procedures she endured. She treated this as an investment in her future. She learned, whether rightly or wrongly, that good looks were the "be all, end all." It was the nature of the beast in an appearance-conscious society.

"The one thing, the only takeaway I learned from my parents," Nadine said, "was not to spend money I didn't have. They constantly chanted save, save, save."

As she saved enough money for each surgery, she scheduled the appointment to have the procedure performed. "I had the reduction mammoplasty first because my health insurance covered the majority of the cost since my size forty-four, double D breasts on a five-foot-five frame were causing tremendous strain on my spine."

The girls stared at two tiny protrusions. Jackie wanted to ask, but dared not, "did you request that your tits be chopped off completely?"

Nadine said, "Then, I endured chemical peels and laser scar removal to clear the scars from teenage acne and puss-filled pimples." She looked at Ruby's unblemished skin and set down her bottle of Moët and ran her hands over her smooth face. "It's too bad there wasn't a laser to zap the scars from my heart."

For a passing moment, a nanosecond really, and one couldn't be absolutely sure because it disappeared as suddenly as it had appeared, the girls detected a smidgen of sadness.

Nadine wiggled her nose. "The Rhinoplasty took the lump out of my nose and shortened it. The final result"— she turned her head to give them a side view—"is a white person's nose that resembles a ski slope. And, not that I needed it, I only wanted it done since it was the in-thing at the time. I had implants ...."

The girls' eyes went to her flat chest.

"Eyes up here, girls ..." she patted the sides of her face, "inserted to give me high cheek bones."

Whew! Jackie thought, but didn't express, because if those nubs on her chest were implants, she better sue that incompetent doctor.

Once all the surgeries were completed and the swelling had disappeared, Nadine loved the new and improved person she had been transformed into. Her personality got bolder, and her attitude and behavior more assertive after each and every costly procedure. "I even requested my doctors turn me into a Halle Berry lookalike," Nadine said.

"Here, here," Ruby raised her bottle of Gosset.

The others looked at Nadine with a "you've got to be kidding look."

"I was dead serious," Nadine said. "And my doctor, along with his surgical team, was as equally dead serious. He told me I didn't have *enough* money." She stifled a giggle and gave the girls a look that dared them to snicker.

It didn't work.

"That's okay," she said. "The doctor's friendly sarcasm was nothing I couldn't deal with. He turned this ugly duckling into a beautiful swan." She stood up, twirled around, and walked the length of the veranda like a runway model, smooth and graceful, posed for them, and walked back. She went to her purse and pulled out a before photograph and handed it to Jackie. "How you like me now?" she asked in a singsong-pitch.

The girls passed the picture around and each looked at it expressionless. They didn't verbalize what they all thought. The surgeries were well worth the money, every blessed cent she spent.

Nadine paused and contemplated whether she wanted to divulge anything else. She decided she had gone this far, taken the risk, she just as well go all the way. After all, who else besides her psychiatrist would she ever be able to ramble on like this, nonstop; and this session was free of charge.

"I also spent years in therapy and thousands of dollars to readjust my hatred of myself," she said. "I was one depressed puppy. I even tried taking my life in my twenties."

She heard an outcry, which she disregarded.

"Took about ten over the counter sleeping pills, you remember Sominex, and went to sleep. I woke up refreshed, feeling better than I had in years. *What the F?* I guess I had gotten a bad batch or maybe I just killed off one of my nine lives, who knows; but that was a sign. Obviously, it wasn't my time to leave this good old earth."

The girls couldn't tell whether Nadine was joking or not so they didn't know whether to laugh or cry.

"I was an adult before I realized I wasn't an albino," she said. "Now, when I look back, and it took my psychologist, yeah, I had one of those also, to get me to recognize that people were ignorant of my beautiful ivory skin tone."

Nadine drained her bottle of Moët.

Unlike the ugly duckling tale about personal transformation for the better, she experienced no such triumph. She had a gripe to avenge and took advantage of her newfound beauty. She turned into a raving lunatic.

Everyone that ever called her a name or disparaged her, she never forgot and exacted revenge. She took her rage out on her parents, siblings, relatives, and coworkers. Even though her childhood friends had not ridiculed her face-to-face like everyone else, she hated them for their pity parties.

"I treasure the times when I return home on those rare occasions I visit," Nadine said. "They don't know it's me so I torment everyone in that piss-poor town. I'm worse than the wicked witch of the west in Oz," she said, screwing her face up into a mangled mess. "I can't tell you what malefaction I did the last time I went home because I'd have to kill you if I did." Her words sounded threatening and evil. "But, I'll tell you this. Hell hath no fury like a *bitch* scorned."

The girls didn't take her seriously, but the vindictive look in her eyes told them otherwise. No way was she kidding.

Jackie interrupted. "Nadine, you're beautiful. You're the poster child for cosmetic surgery."

"And Halle has nothing on you," Ruby piped in.

She was either drunk or delusional.

The girls didn't know which and didn't really care.

CHAPTER 7

AT LAST, JACKIE'S TALE

After a week of listening to the other girls' sagas and consuming nearly half of her case of Mumm, it was finally Jackie's turn.

"I have a dream," she repeated. "But first some background."

She escaped East New Orleans and journeyed to Washington, DC, in the seventies. The move had a topsy-turvy effect on her. The nightlife and street life beckoned her to taste all the nation's capital forbidden fruits. Everything was new, fresh, scary, and daring, all at the same time, and nothing was off limits in her newfound freedom. The obedient young girl from down south turned into an audacious woman up north.

"I felt as if I had landed on another planet instead of just moving a thousand miles. Nothing, and I mean nothing in DC resembled anything in Louisiana."

Jackie paused to reflect on the things she had witnessed and been a participant. There were nightclubs on every other block. And, as much time as she spent in Rands Nightclub at 14th and Eye Streets—she was there seven nights a week—the club should have charged *her* rent. She couldn't answer how she was able to get up every morning during the workweek and make it to her job by eight o'clock after partying 'til well after midnight. Rands was the place where blacks went to dance, drink, and grind.

"The grinding felt oh so good," Jackie said. She jumped up from her chaise and grabbed Nadine's hand, snatched her forward so their bodies touched, and began imitating a slow dance grind—moving up and down in a synchronized movement.

Bernadette said, "Oh no, you have to let a New York girl show you how to grind." She grabbed Jackie from Nadine, put her thigh between Jackie's legs, and they both dipped low to the floor and rotated their hips in a vulgar, erotic display.

The girls howled.

Jackie caught her breath and described the nightlife scene. "There were so many prostitutes: young ones, old ones, really old ones lining the streets looking for their next payday. The pros would be decked out in stilettos, and wore miniskirts that barely covered what my momma called their hind pots. They would scurry like rats when the police appeared, hiding in corners until a John drove up to inquire about sexual delights. I was dumbfounded that I was not mortified by this degrading behavior—just the opposite. I got a thrill out of being at the center of the action and DC was an action-packed city back then."

Jackie stopped and eyed Bernadette's three-quarter full Henriot.

"No, you can't have any of mine," Bernadette said, hugging the bottle. "Get your own bottle," she giggled.

Jackie stuck her tongue out at Bernadette, looked at her own almost empty bottle, and continued. "There were pimps galore. They dotted the entire Northwest corridor of DC and appointed themselves the weirdest, most ridiculous names that I had ever heard in my life. Animal names like Black Cat and Pure Dog. Fake titles—Sir George and King John. Even candy names were part of the equation: Delicious, Good and Plenty, and Mr. Good Bar. There was even a Cash Money. Go figure. I guess he needed to capitalize on the essence of a prostitute handing over her hard-earned take to him."

Ruby noticed that Jackie appeared catatonic as she was reliving that part of her life. She was in a dreamlike state; her eyes were glazed over and there was a peacefulness about her. Ruby had the impression that Jackie treasured and missed this long gone part of her life.

Jackie didn't miss a beat and couldn't help comparing the pimps' garbs to the New Orleans Mardi Gras Indians' spectacular, handmade costumes. "Pimps thought they looked good in their outlandish, bright, color-coded ensemble. They wore hats that the church-going women of New Orleans, the ones who only crossed a foot over the threshold on Easter Sunday in their 'dressed to kill,' brand spanking new outfits, would have envied."

The brim of a pimp's hat extended out at least a foot and was embellished with fake fur or an oversized ostrich feather. The hats were worn tipped downward and slightly to one side.

"And those platform shoes...," Jackie screeched, and shook her head, "yes, it was exactly like Huggy Bear in *I'm Gonna Get You Sucka*, and thank God, no gold fish."

Jackie ceased talking and started laughing uncontrollably. It was contagious and the girls started cackling too. After a couple of minutes, Jackie got herself under control and continued. "They looked like Dracula with their maxi-length coats fanning out behind them as they limped with not-needed walking canes—shame on them for impersonating the disabled."

She erupted into hysterics. This time, tears streamed down her face. Recreating that time period was funny as heck; but back in the day when she was gripped in the epicenter of it, Jackie was fascinated and sucked in by the sights, smells, and sounds of it all. She looked up at the girls to see their reactions. They were in stitches.

"The icing on the cake," she said, trying to restrain another outburst, "was the massive 14 carat gold chains swinging from their necks and the rings decorating several fingers. And you could always tell the pimp wannabes; they donned silver jewelry."

She looked at her now empty bottle of Mumm and went to the refrigerator to get another bottle. Without turning, she asked if anyone needed a bottle. Before they had an opportunity to decide, she loaded her arms and carried five bottles back to the room. "We probably should call room service and order dinner in," Jackie said.

They all agreed.

As they waited for the food to arrive, they took in the breathtaking views of idyllic Perivolas. The resort was a combination of tranquility and beautiful architecture with an inspiring land and seascape.

The view, this place, presented Jackie with a fleeting idea. But, it wouldn't come into focus. It simmered at the edge of her consciousness trying to break the surface; then, it would vanish beneath the waves of her drunken state until the idea itself was forgotten.

They looked at the terraced gardens spilling down the slopes to the pool that had no edges and blended into the blue horizon. A sound broke the quietude and they thought the server had arrived. "That was fast," Jackie said.

It was not the door bell. It was the toll of church bells.

An hour later there was a soft knock at the door. The platters of seafood, pasta, salad, and fruit had arrived.

They ate in silence, enjoying their meal.

After dinner, Jackie picked back up in her storytelling exactly where she left off, as if there had never been a dinner break. "Everything was so out of the ordinary and I saw tons of what can only be described as colorful street entertainment."

Jackie had encountered all kinds of weird characters in DC.

"I was most flabbergasted by the drag queens. They were the life of their own parties. Now that I think about it, they deliberately overdressed to compensate for the penis between their legs. There was always some kind of nightly audition, an informal contest to determine who among them would be crowned best dressed drag queen that night."

The girls were staring at her, astonished that this was the same Jackie they had known for eons. Never, not once in all the years they had known her, had they glimpsed, or more accurately heard, her self-disclose personal details before.

Jackie noticed. "Yes girls, I was in the thick of it, and quite frankly, I loved every minute of it too, in case you were wondering." She smirked and continued on. "Every facet of those queens' appearance was scrutinized by one another. Who wore the highest heels? Who sported the tallest hairdo? Who squeezed themselves into the tightest dress with no hint of a bulge out front?"

The girls dismissed their astonishment and fell to the floor, doubled up. She joined them in the merriment.

Jackie viewed these talent shows as bizarre comedies. In order for a drag queen to win the contest, her makeup had to conceal the five o'clock shadow and a scarf wrapped around her neck had to hide his Adam's apple.

Jackie continued her long-winded tête-à-tête nonstop.

"I am harboring a secret," she said. "Those queens were a blessing in disguise, my guardian angels."

The girls perked up.

"After living in the city a few months, I wanted to try something different." Jackie described how she ended up sitting on the side of her bed shivering violently, not because she was cold, but because she had just gotten the living crap scared out of her. Well more to the point, almost strolled off in a police car in handcuffs, and being slapped with a ten-year criminal record for a one night, dumb-ass lark.

"It was in the wee hours on a Saturday night, it may have been Sunday morning, when I got the stupid idea to pretend to be a prostitute. I put on bright red hot pants, high-heel clogs, and a tight-fitting bodysuit that snapped at the crotch, showed cleavage, and emphasized my breasts. I teased my shoulder-length hair in the style of the Supremes and wore hollow, fake gold, large hoop earrings. I sashayed down Fourteenth Street and passed a group of drag queens, maybe five or six, chattering about something. It was difficult to decipher. One of them started singing. 'You shake it girl. Shake it to the left and shake it to the right; shake it to the one that you love the best.' The queens began hooting as they grossly mimicked my switching, their hips swaying from side-to-side in an exaggerated manner. I stopped and grinned from ear to ear, thinking I had it going on. I kept on strutting until a Ford Sedan pulled up alongside me."

Jackie was getting drunk from the champagne, but not so drunk, because she noticed that the girls were immersed in her story and they looked captivated by this secret she was divulging.

"Before I left my apartment, I had already decided on an amount I would charge if I was so lucky to entice a John. I walked over and leaned against the car. He leaned over in the seat to roll down the window. I looked at this white man about fortyish with a head full of thick red hair and devilish green eyes, dressed in a patchwork shirt and Levis, with a pudge overlapping his belt, and thought, 'he looks decent enough for my first try.' After all, I did not have a clue of what to do. He asked, 'how much,' right off the bat. There was no good evening, how are you this fine night. No chitchat. Nothing! Well okay, I thought; maybe this was the way it was done. Girls, before I could open my mouth and quote twenty-five dollars, I heard loud, blasphemous screams from the queens. I spun around to see what the racket was about. 'He's a cop! It's a cop, girlfriend! Run!' I heard the order loud and clear."

The queens' warnings were shouted over and over again but Jackie heard nothing after the first one.

"To this day, I have no recollection of how I got back to my apartment. All I remember is fumbling with the key to get the door unlocked. My face was soaking wet, but I did not recall it raining. I struggled to walk the two feet to the bathroom, turn on the light, and look in the mirror. A hideous vision returned my stare. The mascara that I had applied so meticulously one hour earlier was now mixed with tears running down my face. The face in the mirror looked as if it had seen an apparition. I walked back toward the sofa and mechanically pulled out the bed. I remember going back into the bathroom but avoided the mirror. I opened the medicine cabinet, grabbed the bottle of Tylenol, and wished it had been sleeping pills."

Jackie glanced at Nadine and mouthed, *I know how you felt.*

"I walked back to the couch, turned off the bedside lamp, and without removing my whorish clothing or shoes, I slid under the top sheet and blanket without folding the bedspread to the foot of the bed as I had been conditioned to do, and curled into a fetal position, holding on tightly to the bottle of Tylenol. I pondered how I could have been so foolish. I laid there for a few minutes before kicking the covers off and getting back out of bed. I dropped to my knees and thanked God that my moralistic parents would never know that their only daughter was prostituting her body. It would not have mattered to them that it was my first outing and no sexual act had been consummated. I bowed my head and said the bedtime prayer that I had not articulated since I was a teen.

"Now I lay me down to sleep
I pray the Lord my soul to keep.
If I should die before I wake
I pray the Lord my soul to take.
If I should live for other days
I pray the Lord to guide my ways.
And even though I had forsaken the Lord, I added another line. Thank you God for the drag queens."

Jackie took two tablets with a glass of warm water. She learned something else that night. She was more scared to die than she was scared of her mother.

Before the girls could comment, Jackie abruptly changed the subject and announced unexpectedly, "I wished I was a man. I was jealous of those pimps and envied their lifestyle. They had all the power and control."

She saw the girls opened mouths and disgusted looks. She couldn't discern if the looks were intended for her or her anecdote.

There seemed to be no end to Jackie's reverie so they decided to get a breath of fresh air and wander into one of the villages and pick up again the following day around noon.

As they strolled into Oia, a beautiful village on the dramatic island of Santorini, the girls were awe-inspired by the magnificent sunset, which displayed a range of colors, seemingly from an artist's palette.

* * *

When they returned from Oia, they went to their own rooms to retire for the night. As Jackie was preparing for bed, she contemplated the story she divulged earlier that day. For reasons she could not explain, it could have been attributed to her wanting to get as far away as possible from her strict upbringing, the colorful lifestyle she had grown accustomed to in DC appealed to her. It was fascinating.

* * *

Washington, DC, was light years ahead of East New Orleans, which occupied a large section of the city east of the Industrial Canal and north of the Mississippi River Gulf Outlet. Although developed as suburban-style living inside the city limits, it experienced little urban development. The only appealing thing about East New Orleans was its uncluttered visual appearance. Buried utility cables lent to a distinct town of no visible wires for street light signals, no twisted mess of power lines, and no large areas covered with leaning utility poles. Interstate 10 was the main auto route, but passersby drove straight through because there were no restaurants, gas stations, or a shopping strip. Matter-of-fact, if plans called for driving through East New Orleans, one had better gas up first.

The town was downright boring. The only thing blacks did for recreation was travel to Lincoln Beach amusement park. There was nothing else in East New Orleans for an adolescent black girl to do to amuse herself. Her mother wouldn't allow her to date, talk on the phone, or wear makeup. The only so-called entertainment she had was attending morning Sunday school and one o'clock church service. When she turned fifteen, she stopped believing there was a God. She knew that if she uttered that piece of vile sacrilege to anyone, she would be struck by lightning, and it wouldn't be from God. A wrath from her mother, greater than even Satan could emit, would have broken lose inside their house and exorcised that demon right out of her.

She thanked her lucky stars that she made it out of that godforsaken, country-bumpkin place of a town, away from the strict rules and upbringing of her straitlaced parents and the prying eyes of nosy neighbors who behaved as if they were her momma too.

Within a month of moving to DC, Jackie fell into the arms of Sir George. She did not reveal that to the girls. It wasn't relevant because no matter how much she despised her straitjacket upbringing, her domineering mother prepared her for the ills of a man, especially men who thought it was their god-given right to exploit women.

Watching her mother in action, Jackie learned that women could gain the upper hand in any situation.

Her mother was a statuesque woman who easily stood a full two inches taller than her father, in stocking feet. She was a good, religious woman, nobody could argue that. She bore her husband four children, all exactly three years apart, as if she had planned it that way. Three boys and one girl, and Jackie was the youngest.

Her momma's words were law in their home in the house daddy built. There was no negotiating; even her daddy followed the rules the majority of the time. He had a daily routine—he worked six days a week as a janitor in one of the warehouses across town, handed over his weekly paycheck to momma in which she doled out a few dollars back to him, stepped aside, and allowed her to take reign.

On weekends though, he was the master-in-charge and momma knew intuitively to leave him alone. He would sat out in the front yard on a rickety bench with his brothers who lived on the same street and they would each have their own bottle of liquor, usually Jim Beam or Smirnoff, and drink to their hearts content. When one greedily slurped his bottle dry before anyone else, they shared the remaining bottles. They would each pour a little liquor from his bottle into the empty one and then line up the bottles to ensure each had an equal amount. The guzzler knew not to pull this stunt more than once. It was a known fact that each kept count and took turns in this little back-and-forth drinking scheme.

And thinking mom or the town's people were unaware of their sightseeing antics, they watched all the young ladies who walked by and commiserated about their own woes. This was the only time her daddy ruled.

Jackie's foundation was grounded and molded by her momma. So, no matter how many times Sir George asked her to turn tricks for him, and he had all kinds of maneuvers up his sleeve, she would say, "only if you will turn tricks for me too." It wasn't long before the relationship's raging fire was doused with cold attitude. His stable of three prostitutes was complaining bitterly and loudly about this young newcomer who thought she was too good to stand on the street corners of DC and sell her goodies for their man.

* * *

Jackie had knocked back almost two bottles of champagne the evening before and the alcohol finally knocked her out. She didn't wake up until two-thirty the following afternoon. When she sauntered out onto the veranda, Bernadette said, "Girl, we kept checking on you. I thought your ass was dead until I heard you snoring. You snore like a man."

"Real sexy," Nadine said.

Jackie shielded her eyes from the intense sunlight and saw a silver tray of food and pointed at it. "For me," she asked. The girls nodded. She lifted the lid salivating for back home favorites—Belgian waffle with one pat of Land O Lakes butter, two packets of Aunt Jemima syrup, and three strips of Applewood smoked bacon. She frowned. Instead, there was Mediterranean cuisine: quinoa with walnuts and cinnamon, salmon frittata, and Greek yogurt parfait. *At least there is a carafe of piping hot coffee.*

"Ah, poor baby," Bernadette simulated whining when she saw the disappointment spread over Jackie's face. "You can take the lady out of the Deep South, but you sure can't take the Deep South out of the lady."

Jackie ignored her and gulped down the food as if it was her last meal before execution and asked if they wanted to go down to the beach.

"Later," Ruby said. "We still haven't heard about your dream."

She took a sip of coffee. "We are between forty and fifty years old, am I right?" Jackie said.

They agreed.

Jackie knew this to be a white lie, especially on her part. If anyone asked directly, which she knew no one would dare, she was a teensy-weensy bit older than fifty. "Well, I have reached a point in my life where I want to be the monarch. I want to be in control of my own destiny. I am ready for a change and the time has come for me to make a move."

She put up her index finger. "One, as a Real Estate Agent, I have done extremely well over the last fifteen years."

She stuck up her middle finger, forming the peace sign. "Two, I have been able to squirrel away enough money to purchase my dream home."

She held up her bare ring finger. "And three, I do not want to wait until I am sixty-five to retire. I want to retire right now, today!"

All of the girls could empathize with her on that point.

"I am going to start searching for a home soon since the market is still weak. With a lot of luck I think I should be able to find exactly what I am looking for."

Laura raised her hand. Jackie pretended not to see it.

"As soon as I find the right property, I promise, you all will be the first ones I contact to share the remainder of my dream."

* * *

On the last night of their vacation, the women wrote the name of a country each wanted to visit for their September 2014 escape, and threw the folded pieces of paper in the center of the coffee table amid the array of empty champagne bottles.

In the morning, they asked the room attendant to clear everything from the table except one piece of folded paper. When they returned from their morning swim, several laps from one end of the seemingly edgeless pool to the other end, they gathered around the coffee table and Ruby opened the single piece of paper. Each crossed her fingers that her spot would be the chosen one.

Ruby started grinning. "See you in South Africa girls," she said. The room filled with "whoopees." She thought the girls were dancing around because they were excited by her selection. She started crying. "I can't believe I'm scratching this off of my bucket list."

The girls stopped gamboling, looked at Ruby bewildered, then at each other, and pointed at themselves. "I wrote South Africa too," each woman said almost simultaneously. The five associates danced and hooted around the room as if they were at a jamboree.

When the hour came to depart Santorini, the women disembarked the same way they had embarked.

"We sing our song of freedom.

We got away from boredom.

Gracias, Gracias.

We all do the hug."

They all huddled, closed in together, and did the group hug.

CHAPTER 8

IAN FERGUSON

Ian's memory returned in bits and pieces. He recalled the horrible argument that started with his wife. He didn't want to remember but it came flooding back.

Ian wanted out of his seven-year marriage badly and it wasn't due to the seven-year itch or turning fifty syndrome either. Evelyn was a cold-hearted bitch, with a capital B. She treated him like a chump and he couldn't grasp why. He knew he was a good man, a good husband, albeit pussy-whipped, according to his buddies. *But, is that any reason for a wife to take advantage of her husband.*

He had never been the one to call it quits first in any relationship. He always allowed women to break up with him. That way, he felt absolved of any guilt that he couldn't make the relationship work. He didn't have the druthers or know-how to break up. There wasn't a manual providing step-by-step instructions. And, he was always the one that got hurt anyway, so he just gave women enough rope to hang themselves, which usually they did. So once they took off, good riddance!

His friends were right though. And, if that was the term for the terminal sickness he had, then so be it.

Because having sex with Evelyn was a mind blowing, one-of-a-kind experience.

Over the years, he was the recipient of hundreds, possibly even thousands of blow jobs and none was of the sensuousness of his wife's. It was obvious she loved giving head and as far as he was concerned, she loved giving him blow jobs. She knew how to wrap her full, succulent lips around his Johnson and lick it like a lollipop. She had this way of nibbling it and tugging it this way and that way until it erupted. She could make him holler with ecstasy within five minutes of commencing the act. Each and every time he gasped the same words, "This is the best head I've ever had."

He even bragged to his boys that his old lady gave the best blow jobs ever. Sadly, this was the only time he and his wife had any type of real connection. This piece of info he didn't share with his boys. He kept that locked in the vault.

He had a sneaking suspicion Evelyn was having an affair. Every day she had somewhere to go or something to do. She was either taking a photography class, a Zumba dance fitness class, or a pottery class. Now, she was contemplating returning to school to get her second Master's. It never ceased to amaze him that she would find anything to do in order not to spend time at home with her husband.

He was lonely, and desperately wanted and needed companionship. He wanted to be loved. He deserved to be treated better. *How difficult could that be?* He begged his wife on several occasions to spend more time with him but to no avail. They constantly argued about it. She accused him of smothering her and he accused her of alienation of affection. The quarrels escalated to full blown crescendos, regardless of how innocuous the colloquy began. He vividly recalled the explosive argument, word-for-word.

"Honey, you're not going to believe this. I was able to get a hold of tickets for the Kennedy Center Alvin Ailey's performance, the one you've been dying to see." He was beside himself with excitement that he had scored the tickets. A coworker was unable to go to the sold-out show so he sold the tickets to Ian, and not at a discount either. The tickets were expensive, but cost didn't matter. It was something his wife kept talking about for weeks on end. "We could eat dinner first at Kinkead's and then head over to the show."

"When?" Evelyn asked from the bathroom in a flat tone.

"Next Saturday night at eight."

She came out of the bathroom with a hot curling iron in her hand, and looked at him. "Ian, you should have discussed this with me first before purchasing the tickets. I already have plans with my girlfriends."

"I wanted to surprise you for your birthday." He was deflated and felt the familiar sign of aggravation rising.

"Well, I'm sorry. I can't go," Evelyn said pointedly. "They made these plans months ago."

"What plans?" he yelled. "Cancel them! I'm almost certain they would understand that your *husband* wants to celebrate your birthday with you."

"No, they won't understand, Ian, and I don't want them to cancel," she screamed back. "We're going to New York to celebrate my birthday. They got tickets to *Motown the Musical*."

He couldn't believe he was hearing her correctly. Other women dropped their girlfriends in a heartbeat, at a moment's notice to do something with their significant other. Maybe that's the problem, he thought. Maybe he wasn't Evelyn's significant other. He was her husband alright, but not significant. And he wasn't going to be fooled any longer because her girlfriends weren't her significant other either.

"Evelyn, I'm sick and tired of you always putting others ahead of me. We don't do anything together anymore." He watched as she screwed up her face and turned back toward the bathroom. He couldn't believe she turned her back on him while he was talking. "The only thing you do for me is suck my dick," he said, at an earsplitting volume that he couldn't believe came from his mouth. The last sentence echoed as it reverberated off the walls.

Evelyn stopped in her tracks before she crossed the threshold of the bathroom and turned slowly, deliberately, to meet his anger head-on. Her homicidal stare could only be described as the beginning of a tornado that had been unleashed and couldn't be corralled. At that very instant, he realized he had gone too far. He knew if there had been a gun, a knife, any weapon at all that she could have gotten her hands on—the curling iron was tangled in her hair—he would be a dead mother fucker right about now.

He scanned the room to find the quickest way around her and out of the house. But, it was too late. Of all the arguments they had regarding her not spending time with him, this was the first time he had stooped to this deplorable level.

"Suck your dick!" Evelyn blasted him. "Is that what you have the audacity to scream at me?" Tears gathered in her eyes, which she wiped away before they could spillover. "Suck your dick." The dam broke. Tears rushed like a downpour out of control. "Well, I hope you enjoyed the last time I sucked it because you'll never get it sucked again, not by me anyway."

He was too shaken to mutter an apology, whether he was sorry or not. He thought it best to keep his mouth shut; he had already said too much. He had never seen this side of Evelyn before. A large vein was visible and rapidly pulsating from the side of her neck. Her eyes looked bloodshot. Those luscious lips were now a snarl. Her entire stance was attack mode and he was in her line of fire. There was no turning back. He had crossed a line that no black man should ever cross with a black woman.

He began to speak instead of listen to the warnings in his head. "Why is it that you prefer your girlfriends to me? I don't understand that," he mustered the courage to sound mad.

"Because they don't snivel, whine, beg, and plead every single day for my undivided attention." She paused to catch her breath. "I dread coming into this house, our home, because I'm sick and tired of having the same discussion over and over again. And you say you're tired.

Look in the mirror, Ian," she screamed even louder. "Would you want to come home to that?"

Ian was dumbstruck. *Is that how my wife sees me?*

"All I want is for you to be a wife," Ian said dejectedly. He felt like a fool.

"And all I want is for you to be the man I met, the man I fell in love with, the man I married. Not the man standing here before me." The words were no longer screams because her voice was hoarse. "Ian, you had friends before we met. You had a life. You enjoyed watching sports with the guys. You couldn't wait to go out after work for a beer or two. You got a kick out of playing poker all night." Evelyn exhaled. "I had a life too, Ian. And, just because we got married doesn't mean we have to give up the things we enjoyed that were important to each of us. You may have forfeited your way of life. I didn't."

"So what are you saying?" Ian asked.

"I'm saying that I'm still going to be me."

Ian changed tactics. "Are you having an affair, Evelyn?"

"Oh grow up, Ian."

"Why are you avoiding the question?" His rage was returning. "Are you having an affair?"

"Yes, Ian! I'm having an affair," she lied.

He turned abruptly and exited the house. He had to get out of there before she saw his shame and humiliation. He had to leave before he really hurt her. He was seconds away from stomping her.

* * *

Lying there in a mysterious bedroom, Ian realized that his dysfunctional and non-affectionate marriage had become a noose around his neck. Sometimes when he was alone, sobs would get caught in his throat. He was so depressed. He couldn't talk to Brian, his best friend and best man at his wedding, about something so asinine. Brian wouldn't understand how a woman, any woman for that matter, could have a leg up on a man, and especially that man being his friend.

CHAPTER 9

EVELYN FERGUSON, IAN'S WIFE

Evelyn couldn't believe the words she had spewed at Ian. Yes, she felt that way, but she didn't mean to say it with such venom. But Ian had gone too far, she rationalized. She had never in her life been spoken to like she was some kind of whore. *Who did he think he was anyway to speak to me in such a derogatory manner? So what if he is a good man.*

Evelyn needed breathing room. That's why she signed up for all those activities. It was either extraneous activities or an affair and she wasn't that kind of wife. Ian wouldn't listen though. He didn't take her seriously. No matter how many times, and there were many, she tried to have a discussion with him about needing space, he always turned it around and put her on the defensive. It was like talking to an idiot, she reasoned. Evelyn felt smothered, like she was drowning. She abhorred this feeling, and loathed him for changing into the man he had become.

Still, she was sorry that the argument had escalated viciously and ended on the tone it had. He had never looked so confused and downtrodden, like someone had extinguished his fire. *Why was I so blind not to see how excited he was about those tickets?* Then, just as quickly as the thought surfaced, she pushed it back down. *No, I'm not letting him turn this around and make me the villain.*

She was troubled by how he left the house though. He was really angry and in a rage. Usually, he would go to his study after an argument. She assumed he left in fear of wanting to beat her to a pulp.

Since her birthday was only two weeks away, she called one of her girlfriends and told her about Ian and their blowup, and asked if she could stay there for a couple of weeks until things at home cooled down. Evelyn said she would be there within the hour. She packed two overnight bags and waited for Ian to come home to tell him her plans. She thought that was the least she could do.

Ian didn't show up that night, the next night, or that week. He didn't call either. He must be really mad, she thought. His boss called and was annoyed. Ian hadn't been into the office in a few days and had stood up a client that morning, which was out of character for him. She began to get worried. Ian wasn't somewhere blowing off steam. He had been missing since last week.

Where are you, Ian? Evelyn said to herself. She was scared. She prayed that Ian hadn't gone and done something stupid like commit suicide.

Evelyn dialed nine-one-one.

CHAPTER 10

JACKIE TRUMPLETON, REAL ESTATE AGENT: Phase One

Jackie Trumpleton's long-held dream was within reach.

Phase one was successfully completed. Since joining Retro/Max–DMV in 1996, she became an overnight success. She was a multi-million dollar Real Estate Agent and had plaques lining the walls of her office to prove it. She made a killing in the real estate market; and during the housing peak, she nearly tripled her earnings.

Being a successful agent wasn't easy. It required an ironclad commitment twenty-four hours a day, seven days a week, three hundred sixty-five days a year.

She loved challenges and thrived on assisting first-time homebuyers realize the American dream of homeownership. Buyers appreciated her dedication, welcomed her guidance, and depended on her for expert advice and counseling. Without a doubt, buyers were her niche.

Jackie reminisced a time about two years ago on Christmas Eve as if it had happened yesterday. She was in the office doing dreaded floor duty when an African-American couple came in, seemingly in a panic. Jackie showed them to the conference room where their story hurriedly poured out. The woman thrust a letter into Jackie's hand and commenced to explain.

"We have 'til the end of the year to find a house," she said excitedly, "and to have, I don't know, some kind of rattle contract in place." She looked over at the man. "What was the term the lender used, Tony?" she asked.

"I think she said a raffle contract, something like that."

"A ratified contract," Jackie said, amused.

"That's it, yes," the woman concurred.

"Okay, what are your names?"

"I'm Connie Murray and this is my hubby, Anthony, Tony for short."

Jackie hoped her facial features didn't display the shock she felt, as she wondered how Connie could attract such a good looking husband while she had yet to have been married once, not even coming close to finding a suitable beau.

Then, he smiled.

Yuck!

Jackie relaxed. She recalled a statement from a former boyfriend made many years ago why she'd never get or keep a man. "Your standards are set way too high," he admonished.

If lowering them meant settling just to say I have somebody, Jackie surmised, having a man who hadn't sat in a dentist chair in god knows how many eons, she'd go through the steel doors of purgatory before she'd lower her standards one iota.

"Okay, let's see what you have there," Jackie said, accepting the folded letter the wife offered. She scanned the letter and realized that the prospective buyers were sincere. She reread the letter, this time slowly, carefully. The letter was from the Virginia Housing Development Authority, the VHDA. The buyers were preapproved for a first trust of one hundred twenty-five thousand dollars. And true to the buyers' words, a ratified contract had to be in place by year's end. *Not only is that in seven days,* Jackie frowned, *it is also counting Christmas Day.*

"When did you receive this letter?" she asked, even though it was clearly dated December nineteenth.

"Only a few days ago," Connie screeched.

"Calm down Con," Tony said, rubbing her back, feeling ill at ease that his wife was so riled up.

Connie pulled away from him and whispered, albeit loudly, "you calm down."

Connie was visibly exasperated, excited, and frustrated, wound up into a ball of rubber bands ready to snap, crackle, pop—one rubber band at a time. Her husband, on the other hand, was cool as a cucumber. He sat back and allowed Connie to do all the talking.

"We applied for this loan over a year ago. Until we received this letter, we thought buying a home was a pipe dream, not an American dream."

After summing up their wish list to Jackie—a detached, four bedroom house with two full bathrooms, and a large yard in Alexandria, Virginia—she had to bring them back to earth gently. Buyers' eyes were always bigger than their pocketbooks. She informed them that the search had to be as far out as Woodbridge in order to find the price range in which they qualified.

"Where *is* Woodbridge? I've never heard of it?" Tony said.

"No more than eighteen miles south of here," Jackie said, not mentioning that during rush-hour traffic Monday through Friday, and from sun up until sundown on Saturdays with construction for a hot lane, the simple straight shot on Interstate 95 in either direction, north or south, could easily take an hour. During non-rush hour, it was a trouble-free, twenty-minute straight shot.

Tony exhaled noisily. "So, in Timbuktu," he pronounced the three-syllable proper noun as if it was three separate words. He looked at his wife. "You're not dragging me out to no man's land, Con. This was your plan all along to get me away from my friends. Who the hell will visit us way out there?" he wanted to know.

"That's the problem, Tony, your Heckle and Jeckle friends."

Jackie interrupted their argument by coughing.

She jumped on the computer, pulled up the MRIS database, and did a search. Four homes came up and she called the sellers to see if they could view their homes that afternoon. Three said yes and one exclaimed, "It's Christmas Eve for goodness sake," and wanted to know if they could come the day after Christmas.

"Anyone who wants to look at homes on Christmas Eve," Jackie assured the Murrays, "is viewed as a serious buyer." The first two homes were dumps. Jackie was amazed at some of the houses she had shown over the years. Sellers expected top dollars but some wouldn't perform simple chores like wash dishes, make beds, empty trashcans, pick up clothes, and clean the bathroom, not to mention remove clutter and trim shrubs.

The last home seemed to have been built for the Murrays, even though it was constructed in the sixties. It was a totally renovated rambler with a finished basement and met all of the buyers' requirements. "This has to be a present from Saint Nick himself," Jackie said to the Murrays. She ignored that Tony was sullen and still under the spell of an oncoming temper tantrum. She called the Sellers' agent right away, impressed he was working on Christmas Eve too, and explained the buyers' precarious predicament.

He was tickled that he was getting a full-price contract the day before Christmas. This was a wonderful gift for the sellers because the house had been on the market ninety-nine days.

Everything was a go or so they thought. The house passed inspection, there were no termites, and the closing date had been scheduled. With no warning, VHDA's underwriter declined the mortgage.

Jackie couldn't follow the words Connie was yelling into the phone. She couldn't tell what Connie was upset about. She heard a lot of huffing and puffing, snorting and sniffling. When she first met them, she thought Connie suffered with asthma; but after a second meeting, she came to the conclusion that the panting was due to a lack of oxygen caused by the truck-size spare tire around Connie's midsection. The woman was not even five feet and when she sat, the tire separated into three distinct, thick hula hoops. Connie easily tipped the scales at three hundred pounds and that was only because it was the maximum weight a home scale could bear.

"We can't get the house," Connie cried.

"What?" Jackie said. "What are you talking about Connie? Take a deep breath and please"—she didn't say for god's sake—"calm down, and tell me what is going on." Jackie thought this was another episode of what happened a couple of weeks ago. Tony and Connie had gotten into a huge argument and decided neither wanted to buy a house with the other. They had marched into her office unannounced to inform her that they weren't going through with the purchase of the home. Right before Jackie's eyes, Connie ripped their copy of the contract in half. "Cancel the contract," she had yelled.

"Our loan was turned down," Connie shouted. "How could you let this happen? I thought we were approved."

Jackie had the distinct impression that Connie was blaming her for the rejected application. She heard Tony in the background using some very disgusting, derogatory language. She wondered if he realized that she could hear him over Connie's yelling or if he just didn't care. "Fuck them and fuck her," she heard him yelling. "I didn't want to move to the boondocks anyway."

Was this the same well-mannered man I met on Christmas Eve?

"I have not heard anything," Jackie said. "Let me check into this and get back with you."

"Please," Connie begged. "All our hopes and dreams are tied up in this house." Jackie could only speculate where those hopes and dreams were two weeks ago when Connie was ready to abandon the house on a whim.

After being transferred to three different people and kept on hold for what seemed an eternity, Jackie finally got through to the underwriter who explained that the Murrays were turned down because they didn't have the traditional credit history.

"You have got to be kidding," Jackie said. "Why was this not an issue at the beginning of the process?"

"Apparently, somebody missed it," the underwriter said indifferently.

"Can we appeal the decision?"

"I don't know what good it would do. The decision has been made," the underwriter said.

Jackie never forgot the words of a CEO she worked for many years ago. *Never let an underling tell you something can't be done. Ask for his or her supervisor, and if still no satisfaction, ask for the supervisor's boss and keep going up the chain if necessary until you speak to someone who "can" make the decision.*

Jackie typed a letter to the executive director at VHDA explaining in detail the Murrays' journey to home ownership. She kept typing as the hands on the clock struck midnight. She disregarded the throbbing pain in her wrist reminding her of the carpal tunnel surgery she kept neglecting to schedule. She asked VHDA to reevaluate its decision. "Aren't first-time homebuyers, like the Murrays, the quintessence of homeownership?" the letter concluded.

Ten days later, a decision was handed down. The Murrays' mortgage was approved.

Endings like this were Jackie's crowning glory.

* * *

It had taken Jackie almost twenty-four years to find her niche.

She had held many different positions, but the glass ceiling in each might as well have been Mount Everest because she never reached the top. There were always obstacles. She was viewed by her superiors as aggressive, opinionated, reckless, and impatient—descriptors that made her un-promotable and unapproachable. Many times the obstacles were her own, which she viewed as being assertive, a forward thinker, and a decision maker.

Becoming a real estate agent was the best career choice and move Jackie ever made. No more bosses, no more obstructions, no more boundaries.

Now, she was free to do things her way.

CHAPTER 11

ARLINGTON POLICE DEPARTMENT

You could hear the thunderous male guffaw before the elevator doors fully opened on the sixth floor of the Arlington police department. It was as if Lieutenant Neathers and Sergeant Gable were entering the final inning of a baseball game that had exceeded three extra innings. The closer the men got to their cubicles, the louder the sound escalated.

The station was no different from any other police station throughout the DMV (District of Columbia, Maryland, and Virginia) metropolitan area. Cheap desk, cheap chairs, cheap carpet, and the stench of week-old coffee. The one saving grace in this particular station was the camaraderie amongst the blues. They got along and enjoyed working with one another. A code of ethics wasn't needed to tell them to watch each other's back. It was a foregone conclusion that they would, no matter the sacrifice. They were family.

The sergeant and lieutenant heard this mirth many times before, but on this occasion it sounded entirely different. Something was happening that was downright hilarious and they wanted to see what the commotion was all about. As they turned the corner, they bumped into a rookie who was doubled over, gasping for air. He tried to say hello but no words came forth.

The commander was sitting at his desk in one corner of the room slapping the top of his desk hard with the palm of his hand. The sergeant couldn't see his face because it was turned away from them.

The lieutenant looked over at the captain and noticed that he had lost composure too. He was chuckling so hard that fluids exited his body. Tears squirted from his eyes, snot ran from his nose, and saliva sprayed from his lips. The captain removed a vile looking handkerchief from his back pocket and dabbed it all over his face.

The only female, Detective Lindon, refused to participate in this belly laughing. She was the most composed and acted the most civil. But, the hilarity of the circumstances had become contagious and she could not escape it. She squirmed out of her chair and walked with her legs tightly crossed to the ladies room, praying she would make it before she peed in her pants.

"What's so funny?" Neathers asked.

There was so much ruckus that the officers didn't notice or hear him. It didn't seem like the cachinnation would ever subside.

"Hey guys," Neathers repeated louder over the uproar. "What's so damn funny?"

Everyone looked toward Neathers and Gable. It took a moment before anyone could respond intelligently. "Well, give it up," he said.

"Okay lieutenant, okay. You're not going to believe this one," Officer Cooper said. He grabbed some papers from his desk and riffled through them. "Listen to this. We got a nine-one-one call from a man claiming that he had been abducted. We thought it was a prank."

"Abducted by aliens, I suppose," Detective Lindon joked. She had returned to her desk from the john. She had not peed her pants.

"What?" Neathers and Gable asked in unison. "Come on guys," Gable said, "pull yourselves together and give us the four-one-one."

"Serious Sarge," Cooper said, "we got this call from a Clyde Hariston and his wife claiming that he was abducted two weeks ago, held against his wishes in this mansion, and get this, raped by an unknown assailant."

Gable's eyes opened wide, not comprehending. "He was raped by a man!"

This caused another outburst, but this time at Gable.

"No, no," Cooper said, shaking his head. "A woman."

Gable was incredulous. "Do you think the wife actually believes that poppycock?" he asked.

"Oh god, why can't such miracles be bestowed upon me," the captain said, exaggerating the words as he returned the gross looking handkerchief to his back pocket.

"Amen!" There was boisterous assent from the male police officers.

The lieutenant and sergeant gave each other a "are you kidding me look" and shuddered. It was obvious to everyone in the room that no woman would come within fifty feet of the captain voluntarily.

"I dream for that kind of fortune," Cooper said.

Lindon rolled her eyes and shook her head.

"Did anyone take a report?" Gable asked.

"Of course I did," Cooper said, as he fanned the papers in his hand. "It's all right here in black and white. This is proof that I did not make this story up."

"Did anyone speak to the husband?" the lieutenant asked.

"Nope," Cooper said. "His wife wants someone to come to their home and take a statement. According to her, he's too shaken up to come to the station." Cooper continued, "I bet he's trembling alright. Probably petrified his wife will find out who he's been shacked up with for a couple of days."

CHAPTER 12

JACKIE TRUMPLETON, REAL ESTATE AGENT: PHASE TWO

Phase two was finding her dream home, and location, location, location was everything.

Even though the real estate market was continuously plummeting, Jackie decided this was an opportune time to become the broker of her own real estate company. She had to find the right property for her venture. She knew what she wanted and spent weeks searching. She needed a large house that could be a combination home and office. Privacy was of utmost importance, even if it was contradictory and detrimental to the visibility of a real estate company.

But every time she thought she found the right property, zoning laws were an issue. It would be either residential only or commercial only. She considered whether her dream home existed. Jackie was determined not to become despondent. *Good things come to those who wait; patience is a virtue*, she constantly reminded herself. She kept up the due diligence and searched religiously.

Then one day during her walk-jog-pretend run, she passed a closed, assisted living facility at the end of a cul de sac in Occoquan, Virginia. *How many times have I been near this building in the last year? At least fifty.* Her mind started racing. She took the earplugs to her iPhone out of her ears and turned off the music to really examine the property. It is perfect, she said aloud and then looked around quickly to see if anyone heard or saw her talking to herself. She was alone in her daydream.

The building didn't have a for sale sign on the property, but so what. She thought it was too large for her plans, but that was okay. As she continued to mull over and assess the shell of the building, all her dreams started connecting like the innies and outies of a jigsaw puzzle. The property was enclosed inside a black, wrought iron fence, and was adjacent to the Occoquan River, which gave the property an island-like ambiance. As she semicircled the building, there was plenty of parking on the side, away from busybodies. Tall, mature trees stood forty to fifty feet on two sides of the property and a humongous weeping willow, at least sixty feet wide, sprawled the front lawn. The location was perfect.

She squinted to read the papers on the windows of the double doors. She was hoping against hope that the building was not going to be torn down and something like a Public Storage facility built in its place. Ever since the real estate market fiasco, homeowners were being foreclosed left and right, and storage facilities were popping up like 7-Elevens, one everywhere you looked, which became a temporary shelter for displaced owners' furnishings and personal belongings. Of course that was a foolhardy assessment. There were only million dollar homes on Poplar Lane.

She didn't want to complete her walk-jog-pretend run. She couldn't. She was too excited about her find. She only hoped the property was for sale.

* * *

Finding out who owned the property was akin to looking for a needle in a haystack, only worse. Every call Jackie made thinking this time she had the correct owner of the property turned into a roadblock and disappointment. Either the owner was playing incognito or someone thought she wasn't serious. She needed a plan of attack. When Jackie wanted something, she didn't allow anyone or anything to obstruct her mission.

She called Nathaniel McManus, a balding, stocky white settlement attorney whose only three suits—black, blue, and gray—hung loosely on his frame because they were at least two sizes too large. Rumor had it that he was a much larger man, maybe fifty pounds or more, and after losing the excess weight, refused to buy smaller suits or have the ones he owned altered for fear he would regain the weight. Jackie used him for all her real estate transactions. He was brilliant, tactful, and forthright, and she enjoyed working with him over the last fifteen years. She dialed his office number from memory.

"Nate," she said, after the familiar pleasantries, "I need a humongous favor. I found a property that I am interested in purchasing, but I keep hitting a brick wall." She gave him the address.

After she hung up the phone, Jackie thought about all the vendors she contracted with over the years. It never occurred to her that they were white until her African-American peers blasted her for not using blacks from the community. "It's the right thing to do," they said. She had been color-blind and was mortified by the oversight. She immediately changed the status quo but wasn't happy with the outcome. A buyer, a seller, a vendor, or someone got shafted one way or the other. This reflected badly on her and she wasn't about to deal with any chaos. After one, and at maximum two, neglected or negative incidents, she said, "not on my watch." She wouldn't give anybody an opportunity to strikeout and tarnish her profession, no matter their race. This was her livelihood. And if you displayed that you weren't excellent in every aspect of your business, there was no way you'd bring that nonsense knocking at her door.

CHAPTER 13

HOME OF ROCHELLE & CLYDE HARISTON

Lieutenant Neathers, Sergeant Gable, and Detective Lindon pulled into the driveway of Rochelle and Clyde Hariston's home, located in the secluded Lake Barcroft neighborhood, nestled between Four Mile Run bike trail on the west and Glencarlyn Park on the south in Arlington, Virginia. They drove in three separate police vehicles, something Mrs. Hariston requested not be done because this kind of criminal activity didn't happen in their neighborhood.

Once they entered Barcroft, they were in the midst of tree-lined streets that bordered immaculate, older homes on very spacious lots with manicured lawns and beautiful greenery and fragrant flowers in bloom everywhere. The streets were still, definitely not what they normally encountered when called out on an emergency call.

Well, at least we didn't arrive with our sirens blaring, Neathers thought.

A woman they presumed was Mrs. Hariston opened the door before they had an opportunity to knock.

"Thank you for coming discreetly," she said. She didn't try to hide her annoyance.

"Good evening ma'am," the lieutenant said, ignoring her sarcasm. "I'm Lieutenant Neathers and coming up the sidewalk are Sergeant Gable and Detective Lindon. May we come in?"

She stepped aside, pointed, and said, "My husband is straight ahead through that door."

"We'll follow you," Neathers said. Training taught them never to allow the suspect, or anyone for that matter, to follow them, and never enter a room unprepared. *Only God knows what could be waiting on the other side to harm us.*

Mrs. Hariston's shoulder brushed his arm as she passed him brusquely. He knew it was deliberate but let it slide, only because she was a woman. If it had been a man pulling that trick, he would have shoved him roughly against the wall and handcuffed his ass.

As they entered what appeared to be the living room, Mr. Hariston was sitting in a chair with his head in his hands. He looked up when his wife called his name and then stood. The lieutenant went through the introductions again.

Mr. Hariston said, "Please call me Clyde."

"Okay, Clyde it is," the lieutenant said.

Both men and Clyde's wife sat down while the sergeant and detective remained standing, as if on guard.

"You want to tell us what happened," Lieutenant Neathers began, and opened his small spiral notebook.

Clyde's eyes didn't meet the lieutenant's as he spoke. Nor did he make eye contact with his wife. "I guess it was around six o'clock a couple of weeks ago when I went running in Four Mile Run Park."

"You *guess* it was six o'clock or you *guess* it was two weeks ago? Which is it?"

"No, it was definitely six o'clock and it was two weeks ago."

"And you waited until now to contact the police," Neathers said.

"I was too embarrassed. I didn't want to call at all. It was the wife's idea."

"Six in the morning or evening," Neathers asked.

"The evening," Rochelle butted in.

"I'm training for my third marathon," Clyde continued, "so that weekend was my long run. I run a six-minute mile so this was twenty miles. I had planned to be out for at least two hours. I was about forty-five minutes into my run, when this woman comes out of nowhere and bumps into me, knocking both of us to the ground. I was okay, but she appeared discombobulated. I asked her if she was okay and she said that she wasn't, she felt dizzy. I helped her to a nearby bench. I wanted to call nine-one-one but she quickly recovered saying she'd be fine. She looked fine to me."

"I bet she did," Rochelle said, cutting him off.

"Ma'am," Lindon said, approaching her with an outstretched hand. "Please let your husband talk without interrupting."

Rochelle rolled her eyes and turned her head to peer out the window.

As Lindon watched the Haristons—thin, tall husband and short, fat wife—she kept wanting to chuckle. She didn't know why but she knew it had to do with their image. It was disconcerting and became difficult for her to concentrate. She was glad Gable was there for backup just in case something untoward happened.

Clyde was still talking. "As I stood to leave," he said, "she asked me to stay with her a while. I looked at my watch and noticed my Runmeter had been stopped for fifteen minutes."

"What's a Runmeter?" Neathers asked, acting uninformed.

Clyde gave the lieutenant a patronizing look and picked up where he left off as if he hadn't been interrupted. "It's an advanced iPhone app that runners use to record distance, elevation, time, and speed. I had already lost about two point five miles. I really wanted to continue my run. She told me to go ahead. I remember her saying something cynical like, don't let me put a damper on your plans. I was embarrassed that she noticed my desire to get away; so in order not to look like a complete asshole...."

Rochelle grunted and said under her breath, "that's exactly what you are—a lying asshole."

The detective gave her the "you've got one more time" stare.

If Clyde heard his wife, he acted as if he hadn't. "So, I sat back down and asked how I could help. While she was talking, runners I had passed eight miles back were sprinting by us."

"What did she look like?" Detective Lindon interjected.

"I didn't really notice," Clyde said.

Neathers glanced at the wife and she had daggers shooting from her eyes as she watched her husband relay the story he knew was her second time hearing. It was obvious she didn't believe one word he was alleging.

"So, you're telling us a woman appears out of nowhere and you don't notice anything about her, not one thing," Gable said. His incredulity was evident.

"What was she wearing?" he asked.

"I don't know."

"Did you notice the color of her hair?"

"No I didn't."

"Was she white, black, Hispanic?"

"I don't know. I don't recall anything. Nothing at all." Clyde finally looked up at Neathers. "Are you a runner?" he asked.

"No," Neathers said, staring at Clyde with penetrating eyes.

Clyde dismissed the lieutenant. "Are you two runners?" he asked, turning his attention away from Neathers' glare toward Gable and Lindon.

They both replied no, which was a lie. Gable had run the Boston Marathon twice and the New York City ING marathon once. Lindon had run two half marathons—the Ninth Annual Winnipeg Police Service Marathon and the Calgary Police Marathon. They had no intention of interacting with Hariston about anything that wasn't related to the alleged crime.

"Well, if you were runners," Clyde sounded sarcastic, "you would know that one-track focus. I concentrate on nothing else but my desire to beat my six-minute mile."

Neathers decided to take a more aggressive approach with Clyde because they weren't learning anything new or different about this alleged kidnapping than what had been reported earlier. Neathers thought Clyde's story might be hampered because his wife was in the room.

"Mr. Hariston, do you need your wife to leave the room so you can talk in private? Is that why you're stalling, ducking our inquiries, and giving obscure answers?" Neathers asked.

"It's Clyde," he said, holding up his hand.

"I'm not leaving this room," Rochelle said. "This is my house."

Neathers looked over at Gable and Lindon. "Please escort Mrs. Hariston out of this room—now!" he said.

As the sergeant and detective approached her, Lindon said, "Do we need to assist you, Mrs. Hariston?"

The image suddenly had a name. *Jack Sprat could eat no fat, his wife could eat no lean, and between them both, they licked the platter clean.* "Oh god," Lindon thought, "this is not the time for this silliness. Stop it," she reprimanded herself.

Rochelle stood up angrily, turning the chair over and marched out of the room, grumbling that this was her house and how dare some police officers come into her home and tell her she had to leave the room.

Clyde started, "Look, I'm telling the truth. I really don't know what happened. One moment I'm sitting on the bench and the next moment I'm waking up in a bed with no idea how I got there. I've been going over and over this in my mind and I don't remember anything."

"If you don't remember anything, how do you know you were raped?" Neathers asked.

"I said that to the wife because she kept badgering me about waking up in a strange woman's bed and MIA for two days."

Neathers stared at him. "Huh," he said, acting as if he had no clue what the acronym stood for.

"Missing in action," Clyde said, disregarding the lieutenant's pretend ignorance. "I told her I didn't have sex and if I had, then it would have been rape. That set her off. She demanded I call the police. Said if I didn't, she would, and accused me of not wanting to make the call because I was a bold-faced liar."

"Why would your wife badger you, Clyde?" Calling him by his first name left a bad taste in the lieutenant's mouth—it felt too personal. "Are you having an affair?" Neathers' fixed, ominous stare put Clyde on edge.

Clyde jumped up and so did Neathers. Gable and Lindon approached, standing shoulder-to-shoulder with their boss, ready to restrain Mr. Hariston if necessary. "This wasn't an affair!" Clyde said. "This is exactly the reason why I didn't want to report this."

"Please sit back down, Mr. Hariston," Neathers said, feeling at ease addressing him in a formal manner. "Why don't you just start back at the beginning and try visualizing everything that occurred."

Clyde sat back down. Neathers sat back down, and Gable and Lindon retreated.

"Okay. Like I said, we were sitting on the bench and I wanted to leave but the woman started complaining of dizziness. I asked if she wanted a sip of my water but realized my camelback was dry. She pulled a bottle of water out of her backpack...." He started mulling over something. "Wait a minute. Maybe she wasn't really a runner; she was lugging a backpack instead of wearing a fanny pack."

"Hmm, that's all," Neathers muttered.

"No. She told me my shoestrings were untied. As I bent down, it dawned on me that I was wearing Five Fingers. I immediately sat up and turned toward her to ask what she meant."

Neathers displayed ignorance again and asked, "What are five fingers?"

Clyde gave him that "you're really not a runner look," and said, "They're these great running shoes that look like a glove with fingers, but for toes. They make you feel like you're running barefoot," he said.

Neathers turned up his nose. "Sounds like faggot shoes to me." His goal was to antagonize Mr. Hariston. Neathers didn't succeed.

Clyde continued as if he hadn't been deliberately sidetracked. He had seen many CSI reruns and wasn't about to allow this know-it-all cop get under his skin.

"Dust, dirt, or something blew in my face," he said. "One minute I'm waking up in a strange bed and the next minute I'm back on the trail."

Lindon walked toward Mr. Hariston. "That's it?" she asked. *Jack Sprat could eat no fat. Jack Sprat is a liar.*

Before Mr. Hariston had a chance to open his mouth, she said, "Stop it, Jack!" The command was loud.

"Excuse me," Mr. Hariston said.

The lieutenant gave her a reproving look.

The sergeant gave her an "ah, you're in trouble" look.

"Detective, do you have anything else to ask Mr. Hariston?" the lieutenant asked.

"No sir. I apologize for the outburst," she looked at the lieutenant and avoided eye contact with Mr. Hariston.

The lieutenant turned to Mr. Hariston. "Are you sure there's nothing else you want to tell us?"

"That's all I remember," Clyde said.

* * *

What Clyde refused to disclose to anyone, especially his maniacal wife, that when he woke up, a woman was seated in an oversized chair about fifteen feet from the bed he was lying on. The room was semidark and he couldn't see her face.

He'll never forget her words. The awful news she shared assaulted his senses. She was direct, straightforward, and without empathy. "You were given an *Ora Quick* test ...,"

"A what? You gave me what!"

She ignored him and continued on, "which diagnosed you HIV positive. You need to get retested by a professional," she said.

"What? What the hell is going on here?" he almost screamed. "You tested my blood?"

"No. It was a quick oral swab."

"What are you talking about? Who are you? Where am I?" He was rambling.

The woman had no regard for his discomfort. "You won't do," she said. She stood up and approached the bed. Before he could react, the same dust, dirt, or something was blown into his face again and he woke up on the same bench, with no memory, as if no time had elapsed at all.

* * *

Once the officers were outside, the lieutenant demanded to know what happened in there.

"I'm sorry, sir. This nursery rhyme keeps ringing in my ears. I can't shake it."

"The only one who gives a command when I'm present is me. Understood?"

"Yes sir."

Gable snickered.

"Stop it!" the lieutenant said, and they all went to their cruisers.

With sirens blasting, the noise shattered the stillness, as they exited Lake Barcroft.

CHAPTER 14

CHIEF MAURICE JOHNSTON

When Lieutenant Neathers, Sergeant Gable, and Detective Lindon returned to the police station, Officer Cooper approached them. "Lieutenant, the chief wants to see you pronto," he said.

"Why, what's going on?" Neathers asked.

"Another man has been reported missing."

"What?" Neathers, Gable, and Lindon said simultaneously.

"You've got to be kidding," Neathers said.

"Nope. It's for real," the officer said.

* * *

Chief Johnston was standing with his back to the door looking out the dirty window. There was no view to speak of. Only the side of another brick building straight ahead, an empty parking lot to the right, and rows and rows of bungalows, craftsmans, and cape cods, as far as the eye could see to the left.

He turned when he heard the door to his office open.

"Neathers," he said, "what in the world is happening? Two men are missing on our watch?"

"Well, Chief, we really don't know whether Clyde Hariston was missing or not, or if he just took off for a couple of days."

The chief cocked his head.

"You have to sit in the same room with his wife to understand what I mean. She was prepared to chew him up, regurgitate him, and spit him out like the piece of lying sack of shit he is."

"So I take it you don't believe he was taken against his will."

"No fucking way, Chief!" Neathers said.

The chief gave him that "don't disrespect my title" look.

"Sorry, boss, but Gable and Lindon share my observation too. What have you got? I came right here."

"Ian Ferguson has been missing almost a week. His wife said they had a nasty, low-down dirty fight and he left the house in a rage. She said she waited for him to return because she was going to stay with a girlfriend but he never came back home. She thought he had just gone somewhere to cool off. But when his boss called a few days later inquiring about Ian's whereabouts because he hadn't shown up or called into work, she knew something was horribly wrong because that wasn't like her husband."

The cogs in Neathers' head were spinning. Another husband missing inside of two weeks. That was no coincident.

* * *

"Okay, listen up," Chief Johnston said, as he entered the squad room, which was rowdy as usual during first shift. He didn't know if it was due to the transition from graveyard shift or what, nor did he care. All he was cognizant of was that by the time he was standing in front of the podium, it was like E.F. Hutton, "when he started talking, everyone listened." The chatter ceased on cue, as if someone had hit a mute button, and all eyes were on the chief, who was looking down at a piece of paper handed to him in his unscheduled, early morning meeting by a member of the five-person Arlington County Board.

"We have a second missing man," he said, scratching his head in disbelief. "Who's on this case with Neathers? Can't recall who I assigned to it."

Gable and Lindon raised their hands.

"Oh come on," came a shout from someone in the back of the room. "You really think this new case is connected to the woman's husband who we all know faked his disappearance to cover his whoring around."

Some officers turned in their chairs and looked at one another. You could tell from the nodding of their heads they concurred with this assessment. The officers didn't believe there was any kind of connection, although they thought it was strange.

"Until we look into these two cases to ascertain if there are any similarities," the chief said, "we won't jump to any conclusions about what these two disappearances are or are not. Neathers and his team talked to the alleged kidnapped victim and his wife last night and got nowhere with that. We may need to bring the husband in without his wife and play hardball."

An officer in the center of the room had his hand raised.

The chief gave him the nod to speak. "What's the likelihood that they are connected?"

"I don't know," the chief said. "We need to figure out if the disappearances, kidnappings, or whatever we want to call them are connected. Are they intentional or is foul play involved?"

"So what is your thinking here, Chief—that we might have a serial kidnapper on our hands," Sergeant Gable said, with total skepticism.

Remarks and inquiries started ricocheting around the room.

"When was the last time anybody heard of a grown man being kidnapped?" someone asked.

Another officer remarked, "There's not even a ransom or demand of any kind."

"We need some concrete information," Lindon said.

The chief allowed the informal interrogation and friendly banter among his officers to go on for approximately four minutes before he interrupted. "Officially, it's not a serial kidnapping because only two men have been reported missing. If a third man comes up missing, it could possibly be serial," he said. "But let's not get ahead of ourselves. First, we've got to look into it. Something is going on. We have one man claiming he was abducted and now we have Evelyn Ferguson up in arms about her missing husband. We have to get a handle on whatever is going on before the media gets wind of it. Or ..." he raised his hands and mimicked a conductor, and on prompt, the officers said in unison, "We'll have a circus on our hands."

The chief looked at Detective Lindon. "Get me some stats on missing men ASAP."

"Yes sir, she said."

Before the morning session adjourned, a third man, Joe Bradford, from across the Potomac River in Prince Georges County, was reported missing to the Bowie dispatched center.

* * *

In all their years as police officers, and it was a significant number combined, Detective Lindon, along with her comrades, had not witnessed or heard of a missing adult male case unless it involved a robbery. She was unprepared for the data she collected and discussed it with Lieutenant Neathers and Sergeant Gable before forwarding it to the chief. After their review, the lieutenant gave her the go ahead to share what she found, and they went to the chief's office.

As soon as they were seated, Lindon proceeded. "I got the majority of my facts from the National Center for Missing Adults, which is based in Phoenix. To date, they have tracked about forty-eight thousand active cases. I spoke to a desk person there and was told that about twenty-six thousand of these missing adults are men."

Lindon heard an expletive from the chief and looked up from the papers. "I know, I thought the same thing too," she said. "Who would have known that there are this many missing adult males? It's not like we're in Afghanistan."

"This is incredible," the chief said. "What else?"

"We already know that the majority of adult abductions are usually women taken by men they know. But Chief, check this out, something that really astounded us. About four out of ten missing men are white, three are black, and two are Latino. Right now, we have two missing black men and another black man alleging he was abducted."

The chief shot his hand out, all fingers splayed, and interrupted Lindon. "Stop! What do you mean two missing and one alleged? I thought the count was two," he looked at Neathers for an explanation.

"I guess we should have mentioned that first, Chief. Before we came in here, another husband was reported missing from PG County."

The chief spun around in his chair and slammed his fist into the blackboard.

Neathers, Gable, and Lindon jumped and looked at one another startled.

"How many of those missing men are psychos?" Gable asked.

Lindon snarled at him. "The politically correct term is psychiatric problems," she said. "Approximately forty-two hundred, and there are other subgroups of missing men:

people with drug or alcohol addiction and elderly persons suffering from some type of dementia."

"Good work, Lindon," the chief said.

"Thanks boss. Even with these stats, though, we and the criminal experts know adult kidnappings are rare. When it occurs, it's usually associated with a robbery."

"Do you think these men are still in the area?" Gable asked.

"I don't know," Lindon said. "I hope so. If they have been abducted and taken to a second location, their odds of getting out alive are slim to nil."

CHAPTER 15

JOE & DOLORES BRADFORD

Joe Bradford was thrice married. Over the last eleven years he had way too many extramarital affairs to count while married to his first two wives. Not surprising to anyone who knew him, those marriages ended in nasty, violent, irreparable divorces.

He was currently married to Dolores in what can only be described as a tumultuous relationship.

Joe did not view his behavior or affairs as aberrant or shameful. He believed it was in his blood to be anti-monogamous.

When his first wife confronted him about his cheating ways, wanting to know why he was subjecting her to this mistreatment, he stuck to his guns. "I'm a virile man with an excessive sexual appetite and cravings that one woman alone can't satisfy," he said.

She slapped him so hard, which was totally unexpected, that he would have sworn he saw stars. And before he could recoup, she gave him a backhanded blow that landed him face-to-face with the kitchen's linoleum floor.

When his second wife asked him the same exact thing four years later, he had never forgotten wife number one's reaction to his smart aleck quip. This time he was prepared. "It's not natural to be monogamous," he said, and jerked his head back, ignoring her murderous stare.

Then, he couldn't help himself. He had to ask. "Why is it that women are never satisfied? I give you everything and it's still not enough."

He couldn't keep his narcissistic trap shut. "As long as I'm providing for you and fucking you two times a week," he said, forgetting common decency and respect for the woman he vowed to love and cherish, obviously thinking he was kicking it with the guys, "so what if I have a mistress on the side."

As soon as the words escaped his lips, he remembered that his wife, twelve years his junior, had taken a kickboxing class and before he could react to protect himself or take cover, she was in the air—adrenaline had fueled her—and hauled off and kicked him in his cajones. He was in so much pain, he couldn't even howl, much less move. He laid there for hours curled up in a knot, left abandoned, and cried, holding his swollen nuts.

When Dolores, his present wife, confronted him, he simply said, "I don't know" and he hurriedly crossed to the far side of the bedroom. He needed to explain, but he also needed to be on guard for an attack. "I don't understand why only human beings are subjected to monogamy." All he expected was a rational answer to what his wife and former wives viewed as an irrational question? "My behavior, which you find unacceptable," he measured his next words, "has been a male tradition for generations. It may even be hereditary and handed down through the Bradford gene pool."

He eyed Dolores to gauge her distance.

"My great-granddaddy had two families in the same town, albeit on opposite sides. It wasn't until I graduated from college that I learned he had children practically the same age as grandpa. You knew this because I told you. Grandpa was known as a rolling stone. Only rumors dictated how many homes he actually had." He was trying to be funny. Dolores didn't a crack smile. "And dad had a mistress for twenty-five years and the entire town of Warren County, including relatives, knew of the affair. But mother, she feigned ignorance all those years. Even on her deathbed, she swore that the best part of her life was being married to my father," he said, shaking his head.

He believed Dolores pretended ignorance too, because every single time after one of his cheating, scandalous affairs, all he'd have to do, which wasn't much, was give her a dozen roses, make love to her all night long, and whisper sweet nothings in her ear, and the scattered stars in her world realigned.

She would forgive him.

"If the situation had been reversed," Joe thought, "it was no way in hell he would allow any woman to trample his feelings." He kept that to himself.

The entire time he communicated his logic to Dolores, she didn't move a muscle, didn't flinch, nor did she speak a word. Joe knew from the menacing look in her eyes, he better tread cautiously in the future. *Even an alley cat has only nine lives.*

He figured it was about time to swoon her with a dozen roses and makeup sex.

* * *

Joe's latest conquest was Vicky Jones and she was time enough for him.

After listening to the dreaded recording on Vicky's cell phone, he left a message.

"Hi Sweetie, I'm on my way," Joe spoke into the car speaker phone. "Vicky, pick up." He dragged out her name, "Vickkkkkky honey, please pick up. Okay, you must be out. I was calling to see if you wanted me to pick up something to eat from Whole Foods."

Joe disliked calling Vicky's cell. He couldn't stand the familiar announcement to sound in his ear. *Hi, you have reached Mrs. Jones.* Then unceremoniously, Billy Paul starts serenading, *Me and Mrs. Jones.* Joe despised the message. Usually he disconnected the call before the recording started. He suspected she was flaunting their relationship, deliberately announcing to the world that he was having an affair with another man's wife. He was indignant the first time he heard the message. They argued for a whole week. That was an understatement. They were close to boxing. Vicky could care less about his anger. After all, he was married too.

The second week there was stone cold silence. Since neither would budge on their positions, they resorted to self-imposed timeouts. They retreated to their own homes, their own lives.

Joe relented first. He felt they were both acting childish. He wasn't getting sex at home and now he wasn't getting sex from his mistress. And he bedamn if he was going to be the "first" Bradford man to get blue balls. He had to end this nonsense before it took on a life of its own.

Vicky was tickled to death that Joe caved first. She was only minutes away from being the first to call. The only reason she delayed was because she was going over different scenarios with her girlfriend. *What should I do when he calls? Suppose he doesn't call, should I call him first? How long should I wait before I call him?*

Vicky had gotten to the apartment first. She learned of this lover's haven when their affair got serious. Joe lied, told her that when he got married—he neglected to mention Dolores was his third wife—that he kept his apartment in DC, unbeknownst to his wife, to be closer to his job. Joe bought this lover's nest after his divorce from his first wife for the sole purpose of taking his countless lovers there for one-night stands.

Vicky listened to Joe's message. She had been in the shower when he called. It had been almost an hour since he called and he still had not shown up. She was getting worried. She sure hoped he wasn't in another one of those pissy mood swings because of her phone recording.

She tried calling his cell phone and when he couldn't be reached, she left a message. "Baby, where are you? I'm at the apartment. Call me, I'm concerned," she said.

When he didn't show or call by the second hour, she called his home number. She dialed star six seven before the number to block her number. When his wife answered, she hung up. She waited ten minutes and called again hoping he would pick up. The receiver was picked up but no one said hello. Vicky heard breathing on the line but she didn't say anything either. Then, out of nowhere, a woman screamed, "SLUT, you have the nerve to dial this number! That bastard is dead!"

And the phone line went dead.

Vicky was still shaking thirty minutes later after she heard his wife's hateful barrage of insults. She tried to recall exactly what Dolores had said. Had Dolores killed Joe or was she going to kill Joe? She didn't know. She wavered whether or not she should call the police. She tried Joe's cell again and heard only his recording. After fifty minutes, almost three-and-a-half hours since Joe called and left a message, and still no word from him, she dialed nine-one-one and informed the police that Dolores Bradford told her that she murdered her husband, Joe Bradford.

* * *

It amazed Dolores that Joe viewed her as an imbecile, a woman so stupid that she was oblivious to his affairs, one after another. Either that or he could care less whether she knew or not, and it probably was the latter. She had actually given up on their marriage the day following their honeymoon when he flirted with every bikini-wearing woman in sight, while ignoring her. She realized then that Joe was a prick, a self-absorbed man with no morals or conscience.

She seriously considered murdering him but something always deterred her. It was almost as if he was clairvoyant, had a sixth sense that something ominous was about to happen. Every time she contemplated taking him out, blowing his brain to smithereens, he would do something unexpected like bring home her favorite Chinese food— shrimp egg foo young, steamed dumplings, and crab rangoon—or surprise her with two dozen roses, all a different color, except red. He had never given her red roses. *But that's okay*, she thought, *what goes around comes around and that day has arrived. That no good bastard is going to pay for the way he has mistreated me over the last year. The nerve of that slut to call our home.*

Dolores planned to shoot Joe as he entered their bedroom that night, no matter how late it was. *How dare he come to me after leaving that whore's bed?*

She had driven to Costco earlier and purchased one item—red roses wrapped in four cellophane packs containing fifteen roses each.

When she returned home, she urinated in a vase, clipped the stems on the roses, and placed them in the vase. She set the huge arrangement on his nightstand. "After I kill the bastard," she thought, "I'll empty the vase of red roses with piss over his dead body."

* * *

The following morning Dolores got a visit from a captain and lieutenant from the Prince Georges County Bowie Police Department.

"Is your husband home, Mrs. Bradford?" the captain asked.

"No, he is not."

"Where is he?"

"Probably with that whore he's been sleeping with. He didn't come home last night."

"May we come inside?"

"No you may not."

"Is there a reason you won't invite us inside?"

"Do you have a warrant?" She looked at the captain, then the lieutenant. She remembered that the forty-five caliber Glock was still on the bed in plain view. She couldn't recall whether Joe had a permit for it or not.

"I don't but we can come back with one."

"I'm not going anywhere. I'll be here."

The captain heard the scanner go off in the police vehicle and excused himself.

The lieutenant took over. "Mrs. Bradford, we received a report that you informed a Victoria Jones that you murdered your husband last night."

Dolores stifled a snort. She didn't know Joe's new slut's name; now she did. "I don't know what you're talking about," she lied.

"Do you know a Victoria Jones?" he asked.

"She's screwing my no-good for nothing husband. No, I don't know her."

"Mrs. Bradford, please step outside."

"Why?"

He didn't answer. He needed her to step outside her home in order to arrest her on suspicion of murdering Joe Bradford, her husband.

Dolores displayed a poker face and adeptly stepped back from the door. Before the lieutenant could react, she slammed it in his face.

That whore, she thought. *She's dead too!*

* * *

The lieutenant stood at the closed door, furious. He wanted to kick the door in but there was nothing he could do. He had no justifiable reason; and, as Mrs. Bradford noted, they had no warrant.

He heard the captain call his name and walked back to the cruiser's driver side where the captain was seated. The vehicle's door was open.

"Listen to this," the captain said.

The police scanner was turned to the Alexandria, Virginia, frequency. They both listened with disbelief. "Please be on the lookout for Ron Brown, an African-American adult male, between forty-five and fifty, who has not been seen since he left work on Friday evening. He has shoulder-length dreads or braids and a goatee. He is of light complexion, about six feet two, and a hundred eighty-five pounds. He was wearing a blue blazer, yellow

V-neck pullover, blue jeans, and loafers. There's a possibility that Ron Brown could be connected to the missing
men from Arlington and PG County," the dispatcher said.

CHAPTER 16

THE MINI MANSION

The closing date had finally arrived and the settlement process went without a hiccup. Jackie would have been surprised if there had been any surprises. Through Nate and his settlement staff's thorough research and tenaciousness, they found the owner of the closed senior assistant living facility and handled all the details.

After many revised contracts, numerous calls back-and-forth, up-and-down negotiation tactics with the owner that happened to be a limited partnership, and a take it or leave it threat thrown out to Jackie from the sellers, the deal almost aborted. Jackie didn't tolerate ultimatums. She didn't give a rat's ass about cutting off her nose to spite her face, nor did she care about consequences. So, without batting an eyelash, she walked away from the deal. She and the partners were a hundred thousand dollars apart from ratifying the contract, which were monies she would have to put up because the appraisal came in low. Her offer was to split the difference and the partners said, "We are not even close."

Jackie said, "Good luck."

When the limited partnership contacted Nate twenty-one days later, they had not heard a peep from him about the now null and void contract, to inquire if Ms. Trumpleton would reconsider accepting the last offer on the table, Nate followed Jackie's pre-scripted comeback. "She will only ratify the contract at the appraised value."

A meeting of the minds ensued and a deal was finalized to purchase the property.

After settlement, Jackie stood up, thanked Nate for a job well done, "as usual," she intimated, and left his office without so much as a glance at the limited partners.

The whole ordeal—from discovering the property to closing on it—took approximately five months.

* * *

The money was not an issue for Jackie; it didn't even create a blip in her consciousness. The limited partners' condescending attitude was the crippling factor and error.

Not only had she been a shrewd and savvy investor—hoarding the majority of the income she earned from selling real estate—she was also netting a handsome three percent commission on the purchase of the property.

Jackie was in seventh heaven when she looked at her Certificates of Deposit. She had followed Suze Orman's advice to a tee and memorized one of her quotes: *Money is such an amazing teacher. What you choose to do with your money shows whether you are truly powerful or powerless.* Jackie's goal was to be powerful and she reminded herself everyday of her objective, and following through paid off big time.

Finally, more than three decades later, she was going to realize a long delayed, but never forgotten dream. She could scarcely believe that her dream would now come to fruition. *If you can imagine it, you can create it. If you can dream it, you can become it.* She believed William Arthur Ward's quote was meant for her.

Nothing and nobody would ever again control or have power over her destiny. She loved being in control. And this power combined with her dream was about to become a reality.

* * *

Jackie sent a text message to each of the associates eighteen months before their scheduled vacation in South Africa. *Emergency conference call Thursday night at ten Eastern Time. Exciting news.*

The women were stunned about this interruption into their private lives. This was definitely not the norm. It was an unspoken rule, although an informal one, that they didn't converse with one another prior to their reunions. And until now, there had never been a reason to do so.

Bernadette was watching television when her cell phone vibrated. "This must be serious," she said aloud, as she reread the message. Mixed emotions were swirling around in her head. *Emergency. Exciting news.* She had to endure two whole days of anticipation to hear this news. *Bummer.* She wanted to know right this second. She vacillated, went back and forth, whether to contact Jackie or not to find out what was so urgent.

"Wonder what's up," Ruby thought, as she read the text that just popped up on her phone. This intrusion had never happened before. She hoped one of the girl's wasn't cancelling. The text did say exciting news. *But, if it's exciting, why the emergency and why can't it wait until we get together next year in South Africa.* The text was contradictory.

These get-togethers every other year were the only times she was able to let her hair down and have no cares, no worries about anything. It was the one thing that kept her surviving every day. She hoped Jackie wasn't cancelling.

By the time Laura saw the text message, she was too emotionally exhausted to react immediately. Her day was hectic, one emergency after another every hour on the hour, or so it seemed. The entire high-rise complex she managed was under fire. There were leaking pipes everywhere and residents were phoning left and right to complain that water was seeping into their units.

As soon as her engineering crew got one emergency resolved, another one popped up without warning.

The previous week the fire inspector found an underground oil tank adjacent to the loading dock that had been buried for over thirty years. The association would have to contact the Environmental Protection Agency to ensure the tank was up to code and not releasing any hazardous substances into the soil that could contaminate groundwater. If the EPA found the storage tank leaking, the financial burden on the association could be ruinous.

They had already tapped into the reserve funds to replace the roof and convert copper pipes to CPVC plastic pipes.

My building won't win "Best Condominium Association Award" this year. If there weren't enough problems already, there was a scandal about the board president and treasurer. Monies had been embezzled and residents were openly accusing them.

The association is going bankrupt, she thought. Laura felt like crying at the prospect of Jackie cancelling. She needed this vacation more than the girls could fathom.

Nadine, on the other hand, was in a totally different mental state when she read the text. *I hope the vacation is being cancelled*, she prayed. She had just cursed at, and hung up the phone on, the sixth bill collector that day. The harassing phone calls had started promptly at eight-thirty that morning and here it was more than twelve hours later and this one collector had already left seven messages. "This call is for Nadine Douglas concerning nonpayment of your Visa bill. We need you to call 1-800 555-1212 immediately. If we do not hear from you within twenty-four hours, we will have no other choice but to take legal action against you."

If the vacation had to be cancelled, she reasoned, it would be hunky dory because she still had not paid one cent toward her portion of the South Africa trip. This was her fault too and now the total amount for the trip had almost doubled. She was too ashamed to admit to the girls that she was struggling to come up with the funds. Ninety-five hundred dollars was a lot of money on her salary and shoestring budget; she was still paying off the 2012 trip to Greece.

* * *

On Thursday night, exactly at ten, the conference call was connected. There was only breathing heard until Jackie began the conversation.

"Hi girls," she started, assuming everyone was on the line. Each exchanged hellos. "I know this is not the norm," Jackie said, "but I would like to cancel our vacation trip to South Africa next year."

She heard one of them suck in her breath; she didn't know who. Before anyone could say anything, Jackie rushed forward. "We definitely have enough time to get refunds, so we will not lose any money."

She expected someone to interrupt but no one did, so she continued. "Remember our dream to one day retire together," she said.

Nothing. You could hear a pin drop across all the intertwining Cat5 cables.

"Well, we can scratch that off the bucket list. I have found our retirement Mecca."

Bernadette spoke first. "Are you pulling our legs?" she asked, immediately forgetting all about the trip to South Africa.

"What do you mean?" Nadine asked. Her anticipation of the news to come was hopeful.

"I am not kidding," Jackie said. "Day before yesterday, I closed on a house. It is a done deal. Signed, sealed, and delivered." She paused and said softly so as not to appear bragging, "well, it is more like a mini mansion—seven bedrooms and seven bathrooms."

Jackie returned to a normal pitch. "After many near misses and plenty of bumps in the road, I finally signed my Jane Hancock on the deal. I was hesitant to get too excited before all the eyes were dotted and the tees were crossed. You are the first and only ones to hear the news."

"Where? How?" Ruby asked. She knew she was probing; something they didn't encourage. But this was different. This was gigantic, wonderful news that Jackie dropped on them out of the clear blue sky.

Then immediately, everyone broke the rule and even asked Jackie "none of your business" questions.

Jackie didn't flinch.

"How much is a mini mansion?" Bernadette interrupted. "It must have cost a fortune. You have *that* kind of money, Jackie," she said. Bernadette couldn't hide her shock. It was true that they had kept their private lives confidential over the years, but this announcement was significant. Yes, they had many rap sessions about one day retiring together, but Bernadette viewed those discussions as pipe dreams; not something that they would actually carry out. It was just girl talk, or so she had assumed.

Jackie responded. "In Occoquan, Virginia, about twenty-seven miles south of DC. I saved money over the years," she said, without divulging any details about her finances.

My finances are no one's business!

She continued. "Over the next three to six months, contractors are coming in to do some major renovations to remodel and update the place. I have hired designers to decorate too. So girls, since everything will be done in a few months, by the end of August, why not spend our vacation here in Virginia this year. This will give you four an opportunity to see where we will retire and whether you like the place and location. I think you will love it and what I have in store."

"But this year is an odd year," Ruby said. "Are we reverting to annual vacations again, which don't get me wrong, I definitely don't have a problem with changing. This will also give us an opportunity to pay our respects to 9-11 by visiting the Pentagon Memorial."

Nadine piped in. "So, what's our share?" She was anxious since she was already strapped for funds—all those cosmetic surgeries cost a mint—and Jackie had the audacity to change plans midstream and sprang this news on them with no pre-warning.

Jackie replied but Nadine wasn't sure she heard her correctly. "How much?" Nadine asked again.

"Nada," Jackie repeated, "It is a gift from me to you all."

There was total quiet on the four phone lines.

"Hello, are you all still there?" Jackie asked. She thought the conference line had disconnected. She hoped she had not miscalculated how the associates would take her news. *After all, it was she who dared to live the life she dreamed for herself. It was she who went forth and made her dreams come true.* And since she was happy, she envisioned everyone would be ecstatic too.

There was a clearing of the throat and again Bernadette was the first to speak. "Jackie, we all know you dance to the beat of your own drum. That's why we love you. So, if you're happy, if you're feeling good, then nothing else matters."

Jackie realized that Bernadette had quoted Robin Wright Penn. This simple acknowledgment brought tears to her eyes. "Gracias, Bernadette," she whispered. But Bernadette could hardly hear the thanks because Laura, Nadine, and Ruby were whooping it up.

Jackie told them she would email details and photos.

"See you in Virginia," all four associates said, and the phone connection went dead.

It had been twelve years since 9-11 and they would vacation again in an odd year commencing Labor Day.

CHAPTER 17

RON & RHONDA BROWN

Rhonda Brown was pissed off. Her husband, Ron, hadn't come home again last night. It had been three days since she had either seen or spoken to him.

"I've had it with that no good mutha," she seethed. She wasn't going to accept any more of his lies or excuses.

How did I get here anyway? she wondered.

Her older sister, Dee Dee, broke it down in layman's terms. "He must have a *big* dick!"

Dee Dee could be so crass.

"What else could it be?" she would ask. "You don't need him so either you're pressed or addicted. Which is it?"

Rhonda thought she had found her soul mate. He was the type of man she was always attracted to. Ron was six foot two, had a swagger to his walk, and sported long sideburns and a mustache. She disliked men with no facial hair. *Looked to feminine.*

He had a great sense of humor and was charismatic. No matter where he went, women eyes followed him. It didn't matter whether Rhonda was with him or not, holding hands or hugged up, the women kept their eyes glued on him. She used to be tickled pink by the other women's display of envy and would hold onto him even tighter. *This is my man.* It made her feel special.

Rhonda was average looking, standing shy of five feet, but she had a *Coca Cola* bottle figure. She knew men overlooked her one-size larger than full-size lips because she had big, stand-at-attention boobs, a washboard stomach, and a show-stopper butt.

She reminisced how she met Ron. It was 1980 and her lucky day. She had moved to Atlanta on a whim. Packed all her belongings in her brand new, Phoenix red convertible Volkswagen Beetle and hit the road. Drove through the night at seventy miles per hour for ten hours, only stopping for gas and a restroom break.

Rhonda moved into the YMCA on Peachtree Street because she didn't know anyone in Atlanta—no family, no friends, no distant cousins. She roomed with Stella Colvin from Alabama. They got along great until the day they met Ron and his brother, Allan, at a nearby park. The four of them were teasing, flirting, and joking around, but Ron gravitated, naturally, toward the light-skinned Stella, who had a round baby doll face, *and wouldn't you know it*, luscious-looking, pouty lips. Rhonda cringed.

Allan showed no interest whatsoever in Rhonda. Matter-of-fact, he playfully wrestled his older brother for Stella's attention.

As the dialogue between Stella and Ron wound down, Rhonda's outgoing personality started percolating. Ron asked Stella for her phone number and she gave him the number that all the young women shared—the coin-operated phone in the entry hallway of the YMCA.

As everyone was parting ways and saying goodbyes, Ron jokingly asked Stella to invite him to the Y for a sleepover.

"I'm not that kind of girl!" Stella said.

Before Ron could apologize and say he was kidding, he heard Rhonda say, "I am."

Ron and Allan's attention jerked from Stella to Rhonda.

Stella glared at Rhonda.

"I'm only kidding!" Rhonda said. She was appalled she said something so bold. It was unlike her.

Ron couldn't dismiss Rhonda's repartee. All the way home, even with Allan rambling on about something unrelated, all he could hear were Rhonda's words being frenziedly repeated in his head—"I am. I am. I am."

Stella didn't give Rhonda's immature, irrational declaration a second thought. She knew she was an attractive girl, way cuter than Rhonda and two years her senior. Stella had long, black wavy hair with curled eyelashes to match. She had the beauty but realized her body was no match for Rhonda's. Even though Stella was a few inches taller than Rhonda, she was carrying at least fourteen pounds more, which equated to two dress sizes. Stella never had any problems attracting men so she was hardly vexed about Ron's new fascination with Rhonda. After all, he had asked for her number, not Rhonda's.

* * *

The continuous ringing of the hallway phone woke Rhonda out of a deep sleep.

"Will someone please get the phone," she screamed. *Why should I have to answer the phone? It's never for me.* She hadn't once given out the number since she moved to Atlanta. She didn't know the number even if someone was interested in receiving it. The phone continued shrilling. She turned over in bed and was shocked to see the clock on the bedside table display ten minutes past noon. It took a couple of seconds to realize that she had slept half the day away.

She dragged out of bed and trudged down the hall to the phone, which wouldn't shut up. Now, it sounded as if it was screeching.

"Hello." She was annoyed by this intrusion into her sleep.

"Is Stella in?" the man asked.

Rhonda's heart skipped a beat. It was him. The man they met yesterday. "Daaamn!" she said under her breath.

"Excuse me," he said.

"Oh, I'm sorry." She was chagrined and couldn't believe she had actually said the expletive aloud. *I'm saying a lot of things out loud these days.* She rebounded quickly. "I was swearing at myself because I neglected to look to see if my roommate was in before trekking down the hall to get the phone," she fibbed.

"Is this Rhonda?"

"Yes." She held her breath.

"It's Ron. I met you yesterday."

And Stella. You met both of us.

"Oh hi," Rhonda said. She hoped she sounded detached. "Let me go get Stella," she said.

"Wait, I was really calling to talk to you."

Hmmm. You didn't ask to speak to me.

"Oh?" Rhonda said instead. She could hardly believe what she was hearing. A man actually chose her over the beautiful Stella. She was thrilled. *See momma,* she looked to heaven as if that's where her mother resided. *I can get a man.*

"Are you surprised?" he asked, interrupting her thoughts.

"Yes, and I also don't think it's a good idea because you asked my roommate for her number."

"But I wanted your number."

That day Ron and Rhonda's relationship began, and Stella and Rhonda's friendship ended.

* * *

"My sister is right," Rhonda thought, "the sex is ruling my common sense." But, it didn't answer why she loved this man more than she loved herself, enough to marry him and return to DC in '82.

Ron was a habitual liar and an addicted womanizer. He gave her Chlamydia, a sexually transmitted disease, and still, she put up with him and his antics.

And now this! Three whole days and not a peep from him and we are still considered newlyweds! This was a new low even for him. He had never stayed out more than one night before.

Rhonda had to make some hard choices. She should have left him last month when she found a new phone number in his wallet and inquired about it. *Yes, I knew if I went snooping around, I would find something.*

And he thought he was slick, telling her J.C. was a male coworker.

Yeah right, she thought.

She dialed the number and heard the same words she had heard many times before. The only difference was the bitch's name.

"May I speak to JC?" Rhonda said.

"This is Janine Charles. Who's calling?"

"Ron Brown's wife," she screamed. "Stay away from my husband!"

"Ron's married!" The woman sounded as if she was in a state of shock and disbelief.

Rhonda hung up the phone. That should have been the deathblow. Yet, she fail victim to his pleading and begging—he was sorry, it wouldn't happen again.

But it did happen again.

The next incident was when he didn't pick her up at two o'clock from her graveyard shift at Arthur Yates & Company. She had waited six full hours when he finally arrived disheveled at eight o'clock. Thank goodness all of her coworkers had left—gone home.

Her feelings of panic had escalated in the first hour, around three o'clock, fearing her husband was lying in a ditch somewhere helpless. By four o'clock, Rhonda was approaching disbelief. *Where is he?*

She rode the elevator back up to her office on the eleventh floor to see if Ron had left a message. No blinking red light signaled from her office phone. She called their home and the phone continued to ring. She went to the window and peered down at secluded Seventeenth Street and Connecticut Avenue. There was no movement at all. Of course not, it was four o'clock in the morning.

From eleven stories up, she felt she couldn't breathe. She had been off work for two hours and had not heard a word from her husband.

At five o'clock, she called George Washington Hospital, Georgetown Hospital, Howard University Hospital, Southern Avenue Hospital, and Holy Cross Hospital—every blessed hospital in the city to find out if anyone named Ron Brown had been brought into the emergency room.

Nothing.

At six o'clock, Rhonda called the D.C. Police Department to make an inquiry.

Had he been arrested for driving under the influence? Had he been in an auto accident?

After four hours of waiting and no clue to where he was, and why he had not picked her up from work, Rhonda was in full blown, homicidal rage.

By seven o'clock, Rhonda's rage turned to revenge.

At eight o'clock, six hours after her shift ended, Ron pulled up to the building.

Rage raised its ugly, unforgiving, diabolical head again.

Ron looked apprehensive as he exited their Deuce and a Quarter. He was wide-eyed like a deer caught in headlights, which scared Rhonda because she didn't know what to expect. He had on the same clothes he had worn the day before when he dropped her off. His usual neat attire was rumpled. His shirttail was out and he had on dark shades at eight o'clock in the morning.

His apologies were frenzied, excessive. His words stumbled over each other.

"Baby, I'm sorry."

The look on Rhonda's face told him it was not nearly enough.

"Please baby, please accept my apology. I overslept."

"Ron," she yelled, "I kept calling the house."

"I wasn't home," his defense came out unrehearsed. They gawked at each other.

"Then, where the hell did you oversleep?" Her screams echoed throughout the lobby of the empty building.

A slip of the tongue, a misstep, and he inadvertently validated that he had cheated again, and again he got caught.

That happened four months ago. And here we are once again at the same crossroads. Three whole days and he has taken my kindness for weakness again.

Rhonda had finally had enough. Her emotions were in overdrive and everything was spinning out of control. She had to terminate this toxic marriage before it totally consumed her or she murdered him, and she leaned toward the latter.

* * *

By nine o'clock the following morning, with neither hide nor hair from Ron, Rhonda scanned the Yellow Pages looking for moving companies with storage facilities. On her fifth try, she was successful and found one that could be at their house by noon.

She waited until five o'clock to call Ron's office to leave a simple message on the machine.

She put her set of house keys in the mailbox and moved out.

CHAPTER 18

A RETIREMENT MECCA

The renovations were materializing beautifully and everything was on schedule for completion. Being a Real Estate Agent made the entire process less complicated. Jackie used the same contractors that she had known and hired for years.

She wanted to ensure the skeleton of the house was up to par before taking on the task of remodeling. All of the problems the two home inspectors encountered, which were few and minor considering the property had been unoccupied for several years, had been corrected.

The master electrician, with assistance from his apprentice, updated all the circuit breaker panels. To their horror and disbelief, even though the master said nothing should surprise him anymore, none of the seven bathrooms had a GFCI reset switch.

"For this to have been a senior citizen home at one time," he told Jackie, "it's pure luck that no residents were electrocuted."

"That we know of," Jackie said.

"True," he responded. They chuckled.

Contractors enjoyed working with Jackie. She had given them many referrals over the years and never once asked for a kickback. They described her to friends and business contacts as "cream of the crop," bar none.

From the day she did a walk-through of the property, she had a vision of what changes would be incorporated to the existing floor plan. She didn't like the idea of a cafeteria in her home so that was totally torn out and the room remodeled. It was turned into a formal dining room to seat sixteen, but not the traditional layout. The room would have a cozy feeling despite its enormous size. There would be a genuine open hearth, wood-burning fireplace in one corner of the room, which required building a foundation to carry the weight of the firebox and chimney. Diagonally across the room would be a built-in, wall-to-ceiling all-glass china cabinet housing her Baccarat crystal vases and Lladró figurines. The cabinet would not resemble her mother's cabinet filled with bone china and silver that made an appearance once a year on Thanksgiving Day.

In addition to a huge, round solid mahogany table in the center of the room with a rainbow of mismatched leather chairs, there would also be two small separate sitting areas in the other two corners of the room. One corner would display a pair of wingback chairs and the other corner would have a pair of tufted, armless chairs. This area would be designed for intimate conversations or reading.

Walls were torn down in the living room, family room, and kitchen to create an open, combined space for social gatherings. There was a total of five flat screen televisions affixed to the walls. A huge, one-hundred-inch Sony was the focal point, and the other four, all Samsung of varying sizes, were sprinkled at different angles throughout the space. Even though Jackie rarely cooked, she had all the white General Electric appliances replaced with stainless steel Jenn-Air. She didn't really like the look of appliances; so, when entertaining, they were all hidden by maple wood, custom sliding doors.

The one thing Jackie loved about the home she grew up in was the wide-plank floors. She had all the carpet in the entire mini mansion removed and hardwood floors installed throughout the top two levels.

In the finished lower level of the house, the base-ment—she despised the name—was completely trans-formed into a gaming oasis. There were areas to entertain any gambling addictions: a wide open space to play pool and a casino room with a poker table, Blackjack table, roulette table, and crap table.

There was a custom wet bar stocked with top-shelf liquors: Appleton, Grey Goose, Hendricks, Patrón, Knob Creek, and Chivas Regal. The wine cellar, hidden from view, stocked the girls' champagnes of choice.

Every bedroom was an en suite with a unique setting and ambiance. When Jackie envisioned having the en suites designed, she recalled the girls' favorite colors and also small, but significant things they had mentioned about themselves over the last twenty years. Those touches had been integrated into each room. The goal was to create a retirement Mecca that was a true vacation refuge encompassing all their desires. So each suite was designed and decorated with that in mind.

One bedroom was painted white with an eggplant accent wall. Matching sheer drapes covered the wall-to-wall windows. The room was filled with white furniture and shades of violet-color accessories throughout—pillows on the window seat, duvet and shams on the bed, and a deep purple, shaggy accent rug under the bed that spread out to the middle of the room.

Another suite was painted bubblegum pink with the exception of the ceiling, which was bright white to match the pristine down comforter and fluffy pillows on the cherry wicker furniture. The wood floors had been bleached white.

The third bedroom suite showed off its pale green walls with hunter green trim and ceiling-to-floor drapes to match. On each side of the bed stood tall curios displaying a variety of artifacts Jackie found while travelling abroad with the girls. French doors led out to a deck that overlooked the dock.

At the end of a long hallway, another en suite was decorated in a tan and chocolate color scheme. On the opposite end was another suite painted black with everything else white: ceiling, woodwork, crown molding, and doors. The headboard and footboard were covered with white leather and the bed covers were black with a blood-red throw folded in thirds across the foot of the bed. Charcoal accessories and a splash of red were peppered throughout the room.

Everything in Jackie's suite, including the bathroom, was pure white with an angelic atmosphere throughout— the walls, ceiling, floor, furniture, accessories, bed coverings, and knickknacks—as if she was bent on exorcising some evil spirit from her surroundings.

The enclosed sunroom was her masterpiece. She wanted to replicate the spectacular views and serenity of Perviolas and she accomplished it. The fleeting idea that had tried to formulate during her drunken stupor while soaking in the panorama of Santorini, the idea she had been unable to grasp, miraculously materialized when she returned home and described her vision to the architect. He succeeded in making her fantasy a reality, but at a king's ransom. The sunroom extended the entire length of the back of the house and was built of glass and steel beams. She wanted the ability during daylight hours to see as far as possible the length of the Occoquan River, boats sailing by, and to enjoy the landscape and greenery her property offered. At night, she wanted to enjoy the sky, the moon, and the stars. The entire sunroom, with the exception of the roof, was tinted turquoise to replicate the clear blue water and beauty of the Aegean Sea.

Also located on the lower level was a separate entrance to her six-room real estate office, which consisted of a large private office that was secured by a deadbolt lock, a smaller interior office for an assistant with no lock, a kitchenette, one unisex restroom, and two conference rooms for meeting clients. Computers, file and supply cabinets, and fax and photocopy machines occupied the open space.

When all the renovations were completed and signed off on, she hung her real estate sign, JOAT Realty, on the lower-level side entrance of the property. If asked, she would inform clients that the acronym stood for "Jill of All Trade." She would say it represented the essence of assisting buyers and sellers in all their real estate transaction needs.

* * *

Jackie sat in her pure white bedroom suite confused. Naming her real estate company JOAT Realty was a conundrum, a mystery of bottled up and mixed emotions. It had nothing to do with her being a "Jill of all trade." That acronym was a sham. JOAT was the first initials of her legal name, the pretentious name she despised all her life.

Her childhood had been insufferable, so it came as a reeling shock when she decided to use her initials in the name of her real estate company. It felt both strange and joyful at the same time.

CHAPTER 19

JACKIE TRUMPLETON'S CHILDHOOD

Jackie had traveled a long distance and come a long way since leaving East New Orleans. It took nearly thirty years, but finally she was at the peak of her game.

She had a name even before she was born, Jacqueline Ophelia Antoinette Trumpleton; and, for as long as she could remember, she was always embarrassed by her name. She believed it to be ostentatious. *Three syllables in every god-forsaken name.* She cringed. *Who in the whole wide world would do that to a child?* There were no other schoolmates she knew of who attended Sarah Reed Elementary or Marion Abramson High schools during her tenure that were saddled with long, drawn out, ridiculous names.

She never had the nerve to ask her mother the origin of the names. It was not because she thought she would hurt her mother's feelings. She knew her mother, without hesitation, would haul off and smack Satan himself out of her for mouthing off, being sassy her mother called it. Jackie would find herself clear on the other side of the room, rubbing the side of her head, and trying not to cry.

The names weren't the maternal or paternal grandmother's names. It wasn't even an aunt or a famous actress name. It was just her name. Her mother acted as if Jackie was born Jacqueline Bouvier Kennedy Onassis, and even she wasn't *born* with the three-syllable names. She married into the last two surnames.

And the way her mother yelled her name when she was mad at her, punctuating every syllable as if she knew doing so would make Jackie cry, which it did. "Jack-ah-lean-o-fill-ya-an-twa-net-trump-a-ton," her mother would scream. "Didn't I tell you to come in here and dry these dishes that I washed? Get in here now!" Her mother would shout so loud that the entire neighborhood heard her. *It was sooo embarrassing.*

Jackie swore that the minute she graduated high school and ran from that town, the first thing she would do was legally change her name.

When she turned thirteen, the year she started smelling herself according to her mother, she asked Aunt Bessie, her favorite aunt, where her name came from. Of all the aunts, and there were many, Aunt Bessie was the kindest, most gentle relative Jackie had ever known. She couldn't believe her momma and Aunt Bessie were sisters—they were as different as day and night. She loved her Aunt Bessie and pretended that she was her mother instead. This was a secret she kept to herself.

Aunt Bessie was a heavyset woman with a freckled, smiling face that displayed dimples. She walked stooped over due to the weight of her large, pendulous breasts. And because of this strain, she did more sitting than standing or walking.

She pulled Jackie in close into her humongous bosom, sat Jackie on her wide lap, and spoke to her in a conspiratorial tone. "Child, your momma kept praying the stork would drop a baby girl, but every single blessed time a baby landed, it was a boy," she whispered. "That stork had a mind of its own, like you I might add, and was determined it was going to do things his way. Three boys dropped before the stork got it right." Aunt Bessie closed her eyes and stopped talking. Jackie thought she had fallen asleep, as she sometimes did. "Lordy, lordy," Aunt Bessie shouted, startling Jackie. "I have totally forgotten why your momma gave you those glorious names. But she had a good reason for doing so, I can tell you that."

"Do you think it had something to do with Juan, Oliver, and Andrew?" Jackie asked innocently.

"Oh goodness gracious, yes," Aunt Bessie said. "I remember now. She wanted your name to have the first three letters of your brothers."

"But Aunt Bessie, why such a long sounding name?"

"Go on child, that's enough questions for one day."

Jackie never got an answer.

When she migrated north, she only used Jackie, like Cher or Madonna, and rarely spoke her full name verbally. It was only disclosed for legal purposes, only written on legal documents.

She took great pains to disassociate herself from her former life. She wanted all her childhood memories, both the good and the bad, dead and buried.

CHAPTER 20

ABDUCTION OF JOE BRADFORD

The abductor's latest conquest, Joe Bradford, was difficult to discipline. He wanted to be in control of his predicament and when he grasped that wasn't part of the plan, it wasn't allowed, he became forceful in his approach.

His reaction wasn't part of her plan either, so she had to figure out a way to get him under control or he would have to leave.

The first time she entered his room, he demanded to know where he was; and, of course, he had every right to be angry. She tried to get him to sit down by using coaxing words, but he acted like a caged animal although the room was easily thirty-by-thirty. He was so agitated that he either didn't notice or didn't care that she was wearing a mask.

"You have five seconds to let me out of this room," he said, looking at the second hand on his watch.

"What is the alternative if I do not?" she asked.

He crossed the room to the other side with unbelievable speed. But she was prepared for him. By the time he reached within an arm-length of her, he felt a mist on his face.

That's the last thing he recalled.

When Joe stirred, god knows how many hours later, it was to the aroma of country ham, homemade biscuits, grits, and fried apples like his momma use to make when he was a young boy. He opened his eyes and through his daze, he saw three or four women standing before him of varying physiques and heights, and skin tones of every type of chocolate he could imagine—dark chocolate, milk chocolate, white chocolate. They were ensconced in bejeweled masks and dressed only in lingerie. Each was holding a dish of the cuisine that smelled so appetizing. He couldn't help speculating whether these mouth-watering women would taste sweet, semisweet, or be unsweetened like the woman he shouted at earlier.

His memory returned. He wondered if one of them was her until he heard her from the opposite side of the room.

"Are you hungry?" she asked.

He turned quickly to confront her. He froze in place.

The woman, almost totally naked and faced away from him, had one leg up on a chair and was leaning slightly forward. She was holding what appeared to be a riding crop. All she wore was a red lacy garter belt, thigh-high sheer black nylons, and five-inch "come fuck me" high heels. Her crotch and derrière were fully exposed.

Joe turned sheepishly toward the other women, and to his disappointment, they were no longer in the room. He wasn't sure if they had been an illusion, but seeing the dishes of food spread out on the table gave him a sense of balance that he wasn't hallucinating.

He quickly turned back to see if the near-naked woman was a figment of his imagination and was delighted to see that she was not.

She was now facing him and an exotic mask was hiding her features. He started toward her and stopped fast in his tracks, not wanting to be maced again. He instinctively knew it wasn't mace because he didn't experience any severe burning sensations; but, something had been sprayed in his face and the next time it just might be pepper spray.

She spoke first. "If you remain in control of your behavior, I would like to talk to you on a serious note. I have a proposition."

Joe was dumbfounded. She wanted him to remain in control while she was standing before him practically in the buff, literally bare-assed, posing provocatively.

Well, two can play this game, he thought. He turned away from her and walked toward the bathroom removing pieces of clothing until he was down to his trunk-style briefs. This was the only type of underwear he wore because he needed the extra jock support for his hefty package. After seeing her in that sexy garter, his package was straining against the material. He stood in the doorframe to the bathroom and turned toward her.

Her eyes shot directly to his groin.

I've got her. That's Bradford magnetism. He grinned.

Just as quickly, her eyes shot to his face. "Shit," she groaned, dropping her head. *He saw me. He caught a glimpse of my Achilles' heel.*

He waited for her to raise her head. When she did, he slowly removed his briefs but his body was turned at a ninety-degree angle so she was unable to get a peek at his bulging package. As he strode into the shower, she had a front row seat to his muscular buns.

The rainfall blasted him full force. He lathered soap up and down his body and was pondering how he could seduce her in order to get a leg up on this seductress. Clarification like one's ability to sing while showering. He decided to ignore anything she attempted that would lead to a sexual tryst. He exited the bathroom the same way he entered, butt-naked, except this time, he was exposed full frontal. She couldn't control herself. She had to look and it was obvious he was turned on.

She silently thanked Weight Watchers for her re-sculpted figure. It had taken ten years to get off of the weight-gain, weight-loss roller coaster. She was assured that when she rejoined for the fifth time in nine years, she wasn't an anomaly. So, she promised herself for the umpteenth time that this time, if for nothing other than health reasons, she would keep the excess weight off.

Standing in front of this man, in little more than a garter, and realizing that he desired her even if he pretended not to, though it was clearly visible in his eyes, she knew that this time she'd be able to keep the promise.

She had not moved from the spot where she was standing prior to his going to take a shower. They both looked at each other and she cracked her whip.

He jumped, startled. He had forgotten all about that crop. He gave her a look and chose his words carefully. "If that whip touches me, we'll have a problem," he said.

She looked at him squarely and said, "We?"

"You don't want to try me," he said.

She advanced aggressively and so did he. Before she could raise the whip again, she found herself pulled in close proximity to him and her arm bound behind her back.

"Ouch," she said, and dropped the whip.

His package was squarely against her sheath. As she struggled to move away, her pelvis ground into his.

"Stop," was the only word she was able to say. It was so meek, he barely heard it.

She couldn't believe she was in this submissive position.

"Um, um, I don't think so," he said, enjoying her squirming and the stimulation it was sending to his manhood. The juices flowing from her were drenching him. He bent down and whispered in her ear. "Touch me."

She obliged and ran her free hand down his thigh and grabbed between his legs.

It wasn't what he expected. It was rough and caught him off guard. He fell to his knees situating him face-to-face with her secreting love canal. He didn't know whether her tactic was deliberate or not but he decided to take advantage of this opportunity. He let go of her wrist and grabbed her butt with both hands and pulled her torso toward his face. He inhaled the scent and nuzzled her center.

She said stop again and it sounded even weaker than before. She grabbed his bald head and leaned back. When he started to move up, she gently shoved him back down. She opened her legs wider and took her hands to expose her jewel.

It was a heavenly sight to Joe. He replaced her hands with one of his and held the hood retracted. He lowered his mouth and fully engulfed her canal. His tongue circled her jewel and he felt it swell. As she writhed above him, his fingers searched her canal for the source of the spasms. She started pumping against his fingers. She was in a frenzy and he kept licking her jewel. She screamed so loud that if he had been close to her mouth, his ear drum would have busted. She tried to get away because the spot was super sensitive. He held her close, removed his tongue, and started blowing gently on the spot. Another orgasm erupted from her body.

She leaned into him for support, speechless, as her body pulsated a full five minutes before subsiding. She started trembling. She was blatantly aware that he could have dislodged her mask at anytime during this sexual escapade, yet he didn't.

When he realized that the heaving was from sobbing and not climaxing, he pulled her down into a seated position, moved behind her, and pulled her into his arms. They stayed in that position until she regained her composure.

She was embarrassed and could not believe she had lost total control of the situation. She thanked God that she was sitting with her back to him. It was no way she could face him at that moment. The mask hid her face but could not conceal the raw emotions that he witnessed.

She tried to pull away but he held her close. His head was lying in the center of her back, and his arms and legs were wrapped around her, imprisoning her.

She spoke. "May I get up?" She paused. "Please."

He released his hold.

She stood up and realized one of her legs had fallen asleep. She turned around to shake it, stumbled forward, and landed in his lap. She was facing this dark god and he had an erection. The right side of her brain was telling her to enjoy the pleasure she was feeling; but the left side, the analytical side, was telling her to get out of that bedroom. The right side won when she felt him inside her. She couldn't believe how easy it was since he was well endowed. He held her in his lap so tenderly and he was doing all the moving. She just sat there like a bump on a log and embraced this wondrous sensation. She kissed him and loved the feel of his tongue going slowly in and out of her mouth. She reciprocated with her own tongue. She loved the feel of his lips on her lips. He flipped her over smoothly, onto her stomach, without missing a beat. He raised her arms above her head and he worked his body up and down.

Then, he pulled her up doggy style. Finally, she was in rhythm with his movements as they gyrated together. He loved the tightness of her love canal and she knew how to work it because of the Kegel exercises she did every day, sometimes twice a day, no matter where she was—in a meeting with a client, at the grocery store, or window shopping. She could tell he enjoyed it because each time her womanhood tightened, clamped down on his love muscle, he nibbled her ear and gasped "oh baby." And, right before he expended his love and filled her up, he exploded with screams of his own.

CHAPTER 21

A MEDIA CIRCUS

Chief Johnston of the Arlington PD was correct. The media was riding the missing men carousel; it *was* a media circus. It was similar to Cleveland but with a twist. Four African-American men vanished without a trace.

They had only publicized three names to the media. But in reality, they were aware of a possible fourth man missing who could be the next victim. They decided to keep that from the media for the time being until they got confirmation.

Since there was no evidence regarding what happened to these men, speculation spiraled rampantly and relentlessly. Every local TV station and newspaper ran the story. Television stations were comparing the situation to Ariel Castro who held three women hostage for ten years.

"Are we looking at a situation where we'll never know what happened to these men?" a reporter asked. "It has been two weeks and nothing."

Newspapers were hesitant to equate the circumstances with the House of Horrors where convicted sex offender Anthony Sowell kidnapped, tortured, and murdered eleven women and buried them in his backyard.

"Our thoughts are with the missing men," one newspaper article stated. "We pray that where ever these men are, they are alive, safe, and sound."

"Three adult men are missing," the channel 4 news reporter said, reading from a list. "Ian Ferguson from Arlington, Ron Brown from Alexandria, and Joe Bradford from Bowie." The reporter embellished the remainder of the story because he had no confirmation of the subsequent statement out of his mouth. "There are actually four missing men but the first man's name is being withheld and he is in protective custody for his safety."

Channel 5 interviewed Evelyn Ferguson, who could not stop crying. "Ian," she said into the microphone, "if you are watching this telecast, please know that I am so sorry and I just want you to come home. There's nothing we can't work out." She handed the microphone back to the reporter and disappeared into the crowd.

"As far as we know, the FBI has not been contacted yet," the reporter from Channel 7 News said. "When we asked for a statement, we were told by Supervisory Special Agent Lawrence Madison that in missing person cases, the FBI makes their facilities available at the request of a state or local enforcement agency. When asked if such a request had been made by either Arlington PD, Alexandria PD, or Bowie PD, I was told that the FBI cooperates with all requests and that was all the information they would divulge at this time. It appears that local enforcement agencies have not reached out to the FBI."

Channel 9 News was the only station with a totally different angle on the missing men. "There is a strong possibility that in the case of Ian Ferguson, he may have left on his own accord because he and his wife had a horrific fight and he walked out." The reporter paused. "Foul play can be attributed in Joe Bradford's case because according to his mistress, whose name is being withheld because she is also married, told cops that Dorothy Bradford admitted she had murdered her husband." The reporter asked a Bowie police officer for confirmation of this report.

"We are still investigating the accusation," the officer said.

When the reporter tried to push for additional information, the officer replied, "No comment."

The reporter went on to say that experience has taught authorities that only a handful of missing person cases turn out to involve foul play. "Statistics show that a large number of adults who disappear do so on their own accord. It can be due to a soured relationship or financial difficulties. Only time will tell if either of these is true or false."

All the TV stations ended their piece in the same manner, sounding like a recurring recording. "We'll keep you up-to-date as soon as we get more details."

CHAPTER 22

ABDUCTION OF RON BROWN

"Who are you?" the man asked. He sat up and looked curiously around the room. He rubbed his eyes because he thought the woman he was communicating with was wearing a mask, not a scary Halloween-type mask, but a beautifully embellished one.

"Where am I? What am I doing here? How did I get here?" The questions kept spewing forth because he was baffled.

"What do you want?" he asked. He felt woozy, like he had been drugged.

"I will communicate in due time," the mysterious woman said.

"Your voice sounds familiar; have we met before?"

She stood up to leave.

"Wait, please don't go. I don't understand," he said.

"In due time, lover, I will explain everything."

Lover? What does she mean by that? Ron wondered. He needed answers, but none was forthcoming. He didn't grasp what was going on or how he had gotten himself in this predicament. The room was spinning and he was feeling light-headed.

He fell unconscious.

When he awakened, he couldn't discern how much time had elapsed because the woman was still sitting across from him, but this time reading a book. From the distance between her and the bed, he could read a portion of the title, "Confessions of a ...." Before he could read the last word, he blacked out again.

The woman was seated in an oversized chair, one leg curled under her, the other dangling to the floor. While he was asleep, she had been studying the well-appointed bedroom and was proud of what she had accomplished. It was two-o-eight in the morning and she was impeccably dressed, as if she was waiting to meet a high-profile client. Her attire was pristine and epitomized success; not that navy blue pin-striped suit, white shirt ensemble, resembling a "million attorney march" that lawyers religiously replicated. Her attire was a tailored, white Calvin Klein virgin wool fitted dress trimmed with a strip of charcoal gray leather and black, nondescript buttons down the left side. A two-inch wide, red leather belt cinched her waist. Her feet were adorned with one inch pewter-color pumps.

People who interacted with her assumed she was rolling in dough; but truth be told, she didn't pay full price for anything. She despised the six to seven-hundred percent markup on clothes and shoes at high-end stores like Neiman Marcus and Saks Fifth Avenue. She only shopped at outlet malls. On the atypical occasion she did shop at a department store, it was only when she received sale coupons for items marked down at least seventy percent off the original price. She also had a trick or two up her sleeve. If she saw an article of clothing she just had to have, she would sacrifice and purchase it, but never wear it, and hang it in her closet with the price tag still attached. She would return to the store weekly, with receipt in hand, waiting patiently for the item to go on sale. The moment it did, she would pounce on the cashier with her receipt and request a "benefit of sale," a refund of the difference between the amount she paid and the new adjusted price. She had sixty days to take advantage of this maneuver and it was marked in her electronic calendar with an alert for the day before the refund opportunity expired. Then, and only then, did she remove the price tag and wear the reduced-price item. If the item did not go on sale, she'd returned it to the store for a full refund. She preferred St. John, and owned several pieces, which she acquired from consignment shops in Old Town Alexandria and Bethesda, because the retail price on that brand name was highway robbery.

The jewelry she wore was minimal, but exquisite. The half carat diamond earrings, Cartier watch, gold bracelet with one charm, and ring with rubies and diamonds worn on her engagement finger, although no proposal in sight, were all acquired at different times from The Pawn Place in Arlington at a price she considered pilferage. Since she was a regular customer and introduced everyone she knew to the family-owned merchant every time she got compliments on her unique jewelry, the pawn shop owners would give her a referral discount. Regardless, she still haggled, negotiated, and went back and forth for days prior to finalizing a purchase. There were times they were far apart on an agreed-upon price. When that occurred, she would put the desired item in interest-free layaway and retrieve it within a year.

She never, not once, entertained purchasing any of the gaudy jewelry that was so prominently displayed in the showcases.

She rarely wore makeup or had her eyebrows plucked, waxed, or threaded. Her fingernails and toenails displayed no polish, only buffed to a natural shine. She wore her hair in a stylish pixie cut that made her look ten years younger, or so she had been told. Since her hair was naturally curly, she clipped and maintained it herself. She did not dye the few strands of gray because she enjoyed the distinguished look it gave her. Even though she wasn't beautiful by *Glamour* magazine standards, she was stunning when she got dolled up, and she knew it.

She watched the peacefully sleeping man straddled across the bed with the Egyptian, six-hundred thread, top sheet, barely covering his buttocks. When she saw him the night before at a Japanese restaurant in Old Town Alexandria, her heart skipped a beat. She knew instinctively he was the one. She wanted him added to her collection. But she couldn't approach him at the bar. There were too many diners, too many eyes. He looked so pitiful sitting there all alone, drinking far too many shots of Johnny Walker Black. She was astounded that the bartender kept pouring him drinks. But like anything else, the dollar spoke volumes. As long as he was tipping consistently, the sexy, buxom bartender kept pouring.

It was obvious that he was wallowing in some kind of misery, maybe a volatile argument with his wife—she had noticed his wedding band immediately. He was one of two types of men she was seeking.

The first type always had some kind of woman problems, some wifely drama they were trying to escape, drown out in liquor, like her father. And these men always needed a break, a release. She would be the one to fulfill their needs.

The second type was the horny men. They had no drama. All they wanted was to get laid. And those were the ones she needed to fulfill her needs.

So, she waited and watched him, like a cobra. It wasn't long before she struck.

As usual, the take down had been easy.

* * *

When Ron woke again, the woman was gone. He felt alert and more like himself. He looked around the stately bedroom and realized he was in unfamiliar surroundings. He tried to recall what he had been doing before he got to where he was now. Out of nowhere, he was inundated with memories.

Rhonda had left him. He couldn't blame her but he was furious at the way she did it. Destroyed all his clothes—every single piece. She took scissors and shredded the front of every button-down shirt and amputated one leg of every pair of slacks, even his jeans. He counted his blessings that his suit jackets had escaped her vengeance. But, when he turned one over, it was not to be. They had all been stabbed in the back multiple times. She even cut his neckties in half. The only thing she had not destroyed was his shoes. She probably would have too if a chainsaw had been readily accessible. *How the hell am I suppose to go to work with no clothes to wear?*

He was in a murderous rage and there was a nagging thought floating around in the back of his mind that he couldn't grab onto. When it finally came into focus, he grasped the significance of his circumstances. *It could have been me that she mutilated.*

He called the cops who were useless.

"Did you see her do it?" he was asked.

"Hell no I didn't see that 'stank ho' do it!" he screamed. "She's still alive isn't she? She's lucky I didn't come home while she was performing the act. I would have killed that bitch!" He was irate.

"Mr. Brown, have you harmed your wife?" the officer asked.

He couldn't believe it. Now, that Rhonda might be in harm's way, the police were ready to act.

"May we speak to Mrs. Brown?" the officer said.

Ron slammed down the phone so hard, the speaker flew out of the receiver. He immediately left the house figuring they were on their way to arrest him for a murder he hadn't committed, not yet anyway.

He knew he was a raunchy husband and deserved exactly what Rhonda had done to him. From the day he met her, he continued sleeping around. To wallow in his misery, he went to the neighborhood Japanese restaurant, a hole in the wall eatery that served the best Fugu Sashimi he had tasted since he served in the military in Okinawa. After a twenty-minute wait, the buzzer vibrated alerting him that his table was ready.

As he waited in the dimly lit restaurant for his entrée to arrive, he squinted to read the local section of *The Washington Post,* which he bought from the vending machine outside, when he felt a presence beside him.

"Are you eating alone?" the woman asked.

He was prepared to say his wife was joining him. But when he looked up from the paper and saw this striking woman with dark chocolate, velvet-like skin, expressive eyes, and a killer smile standing before him, he changed his mind and said, "Yes, I am. Would you care to join me?"

Without a word, she sat down on the same side of the booth as Ron. He didn't slide over so they were touching, side-by-side, from their shoulders, along their thighs down to their feet. After a few pleasantries and before his food arrived—he was tingling all over at the closeness of her, the smell of her perfume—she pointed out a couple at a nearby table who appeared to be arguing. She whispered, "I bet they'll make up before you can get me into bed."

He pulled a wad of money held by a silver engraved clip out of his pocket and threw a hundred dollar bill down on the table, and they immediately left the restaurant.

Later that night when he woke up, Ron found himself undressed, totally naked.

He couldn't recall whether he bedded the woman or not.

CHAPTER 23

ARLINGTON PD
CONTACTS THE FBI

Arlington's Chief of Police, Maurice Johnston, looked extremely haggard, as if he had been up all night with a severe bout of diarrhea. The uniforms working the case *were* up all night and were downright exhausted. There were now four men missing and not a clue. They had been working this case nonstop and still not one iota of evidence that would lead them to the whereabouts of these men, or link the disappearances in anyway, or what caused the disappearances. There were so many missing pieces to the puzzle that once they thought they found and fitted one piece into place, it only fit because another officer forced it into place, which fell apart as soon as it was reviewed and examined closely.

The chief had even authorized additional man hours to help Lieutenant Neathers and his team get a handle on this. It was not enough. The kidnappings were spiraling out of control. They needed additional man power.

He picked up the phone to call Neathers. Before he punched the numbers of his extension, Neathers burst into his office without knocking, and said, "Turn on the television."

The chief could not believe the words he was hearing coming from the woman's mouth. A middle-aged, average-looking, African-American woman was telling NBCNews4 that her husband, Brian Taylor, who is also a friend of another missing man, Ian Ferguson, has not been seen or heard from since yesterday. When the reporter asked why she didn't notify the police, she started sobbing and said that she was told to wait forty-eight hours, and if her husband didn't come home or she hadn't heard from him, then she should file a missing person's report.

Chief Johnston was stupefied by the news report. He yelled, "Get Mrs. Taylor in here pronto!"

Neathers rushed out of his office.

The chief called another "all hands on deck" meeting. He gave a command to all the officers present and informed them to tell every other officer they come into contact with, that any calls regarding a missing man, woman, child, or dog, he wants to be notified immediately, and only he will make the decision whether a report will be filed or not.

"Is there anyone here who doesn't understand this directive?" he asked.

The chief finally succumbed to the notion that these disappearances were genuine and connected, and that the FBI had to be contacted because the Arlington PD didn't have the resources available to conduct an all out search.

Unbeknownst to the Arlington PD, the FBI had already taken notice.

* * *

Even before the FBI was contacted for assistance, the Critical Incident Response Group was standing by and had already put resources in place to examine the male disappearances. Agents from the behavioral analysis unit, the BAU, were prepared at a moment's notice to travel to Virginia, Maryland, and DC to provide advice and support.

The FBI supported four behavioral analysis units and this particular case fell under two of them: Unit Two specialized in crimes against adults, if this happened to be the case; and Unit Four, the violent criminal apprehension program known as ViCAP, concentrated on missing person cases when there was a compelling possibility of foul play. Both units provided resources focused on serial-related crimes.

At first glance, the FBI was skeptical that these disappearances were a serial crime; but, as more time passed and the number of disappearances increased with no clues, serial kidnapping was now considered a real possibility in this case.

From both the media and informants, they learned there was a total of five disappearances from neighboring jurisdictions: Arlington, Alexandria, and Bowie.

The agents sat around the large conference room table and began dissecting and categorizing what they already knew about the case. "I know everyone's been keeping up with what's going on here around the nation's capital," Supervisory Special Agent Madison said. "We haven't been contacted by any police departments yet, so until they do, let's concentrate on what we have so far."

They turned their attention to the whiteboard where five columns were separated by thick red lines with the names listed in alphabetical order scrawled in bold black letters. At the top of each column were pictures of the missing men, including the one that supposedly got away, extracted from their LinkedIn profiles—Joe Bradford, Ron Brown, Ian Ferguson, Clyde Hariston, and Brian Taylor.

Madison hashed out the similarities. "All are African-American males, between six feet and six five in height, approximate age forty-five to sixty, and all of them are basically in decent shape with no medical problems. They're all married. These men are not low-down, good for nothing troublemakers. They have decent jobs and are from middle to upper-income tax brackets. None has a criminal record; only minor traffic infractions not even worth mentioning. They don't do drugs or smoke, and all are social drinkers, nothing heavy. This is where the similarities stop."

He heard snickering from the back of the room, looked up, and noticed all his agents had turned around with eyes directed at a female agent.

"Did I say something funny, agent?" Madison asked. He couldn't decipher the name on her badge.

"I apologize sir for the interruption. I was just joking around."

"That's not good enough. Please do us the honor and include all of us on the side debate."

The agent looked uncomfortable and regretted being in the spotlight. "I was just asking who in their right mind would kidnap middle-aged married men when there are all these hot, young, single men around, sir," she said.

The young male agents howled like wolves and stomped their feet and the young female agents clapped, and then twirled their fists in the air exclaiming, woo-hoo. The older agents turned their attention back to Madison.

"Who are you?" SSA Madison asked, squinting to read her badge.

"Assistant Special Agent Gonzales," she said.

"So, what category do I fit in?" the sixtyish Madison asked, practically daring her to respond.

She mumbled something neither he nor anyone else in the room could hear.

"That's what I thought," he said. "Unless you have something relevant to impart, I advise you to keep your irrelevant comments to yourself."

Madison picked up where he left off. "We just might have a serial kidnapper on our hands although I don't want to call it that just yet." He pointed to the board. "Ferguson, Hariston, and Taylor are residents of Arlington. Brown is from Alexandria, and Bradford from PG County. This kidnapper, if that's the direction we're going in, is all over the map. There's no rhyme or reason to the pattern, except they're missing. Has anything weird been happening in the District, any word from them?"

"Nothing we've heard about," Special Agent Kelly said. She looked at the other agents in the room. "Hear me out for a minute, guys. If these are kidnappings, I think the order may be wide of the mark. Ian Ferguson was reported missing first, right? Suppose Clyde Hariston was actually the first man gone missing, but Arlington PD didn't know about him until later. Hariston could have been the first one kidnapped."

"I like where you're headed," Madison said. He refused to use the word kidnapping. "If more men come up missing, God forbid, all of these may be out of order." He flipped through his pad. "Did I see a note somewhere that Ferguson and Taylor are best friends?"

"Yes," Kelly said.

"That's why this sticks in my craw. I want to hold off calling this a serial kidnapping. Suppose those two just went off together somewhere—a bromance brewing or a bromance feuding, something along those lines."

After the caustic dialogue with ASA Gonzales, Kelly was hesitant to correct the boss. She tenuously raised her hand and then snatched it back down into her lap.

"It looks like you want to say something, Kelly," Madison said.

"Sir, if you please, bromance is a nonsexual relation-ship between two straight men. I don't think they would go off together."

He looked at her. "Well, a gay relationship then."

The awkward moment passed. "I doubt it," Kelly said. "We haven't spoken to anyone under the radar who indicated anything of the sort."

There were murmurs.

"Anything else?" Madison asked.

Kelly raised her hand again.

Madison acknowledged her again.

"If Clyde Hariston's story is believable, it could be some kind of adult sex ring or male trafficking," she said. "Why else would someone test him anonymously for AIDS?"

The room became silent and all eyes turned toward Kelly.

"You know something that you haven't shared," Madison said.

"I just heard this last night and was prepared to discuss it this morning," Kelly said.

"From whom?" Madison asked.

"I think everyone here knows that Detective Lindon from Arlington PD and I are roommates and we're both runners. Last night she talked about this cuckoo case— her words not mine—they're working on over there. One of the victims, Clyde Hariston, starts complaining to another female runner about this woman who intentionally knocked him down and sprayed something in his face. He swears he woke up in a hotel room and she wanted to have sex with him. When he rejected her, according to him now, she implied he had AIDS by showing him an empty HIV test kit, lambasted him, and called him derogatory names. Before he knew it, he was sprayed again. The next thing he knew, he was back on the trail as if nothing had ever happened."

The agents were hanging onto Kelly's every word.

"He actually told another runner he was tested for AIDS," Madison said. This was an incredible piece of material fact that they needed.

"Practically, yes sir," Kelly said.

"Holy cow!" Madison shouted, "That's a viable piece of information. We need to visit him immediately and find out why he misled the Arlington PD. As soon as we're invited to assist, I want to also interrogate the wives, mistresses, girlfriends, and anybody else that could be a possible suspect. We have cheating husbands and angry wives. That's a recipe for murder. We also need to setup an anonymous tip line as soon as possible, like yesterday. Somebody, somewhere, *knows* something," he said.

"We need a clue, just one clue."

* * *

When Chief Johnston finally conceded that they needed the FBI's investigative skills and operations support, he invited them in so they could coordinate their efforts. The FBI deployed logistics immediately and met with all the local law enforcements involved.

Chief Johnston waited too long to get them involved. Another man, Ben Wright, was confirmed missing, this time from DC.

* * *

Supervisory Special Agent Madison and Agent Kelly went to Clyde Hariston's home to investigate his neglect to disclose his HIV status.

"I didn't disclose anything because I'm *not* HIV positive," Clyde said. He was angry about this intrusion into his personal life.

Madison gave Kelly the nod to proceed.

"Have you been tested by a professional facility and before you lie to us, Mr. Hariston, we will subpoena your medical records, if necessary."

Clyde despised women. They were always threatening him about something or demanding that he do something. *Why can't everyone just leave me alone?* "No, I haven't been tested and I know my rights. You cannot get my health records without my permission. I'm not going to let some lying bitch who abducted me tell me I have AIDS."

Kelly kept a straight face. *When suspects are angry or afraid, they just might say anything.* She had just learned something that the FBI had not been privy too.

"Were you told you had AIDS or told you were HIV positive?"

"What difference does it make? She was lying!"

Madison stepped in to take over the interrogation because Mr. Hariston was agitated and becoming belligerent. He didn't know whether it was due to Kelly's accusations or her tone.

"Okay, we have gotten off track. We have confirmation that you told other runners that a mysterious woman advised you that you were HIV positive. Is that true or false?"

Clyde felt he was being cross-examined. "I'm not going to sit here and be accused of anything," he said, deliberately avoiding the question, while he contemplated what he wanted to disclose. *Damn Rochelle for demanding I make a report, and why couldn't I keep my big mouth shut. I just had to tell somebody.* "I'm frightened to be tested. I don't want to know the results, just in case she was telling the truth."

"Did this woman say or do anything else?"

"Even though the room was dark, I could swear that the woman was wearing a mask. I couldn't see her face; it was partially covered. She also inquired about my sexual habits, sexual history, and sexual preferences."

"Do you think she thought you were homosexual?"

"What are you insinuating? I'm married!"

Madison considered a different angle before responding. He realized that Hariston was under a lot of pressure and at a breaking point. Now was the time to go for the jugular. "Maybe she saw something in your mannerism. Are you bisexual?"

Hariston's reaction had the opposite effect the agent was hoping for. Hariston shut down.

And the two men just stared at each other.

Madison spoke first. "Is there anything else you recall that you neglected—I mean forgot—to disclose to the Arlington PD?" Madison said.

"That's everything I remember," Clyde said.

Before the agents left his house, Madison informed him that they would notify the appropriate health authorities about his HIV status.

Kelly looked at him as if he was a piece of chewing gum stuck to the bottom of her boot. "It's a death sentence, Mr. Hariston, which you could pass on to your wife and other innocent people."

"I haven't had sex with anyone, not even my wife, since that woman spewed that disgusting accusation."

"Mr. Hariston, it is imperative that you make an appointment with your private physician as soon as possible, have a discussion with your wife today, and cease sexual activities immediately. Do we understand each other?" Kelly asked.

Clyde glared at her.

"Having unprotected sex knowing you are HIV positive is a crime. Are we clear?"

"Please leave my house," Clyde said.

CHAPTER 24

ABDUCTION OF BRIAN TAYLOR

Brian bolted upright, unsure of what had awoken him. Was it a sound, a dream, or daybreak streaming in through the floor-to-ceiling windows? He was in unfamiliar territory. Nothing was recognizable in this well-appointed bedroom. The walls were painted dolphin gray with a slate-colored trim. Black and white transparent, checkered drapes were drawn open at the windows, and a navy blue comforter lay folded in half at the foot of the bed. Jazz was playing from a Bose system; he knew that wave sound because he owned a Bose. He didn't see speakers, although he looked all around the room. The music encircled him like a sleeping bag.

He rolled over to the other side of the bed and opened the drawer of the bedside table. He didn't know why he did that but he certainly wasn't expecting to see what he saw. The drawer was like a miniature adult store, overflowing with all kinds of kinky sex toys. He didn't trust his vision. He shut the drawer quickly and slowly reopened it. The toys were still there, some of everything—vibrators, penile toys, anal plugs, and nipple clamps.

Where the hell am I? He didn't know whether he was afraid to know or excited to find out.

Brian started to really take in the interior of the room. He stepped out of the huge round bed and realized, uncomfortably, that he had a hard-on, not from excitement but the urge to relieve himself. He looked around for the bathroom, saw French doors and pushed them open. *Well goddamn, where am I,* he thought for the second time in less than five minutes. He forgot his stiff penis, which was now standing at attention, and backed out of the bathroom. His hands were still on the door handles. He thought his eyes were deceiving him. He closed and opened them again. As he looked around the humongous bathroom, he couldn't figure out where he should do his business. Before him were three choices: a toilet with the lid already up, a bidet, and a urinal. He used the urinal just because; outside of a public restroom, he had never seen a urinal in a house before and this was a new experience.

Brian opened the mirrored medicine cabinet. There was a bottle of blue pills that looked like Viagra and an abundance of condoms in different textures and one size, all extra large. He was amused.

He went to the door of the bedroom and it was locked. He yelled out if anyone was there. He looked out the windows and saw a large body of water. For some reason, one he didn't inherently understand, he remained calm. He wasn't frightened. He couldn't wait to find out what was to come.

Brian returned to the bed and tried to recall yesterday. *What had I been doing?* It hit him like a ton of rocks.

Evelyn had called. She had not been able to get in touch with Ian. When he thought about it, it was peculiar because he and Ian usually spoke every other day. Brian was aware that Ian and Evelyn were having marital problems but it was nothing he and Ian couldn't talk about. He teased Ian a bit about his marriage, okay a lot, but "come on," he thought, "that man is pussy-whipped." He couldn't believe Ian was so gullible. But he would never be so direct with Ian; he kept his opinions to himself. He loved the man and Ian was the best man at his wedding. Ian was a genuine friend who would do anything for anybody.

Ian also knew all Brian's dirt. Brian was the scum of the earth. All their buddies knew it and even Brian agreed with the assessment. But, he didn't care. He loved women and women loved him. He wasn't going to apologize for it. If Brenda thought marrying him would end his lascivious ways, she of all people should have known better. She knew exactly what he was—a man whore. He had not only screwed his wife's maid of honor before they got married, but one of her bridesmaids too. If Brenda had a problem with his behavior, she would have to deal with it. She was no better than him in the relationship destroyer department.

He defended his wrongdoing. He had been in a previous relationship, dating Trish on and off for five years, when she introduced him to Brenda, her best girlfriend. Trish and Brenda were like sisters. However, during one of those off-again, on-again episodes when Trish cried on Brenda's shoulder one time too many telling Brenda all her woes, Brenda swooshed in like the vulture she was and snatched up the consummate player.

So, if women want to be with me, who am I to deny them that privilege, he rationalize.

Brian was a handsome man who worked out six days a week to maintain his awesome body. Women checked out men too, he knew this, and that's why his workout series were brutal, nothing to poke fun at. He lived and breathed the gym—doing reps, squats, lunges, kicks, push-ups, weights—and his diehard exercise regimen paid off.

Evelyn's call had caught Brian off guard. He knew she hated him and unless hell froze over, she would never call him to ask anything about Ian. He knew hell hadn't frozen over so something dreadful must have happened to Ian. He braced for the bad news.

She tried to be polite to Brian; she loathed him and his antics. She could not understand how someone as soulful as Ian could be friends with that despicable human being.

"Hi Brian, it's Evelyn, how are you?" she said.

Brian heard the anxiety and decided to be cordial. "I'm fine, Evelyn, and you."

"Not good. Have you spoken to Ian recently?"

He was cautious. "Not since day before yesterday. What's up?"

She hesitated, deciding how much to reveal, then thought better of it. "You probably heard we had another blowup and he left the house Sunday evening and hasn't been seen or heard from since."

Alarms sounded in Brian's head. He had lied about seeing Ian a couple of days ago because he thought Evelyn was spying on Ian. He hadn't spoken to Ian since early Saturday morning when they played basketball over on East Monroe in Alexandria. So that meant Ian had been out of touch a few days. "What do you mean?" Brian said. He kept his tone even.

"He hasn't been to work all week. When you talked to him, was he okay?" She sounded anxious.

"Evelyn, I think it was more like Saturday or maybe Sunday when I last spoke to Ian and he didn't say anything about you two fighting. Let me call the guys and see if I can find out anything. I'll call you back."

"I appreciate that," Evelyn said, and she truly meant it. She was fretful and it was making her nauseous. She had not participated in any activities since Monday and that amazed her. When Ian was around, he got on her last nerve; but, now that he wasn't there, she realized how much she missed him. There was a void in her life.

Brian listened to the anxiety and tried to still her fears with soothing words. "I'm sure he's fine Evelyn, probably somewhere cooling off, getting his head straight."

There was a lull.

"Brian, I reported Ian missing this morning. I didn't know what else to do and I'm sorry I didn't call you sooner."

Brian was infuriated. *Why would you get the police involved?* "Well, you did what you had to do so no use worrying about that now. I have to find my boy. I'll hit you back as soon as I find out something."

Before Evelyn said another word, Brian hung up the phone. He called her all kinds of dumb bitches. He screamed the words. He couldn't believe she waited a week to contact him. He forced himself to calm down. *Where are you man and why wouldn't you call me if you're in some kind of trouble, no matter what it is?* Deep down, Brian knew why. He constantly badgered Ian about his relationship with Evelyn. Ian had discontinued discussing his marriage months ago and Brian left it alone too. *That's probably why he didn't discuss this latest blowup.*

Brian called their basketball buddies, but they hadn't seen or heard from Ian all week.

* * *

Brian began to recall what happened to him.

That night he went to his and Ian's favorite hangout, Hooters over in Fairfax, to ask around about Ian. That's when he heard the breaking news from the TV above the bar—four men were missing from the DC metropolitan area.

How in the world had I missed news of that magnitude? Brian answered his own question. *I was too busy whoring around,* he silently admonished himself.

He was about to ask the pretty bartender who had been trying to get his attention ever since he sat down at the bar to turn up the volume, when he felt a hand high up on his thigh and a breast touching his arm. He turned to look at the woman who was so forward and was flattered by what he saw. He was use to women trying to make eye contact all the time, but he never had a woman approach him so boldly, and definitely not one as exquisite as this one.

She noticed he was drinking Patrón and asked the bartender to pour him a double shot. The bartender smarted. She was incensed at this interference. Her goal tonight had been to take this fine-ass man home and screw his brains out.

Brian was ecstatic by the intrusion, forgetting all about the top news of the hour.

This is going to be an easy lay, he thought.

That's all he remembered.

CHAPTER 25

INTERROGATION OF THE WIVES

FBI Special Agents Kelly and Coffy knocked on the front door of Joseph and Dolores Bradford's home.

"Who is it?"

"Special Agents Kelly and Coffy, FBI. Are you Mrs. Joseph Bradford?"

"I'm Dolores Bradford," she said, through the closed door.

"Ma'am, may we come in?"

Dolores opened the door about three inches wide and peeped out. "What's this about?" she asked.

"The disappearance of your husband, Joseph Bradford."

She cocked her head to the side considering whether she wanted to let them in or not. *The FBI was friendlier than the Bowie PD*, she thought.

Dolores unlocked the storm door, turned, and walked back toward the rear of the house into a huge, two-story family room. "I was getting ready for bed," she said. "Please sit anywhere." She sat in a recliner as far away from them as possible.

Coffy looked at his watch. It was four o'clock in the afternoon.

Mrs. Bradford wore a tattered robe, raggedly looking slippers, and had pink jumbo plastic rollers in her hair held in place by a bright colored turban. Kelly took note that Mrs. Bradford's appearance was a direct contradiction to her home, which was immaculate.

Kelly moved to a chair closer to Mrs. Bradford.

Coffy stayed put.

"We're sorry about the interruption, Mrs. Bradford, but I'm sure you have heard that there is a total of five missing men to-date." The agent didn't disclose, *and the only connection we have are the wives.* She did disclose, "we know two things: Mr. Bradford had a mistress and you knew about her."

"I was aware he had mistresses. Plural. He's always screwing somebody, but I didn't know this one's name until the Bowie police told me."

"Um hum," Kelly said. "Do you own a weapon?" *Let's handle that before we proceed.*

"I don't. Joe does and I think he has a permit. Would you like me to get it?"

"Please tell us where it is and we'll retrieve it."

"It's upstairs, second bedroom on the right at the end of the hall. It's in the nightstand, bottom drawer near the back. Joe kept it there 'cause he thought an intruder would go to the top drawer first."

Coffy went to retrieve the gun.

"Mrs. Bradford, if you did not have anything to do with the disappearance of your husband or cause him any bodily harm, why did you tell Victoria Jones that you killed him?"

"I did not tell that slut I murdered my husband. I asked her why the hell was she calling *my* house looking for *my* husband. I told her that bastard is dead! It was a figure of speech, nothing else."

Coffy came back into the room holding a Glock by the trigger guard.

"The ten-round magazine is full and it hasn't been fired recently," he said. "But the bedroom is a mess—a broken vase with wilted flowers on the floor beside the bed."

He looked at Mrs. Bradford.

"There's a large, dry, brownish spot on the carpet. I don't think it's blood. It has some kind of odor," he said.

"Are there any more firearms or weapons of any kind in the house, Mrs. Bradford?" Kelly asked. *Better to be safe and on guard.*

"Dolores," she corrected the agent.

"Excuse me."

"I would appreciate it if you didn't address me as Mrs. Bradford."

"And why is that?" Kelly asked.

"I hate that bastard. Honestly, I wish I had killed him. I hope he *is* lying dead somewhere."

Kelly was taken aback. She hadn't expected this abhorrent response. "Did I hear you correctly, Mrs. Bradford? You wish your husband is dead."

"Absolutely." *I asked that dumb twit not to address me as Mrs. Bradford.*

Kelly envisioned the judicial system locking up Dolores Bradford and throwing away the key. "What happened in the bedroom? Did you and Mr. Bradford have a fight? Did you kill your husband?"

"You're not listening to me!" Dolores screamed. "I wish I had killed him. Wish! Come with me, I'll show you what happened in the bedroom."

Kelly and Coffy followed her.

"I wanted his dead body right there," she pointed at the large dry spot on the floor with broken glass splattered everywhere.

Coffy palmed the handle of his 9mm.

There were streaks of some type of liquid on the wall. "I *wanted* to riddle his body with his own gun. I wanted to drench his dead body in roses and my piss because that's how he made me feel for the last couple of years, like nothing but a bedpan of piss."

"That's urine!" he screamed. Coffy could not believe he had been down on all fours sniffing Mrs. Bradford's pee. If he could have shot her there on the spot and gotten away with it, he would have.

Kelly thought nothing could astonish her anymore. This was another episode she could add to her journal of unbelievable things that happen in the daily life of a FBI agent.

As they walked to the cruiser, she told Coffy that he could be the agent-in-charge when they got to Rhonda Brown's house. She had enough of these crazies for one day.

Coffy said, "Let's flip a coin 'cause you didn't roll around in anybody's piss."

Kelly turned her head so Coffy wouldn't see her laughing.

But he heard her.

* * *

The agents had a difficult time locating Rhonda Brown because she no longer lived at the address she and Ron Brown shared. They went door-to-door making inquiries and finally found someone who was willing to provide them with her new address and phone number. They thought it advantageous not to call first, just drive right there since it was less than five miles away in the Del Ray neighborhood. The element of surprise was always the preferred way.

Rhonda heard a vehicle enter the driveway and went to the door. She stepped out onto the screened-in porch as the agents exited the cruiser and ascended the three steps. They introduced themselves, verified their identities, and asked if they could come inside.

There was a street party going on and the deafening sound was the initiation of Agent Kelly's migraine. They noticed as they drove pass houses, some residents were outside gardening, other persons were loitering, and smoke was coming from barrels turned into grills. Even with billowing fumes in the air, they still detected the smell of marijuana. Some residents, or loiterers, were even drinking beer out in the open and the agents knew the red plastic cups contained some kind of alcohol.

Booming hip-hop music was coming from a parked lowrider with a Latino behind the wheel and another riding shotgun, with two black passengers seated in the rear. The car was bouncing to the sound of Dr. Dre, *Let Me Ride*.

The agents had to slow down, practically to a tortoise's pace, in order not to run over the kids who were playing hopscotch in the middle of the street, and no intention of moving out of the way until the agent pressed the horn.

No one in the neighborhood paid the agents any attention. It was as if they were invisible. Once they were inside the house, Kelly called the Alexandria PD for backup, just in case. "This is FBI Special Agent Kelly. I am with Special Agent Coffy at twenty-nine twenty-eight Biltmore Avenue in Del Ray, Virginia. We request backup for a four fifteen violation."

"Are you in danger?" the dispatcher asked.

Kelly responded no. "But, there is loud music playing; I can barely hear you. People are walking around with visible, open alcohol containers. And, there are blacks and Latinos loitering."

"Ten four." The dispatcher ended the communication.

Before the agents could sit down, Rhonda said, "Yes, I destroyed his clothes, but I bought them and I have the receipts to prove it. So, I have the right to shred my own property."

"Mrs. Brown, we're here because your husband is missing and we can't locate anyone who has seen or spoken to him since he left work two weeks ago."

"What ... what are you talking about?"

"Have you been listening to the news?" Agent Coffy asked. "One of the missing men is your husband."

Rhonda's eyes turned into a sprinkler system. She grabbed at her chest and fell to the floor. Agent Kelly rushed to her. "Mrs. Brown, are you okay?"

Coffy looked for the bathroom, found a powder room, brought back some toilet tissue, and handed it to Mrs. Brown.

"Thank you," she said through tears. She had started hyperventilating.

The agents waited for her to gain control of her emotions.

"Can you tell us the last time you saw your husband?" Kelly asked.

"The day I left him—two Fridays ago. I moved out of our home and put the majority of my belongings in storage."

"So, you didn't know he was missing?" Coffy asked, thinking she was lying through her teeth. *These missing men had made the national news. So unless she was living under a rock, she's lying about something*, he thought.

"No I didn't," Rhonda said, looking at Coffy. "I took off and went to Houston to visit my sister."

"Have you spoken to your husband?" Kelly asked.

"No, not since I left him. I didn't know Ron was missing. When I didn't hear from him, I figured he got the message that *this* time I really left him."

"Why did you leave him in such a drastic manner?"

"I was married; he was not."

"What does that mean? You're either married or you're not." Kelly looked at Coffy for confirmation. He shrugged his shoulders.

"Exactly," Rhonda said. "From the day we met, he continued his philandering ways. I assumed marriage would change him. You know what they say when you assume. 'You make an ass of you and me.' I made the biggest mistake of my life."

For a second Kelly felt sorry for Mrs. Brown but could not communicate that feeling. Kelly was there to do a job and Mrs. Brown could be a suspect in her husband's disappearance.

"Mrs. Brown, your husband's assistant played a message for us that you left on his work phone." Kelly looked at her notes. "What did you mean by, and I quote, *'when you get home after five, I left your ass and that's no jive?'"*

"I always threatened Ron that I would leave him. He never believed me. Those are lyrics from a Gap Band song that I use to sing to him. They're not the exact words. I'm not good at memorization but it goes something like this." To their utter amazement, she started snapping her fingers and singing the song.

"Are you saying he *never* called you to ask why you left?" Coffy repeated.

"I have not talked to Ron since I left him."

"Thank you, Mrs. Brown, that's all for now," Kelly said. They handed her their cards and Coffy told her to call them if she heard from her husband or could think of anything else.

Mrs. Brown's water works started again.

The agents looked out the front door and didn't see an Alexandria police officer in sight nor heard any sirens approaching. They walked hurriedly to the cruiser.

No one acknowledged them.

Once seated, Coffy asked, "Do you think she's being truthful?"

"I don't know. The tears seemed genuine," Kelly said. "You think she's lying, don't you?"

"I think that fainting was an overly performed act."

"I'll give Alexandria PD a call and ask them to keep a detail on her, if one is available."

"Yeah right, keep your fingers crossed," Coffy said.

* * *

The following day, the agents went to interrogate Brenda Taylor, Brian Taylor's wife. When they arrived at the front door of the home, they heard a loud commotion, which sounded like dishes breaking.

Coffy knocked loudly on the door and yelled, "FBI."

There was a lot of screaming and cursing, the most foul language he had ever heard. He tried the doorknob, it turned, and he pushed the door open. He and Agent Kelly approached stealthily in the direction of the sound while surveilling their surroundings. When they got to the kitchen, they saw two women standing on either side of the island, one with a butcher knife in her hand and the other holding a frying pan.

Coffy kicked a butcher block of knives behind him. Broken dishes were everywhere.

"FBI, drop your weapons!" Kelly bellowed. The agents had their guns drawn and pointed at the women.

Both women turned and complied with the command. There was a loud clanging sound as the knife and pan crashed to the floor. Kelly went toward one woman and Coffy went toward the other one. They holstered their guns and the women were escorted to the living room.

"Sit down," Kelly said.

The agents produced their badges and introduced themselves. "We are here to talk to Mrs. Taylor," Kelly said. "Which one of you is Brian Taylor's wife?"

"I am," Brenda said, raising her hand. Her face exhibited the bruising of a black eye that was getting darker and a split lip that was growing larger.

"And you are?" Coffy asked, looking at the other woman.

"Trish Morton."

"What is your relationship to Mrs. Taylor?"

Brenda interrupted. "We have no relationship. She's Brian's ex-girlfriend."

The ex pointed at Brenda, "and she's the bitch that slept with Brian behind my back and then married him."

"Your momma's a bitch," Brenda shouted and stood up, preparing to jump the ex-girlfriend.

"Hey, hey," Coffy yelled over top of them. "Calm down, right now, and act like ladies, please."

Kelly grabbed Mrs. Taylor by one shoulder and shoved her back down on the couch. "Okay, we're going to talk one at a time and we're focusing on Mrs. Taylor first." She looked at the other woman. "Don't interrupt."

She turned her attention back to Mrs. Taylor. "Do you know where your husband is?" Kelly asked.

"No I don't. He got a call from Ian's wife, Evelyn. She informed him that Ian was missing and Brian went out looking for him. Ian wasn't at the basketball court so Brian went looking for him later that night in their usual haunts. He couldn't understand why he hadn't heard from Ian. He speculated that Ian and Evelyn probably had a fight—they're always fighting—and thought Ian had gone somewhere to cool off. I haven't seen or heard squat from Brian since. And since the police had me on standby, I went to the media."

"Well, Brian was with me that night," the ex-girlfriend lied, "all night long."

Brenda couldn't see the ex because Kelly had blocked her view.

Coffy warned the ex that if she opened her mouth one more time without their permission he would have her ass hauled off to the police station.

"Well, when will it be my turn to talk?" she asked. Her weave was askew and looked as if it had been yanked out of place and she had four long fingernail scratches down the left side of her face.

"It's your turn now. What's going on here between you and Mrs. Taylor?" Coffy asked.

"We use to be best friends and she starts screwing my man behind my back and then marries him," the ex said.

Kelly tried to process what she was hearing.

"You two were on your ninety-ninth breakup. I thought this time it was for good," Brenda said.

"So that gives you carte blanche to carry on a relationship with him right under my nose," the ex hollered. "It's fifteen men to every woman out here and you couldn't find your own man."

The agents looked at Mrs. Taylor, but made no comment.

"First of all, it's fifteen women to every man but not that it matters. You couldn't make him happy, so I did," Brenda said.

"You tramp," the ex screamed, and lunged toward Brenda.

The agents held both of them down.

Coffy said to the ex-girlfriend, "You must leave this house right now and don't come back. If you do, we're telling Mrs. Taylor right in front of you to get a restraining order."

He looked at Mrs. Taylor. "You may want to get that black eye looked at," and turned to the ex. "We have a first aid kit in the vehicle. We'll give you some antiseptic wipes for those scratches."

Kelly, Coffy, and the angry ex-girlfriend left Brian and Brenda Taylor's home together, but not before a parting shot from the ex. "You know, Brenda, your day is right around the corner. And believe me when I say this. Brian is not missing. He's out there shacked up with *your* replacement."

* * *

"Good grief, all these husbands are whores," Agent Kelly said. "What's up with that? Is it a black thing?"

"There you go profiling again, Kelly," Agent Coffy said.

"I'm not," she said. "It's just a question."

Coffy thought about it. "Yeah, but why are you asking me?"

"Well, you're a black man, aren't you?"

"It eats at you that you don't know my race, doesn't it?"

"No it doesn't. I could care less that you're black."

Coffy grinned. "Oh really now. Well, for your information, not that it's any of your business, I'm not black."

Kelly couldn't hide her shock. "You're not!" she said. She quickly regrouped. "And not that it matters, what are you then?"

"What are you?" he asked.

"White," she said. *You're trying to throw me off kilter and it won't work.*

"You know this how. We look alike if you're profiling based on the color of my skin or my facial features."

"I know I'm white because I just know."

"Um hum."

"Well, are you going to tell me or not?" Kelly asked.

"Nope." He grinned at the idiocy of their back-and-forth conversation. It was the Twenty-first Century and white people still needed to know his race, he guessed, before they could make a determination or assessment whether to socialize with him or not outside of the FBI.

He quenched her thirst but not before he paused for effect. He just wanted to witness her shock again. "I'm white," he said. Sure enough she didn't disappoint him.

"Really!" she said.

He decided to be truthful. "I'm biracial—white, black, and native American, in that order."

"Thank you for not getting upset, Coffy."

"You're welcome, Kelly. Now that you can relax around me, let's get back to the conversation at hand."

"Okay, what's the rationale in getting married if guys still want to play the field?"

"See, you're doing it again. You're making assumptions. Women fool around too, you know."

"I'm serious," she said.

"Well, don't look at me. I'm not married."

"It's a farce and not fair. It's like slapping the institution of marriage in the face."

Coffy decided to give Kelly a lesson on reasons married men and men in committed relationships cheat. "You all punish us by withholding sex and give us ultimatums—either marry me or this relationship is terminated. You women have timelines made up in your head that are inflexible once you enter into a relationship."

"What's that suppose to mean?"

"You sure you want to hear this Kelly, 'cause I'm going to shoot straight."

"Shoot," Kelly said.

"One month into the relationship, y'all want an exclusive.

"Two months in, you start cock blocking."

"What?" Kelly exclaimed, shaking her head.

"Barely three months and a day, you need to hear 'I love you,' cause last month you said it first.

"Going on four months, you start discussing living arrangements, since we're spending so much time together anyway, so you say."

"That's not fair!" Kelly said.

Coffy shook his index finger at Kelly.

"Oh no, you wanted to hear it, you're going to hear all of it. Five months in, y'all want to control who our female friends are, conveniently forgetting that we knew other women before we knew you existed; so you hint something fishy must be going on.

"It's going on six months and now you can't tolerate our male friends, swearing we're hanging out too much, spending too much time together, implying it must be a gay thing just to antagonize us."

Kelly sighed, then frowned, but said nothing.

Coffy kept on rolling. He didn't break a stride.

"Then the holy grail. Seven months into the relationship, you start hinting at marriage." He shook his head.

"Lo and behold, the eighth month rolls around and you don't get your period, it's late, scaring the beejesus out of us."

Kelly wanted to slap him to make him stop talking, but at the same time, she needed to hear the answer from a man's perspective.

"Month nine, you're badgering us constantly about something we did or something we didn't do."

"My god," Kelly butt in.

Coffy wasn't done.

"The tenth and eleventh months, it's one-sided talk nonstop about getting married. Blah, blah, blah." He imitated a quacking duck with both hands.

Kelly couldn't help herself. She laughed at his imitation.

"Then, like clockwork, comes the ultimatum. 'It's been a year and if you're not going to marry me, it's over!' you inform us."

"Wow! Is that how men really think?" was all Kelly could say. She had no rebuttal.

"It's like the twelve *months* of Christmas, except we don't get any gifts," Coffy said. "Only nagging, more nagging, and nonstop nagging. Jesus, if you women would only give us guys a break."

"So, what are you saying?" Kelly asked.

"Whether white or black, we marry y'all to shut you the hell up!"

CHAPTER 26

THE TRUMPLETON BROTHERS

Juan Trumpleton had been concentrating on NBCNews the entire weekend. A story about five missing men from the Washington, DC, metropolitan area caught his attention. A press release was going to be given at three that afternoon by the Arlington Chief of Police because two of the missing men were from Arlington, Virginia.

The news anchor said all the missing men were from middle to upper-class communities and income brackets with jobs and wives. "The police don't know what to make of the situation because they have never experienced this type of crime before. Kidnappings, if that's what this is, do not happen to grown men, not in this country anyway. The police don't say whether foul play is involved or not, and the media can't divulge any information because the police aren't providing us with anything."

Juan sat at the table transfixed and rubbed the side of his temples with his middle and index fingers to relieve the pressure that was building. He succumbed to the notion that this would be a monstrous headache. He knew he had to make the call. He looked for the number because he did not know it by heart. The last time he called any of his siblings was when their daddy got critically ill. The doctors said he wouldn't pull through the night. They asked family members if his papers, his life, were in order. Their father had been transferred to a hospice where Juan, his brothers, and mother were at their father's bedside for seven days and seven nights. The family could not locate Jackie. To this day, three years later, their daddy was still alive, still drinking, and still smoking.

"It's a miracle!" their mother said, praising the Lord.

"What did doctors know," Juan thought. "They were always playing God with people's lives."

He had to make the call, and with misgivings. He called the middle brother, Oliver, first, because he would listen without prejudging him. Juan had been carrying around this burden ever since he first heard the national news about men disappearing.

Juan dialed the number. After six rings, he started to hang up when he heard his brother answer, "It must be something bad if my kid brother is calling." The name Juan Trumpleton had displayed on the caller ID box. Oliver had not spoken to his younger brother in nearly a year.

"Hi Olli, how have you been?" Juan said. He had never called him Oliver because he couldn't pronounce it as a child so the name Olli stuck. Before he could say another word, Oliver cut him off.

"Been doing good, bro. I don't believe it. I must have talked you up, man. You remember, Cornell? He asked about you just the other day and wanted to know the next time we were coming home. I told him I didn't know; that we only talk when somebody back home dies."

Juan listened to Oliver go on and on, waiting for him to shut up so he could get a word in. Of course, he wouldn't be insolent to his older brother by saying anything disrespectful.

He waited for a pause. "Olli," Juan began, trying to sound upbeat.

"Are mom and dad okay?" Oliver wanted to get that out of the way first.

"Yeah, yeah, they're ok," Juan responded quickly. The brothers always asked about their parents first before saying anything else since they didn't speak to one another on a regular basis. With the exception of Sissy, their nickname for Jackie, mom spoke to everyone monthly and then she'd share any updates with each of the brothers.

For some reason, when Sissy left home, she severed ties with the family and no one understood why. Juan was the only one Sissy conversed with, and those were rare occasions. Well, he kind of knew the reason. Sissy felt mom was tough on her just to be mean. When he tried to explain it to her, "Sissy, it wasn't like that. You were the girl, that's all, and the youngest. Mom wanted to protect you."

"That is BS and you know it!" Sissy was adamant and that would be the end of the discussion.

Juan learned at an early age that there was no winning an argument or a fight, for that matter, with Sissy. He'll never forget their first and only fight, which happened on her birthday.

He was thirteen and she turned ten.

Aunt Bessie had just finished plaiting her three long braids—one in the front that followed a path down the side of her face and adorned with an oversized pink ribbon to match the color of her dress, and the other two flowed down her back and curled at the ends. She was as proud as a peacock when she pranced outdoors and went to the swing set with her white Barbie and Ken dolls.

Juan and two boys from the neighborhood were swinging so she went to the seesaw and sat there, and commenced having imaginary small talk with the dolls. For reasons unknown, because Juan had never pulled this stupid stunt before, he grabbed her two back pigtails and started swirling them like Double Dutch.

"Stop Juan," she cried, "or I am going to tell mom." He was messing up her hair that Aunt Bessie had so lovingly groomed.

"Crybaby, crybaby, wipe your dirty eyes," he sang, showing off for his friends.

Something happened. To this day family members said she snapped. Mom said it was the devil.

Jackie jumped off the seesaw and pounced on Juan. She, Barbie, and Ken started wailing on him. He collapsed to the ground. Her right fist holding Ken pummeled Juan everywhere, including the ground; and Barbie was in her left hand seeming to strike him everywhere else her right hand missed. Juan's friends were playacting "duke it out" as if they were Sonny Liston and Cassius Clay.

Juan's screams brought mom, dad, Andrew, and Oliver running from around the front of the house. They thought Sissy had fallen off the swing and broken something because the screams were the piercing sounds of a little girl.

Sissy was beating the dickens out of Juan. Andrew and Oliver were almost knocked to the ground as they pulled the two apart.

Juan had a knot on the side of his head, his nose was bleeding profusely, and he was crying like a baby.

Dad told the two boys, "scat, go on home now."

Not one adult inquired what happened. Mom saw Juan beaten up and Jackie with not so much as a scratch on her, although her new dress was dirty and her patent leather Mary Janes were scuffed, decided it was Jackie's fault. So, while squeezing Jackie's upper arm, mom swatted Jackie's backside with the other hand as they marched toward the house pass Aunt Bessie, who was standing in the doorway looking at Juan, amused.

As Juan passed, Jackie heard Aunt Bessie say, "I betcha that'll teach you about picking on your little sister," and lifted her huge leg and kicked him lightly on the butt, which made him bawl even louder.

Dad said, "Yep, we need to call him sissy," and the two brothers wallowed around in the grass laughing.

Mom turned around. "There's nothing funny about this," she said. "Jack-ah-lean-o-fill-ya-an-twa-net-trump-a-ton needs to learn to be a lady."

"And Juan-trump-a-ton needs to learn to be a man," Aunt Bessie said, giving him the evil eye.

From that day forward, until Jackie moved away, Andrew and Oliver referred to Sissy as Jackie-O and Juan was called Sissy-J; of course, out of mom's hearing range.

Juan knew that once Sissy made up her mind that she was right, the Lord himself couldn't change it. And she wouldn't forgive mom for her harsh upbringing. When Sissy left home, with not so much as a goodbye—mom came home from church and found Sissy's belongings packed in her car—Sissy announced she was moving. When mom asked where, not understanding, Sissy said that she didn't know where and mumbled that she'd send a postcard when she got there. Then, as mom told the story through sobs and a broken heart, Sissy sped off so fast in that Mustang of hers that the car spun around and the back tires spattered her with gravel and dirt.

"It would have hurt no more," mom said through tears, "than if Sissy had screamed I hate you mother. I felt like she was spitting at me."

"So, what's up," Oliver asked.

"Have you seen the news about those missing men up in DC?" Juan asked. Before Oliver could respond yes or no, Juan blurted out, "It's Sissy."

"Whoa, Juan, slow down and back up a sentence. What are you talking about?" Oliver asked, not comprehending this rubbish his kid brother was saying. "What's Sissy?" he asked.

"The kidnappings," Juan said, in a conspiratorial tone. "Sissy's responsible."

"Have you gone mad, Juan, or are you smoking weed?" Oliver asked. He didn't understand this conversation they were having. "Have you said this garbage to anyone else?"

"No," Juan said.

"Well don't!" Oliver instructed.

Juan tried to explain, but Oliver prevented him from saying another word. "Look," he said, "I'll give Andrew a call. I was planning on coming home this weekend anyway. I'll pickup Andrew. Let's meet at Dong Phuong on Saturday night. We'll talk then. And, Juan, I'm serious bro, don't breathe another word of this malarkey to anyone until we get together."

Juan felt reprimanded by his older brother and out of deference to him, he would keep this to himself, at least until Saturday.

* * *

They found a booth near the kitchen that was secluded from other customers. While Oliver and the oldest brother waited for Juan to arrive, Oliver gave Andrew a rundown.

Andrew had the same reaction. "Is he on drugs?" he asked.

"I know," Oliver said. "I asked him the same thing. I told him to keep his mouth shut until we heard where he got this weird notion that Jackie-O has any connection to missing men."

The brothers knowingly smiled at the pet name.

"No, I'm not on drugs," Juan said, as he sat down. The brothers hadn't seen him walk up and Juan had overheard part of the exchange.

The brothers ordered a round of sodas with their meals. No liquor. They wanted to be sober. So, they talked about sports until their food arrived and the waitress left the table.

"Okay," Oliver said, "let's hear it."

Juan told them about a time he had visited Sissy years and years ago. "I came across this journal she was keeping," he said, "and while she was at work, I ran over to Kinkos and had it copied." He pulled five sheets out of a portfolio they hadn't noticed.

Oliver watched Juan intently as he was talking. "You spied on Jackie-O," he said in disbelief.

Juan grimaced as he heard the despicable nickname he had been cursed with all those forgotten years ago. "Read," Juan said, and thrust each a copy, refusing to acknowledge Oliver's glare.

They scanned the pages. Andrew was the first to speak. "Juan, is this all you have to accuse our sister of criminal wrongdoing?"

Oliver agreed. "Please tell us you have more than this, which is nothing more than a girl's confidential journal, which you stole," Oliver said, emphasizing confidential and stole.

"Remember when that pimp brought Sissy home for Aunt Bessie's funeral," Juan said, ignoring both of their questions.

The brothers ignored his question too.

"Come on guys," he said, "think about it. We hadn't seen Sissy in a year and she's dropped off in front of the church in a red Fleetwood Cadillac with a checker board roof and matching seats. It was embarrassing having that pimp car in the procession."

The brothers recalled that time and started jesting. It was funny now, but not back then. Mom had a conniption.

"Well, ever since then, I've been keeping an eye on Sissy."

"So, I'm right then, you're spying on her." Oliver said. "And you've stalked her for what, thirty years," he said. He shook his head. If they had not been in a restaurant and Juan had been any other man instead of his brother making these outlandish remarks about their sister, he would have punched him square in the chest.

Andrew couldn't take it anymore. He reached across the table and grabbed Juan by the shirt collar and pulled his face close to his own like he did when they were teenagers. "Listen here Sissy-J," Andrew had reverted to Juan's cruel childhood nickname, "I don't know what's going on in that brain of yours," he knocked twice on his head, "but you better abandon this bullshit, and get a grip. There is nothing in these personal writings that imply anything about missing men." He pushed Juan back down on the bench so hard that the couple in the adjoining booth turned around to see what was going on.

"Sorry about that folks," Andrew said. The couple turned back to their meal.

He looked back at Juan, "What's wrong with you?" Andrew was incensed.

"Well, I have more," Juan said angrily, starting to regret that he had brought this to Olli's attention.

"What ..., what do you have?" Andrew asked.

Juan pulled another piece of paper out of the portfolio.

"What did you do?" Oliver asked, "ransack her entire apartment? No wonder she moved clear across the country to get away from all of us."

"A thousand miles is not clear across the country," Juan said.

"Oh, you got jokes, do you, at a time like this," Andrew said.

"No, it's just the two of you are beating me up before you hear everything," Juan said.

"I haven't touched you yet," Oliver said.

"Olli, I called you because I thought you would not judge me before hearing everything," Juan said.

"Well Juan, you caught us off guard. We don't talk in over a year and then when we do, this is the topic of discussion."

"I know guys and I'm sorry, but this story on the news, it really got me putting two and two together," Juan said. "When I first came across the journal, I thought Sissy was writing a book. But, when I read the stuff about us, our family, I realized it wasn't fiction. This stuff was for real. Then, I really started snooping around. Guys, sissy has a lot of money, and ..."

"How much?" Andrew interrupted. He had just about enough of Juan.

"She's a millionaire!" Juan said.

Both brothers held their breath. Oliver and Andrew looked stunned.

Oliver spoke first. "Juan, what does being a millionaire have to do with missing men? What's the connection?" *Jackie's a millionaire!* He hid his astonishment.

"She's a madam!" He said this so loudly that other patrons in the restaurant turned and looked at them.

"Lower your voice," Andrew said.

"Didn't you read it in those pages I gave you from her journal? She wanted to be a pimp after she left home," Juan said. His breathing had increased rapidly and his voice exhibited extreme excitability.

Juan realized his brothers were laughing at him. Their facetious behavior toward his serious concerns insulted and angered him, and made him feel as if he were a fool for bringing up this discussion. Their ruckus was so loud and disturbing that diners turned and gave them angry looks. They even heard a toddler ask his mommy what was so funny.

"We're sorry," the brothers said.

"We'll keep it down," Andrew said.

They turned their attention back to Juan.

"Man, you're making a mountain out of a molehill. You're trying to connect dots where there aren't any," Oliver said.

Juan was shocked his brothers didn't see Sissy the same way he did. He had not been prepared for their outrage and denial over his accusations. They seemed offended that he would speak ill of their sister in this manner. He hadn't brought this news to them on a whim. He had kept this information in solitary confinement for years. It was only when this missing men thing happened that he believed there was a connection.

Juan thought he showed his brothers enough proof to validate his reasons for believing Sissy was involved. But, apparently not. And since they were so furious, he didn't dare mention what he considered the coup de grâce. He knew Sissy had purchased a mansion in Virginia. He searched for it on Zillow and although he couldn't find an exact price, comparable properties were priced for several million dollars. Last he checked, Andrew was right about his stalking her, she was having extensive renovations done. *Why would she keep this a secret from the family and why wasn't the family invited to her home?*

"Well, she also established her own real estate company and named it J. O. A. T. Realty," Juan said, in a tone that was defiant. He laid down on the bench because he saw Andrew coming after him again.

"Let him be, Andrew," Oliver said. "Okay Juan, humor me. What has your detective work uncovered?"

Juan sat up. "It's a combination of our names," he said, "Juan, Oliver, Andrew Trumpleton." Juan looked so serious that the brothers' outburst prompted a second round of apologies to diners.

Oliver waved the waitress over to the table. "We'll order a round of martinis now."

"Okay Juan, you really are reaching now," Andrew said.

"And it's the initials of her full name too. Remember, she hated her name, Jacqueline Ophelia Antoinette Trumpleton, with a passion. That's why she calls herself Jackie and the name of her company is no coincident," he said.

"And that's why we call you Sissy-J ...," he started, before he saw Oliver shake his head.

Andrew wanted to beat Juan to a pulp, knock some logic into him. "What does any of this have to do with Sissy and missing men?" he asked.

Juan kept quiet. He wished he could knock the crap out of Andrew and escape repercussions.

"Juan, there's nothing you said here tonight that gives us any indication that Jackie-O, he emphasized the nickname, is, was, or has been a madam. Nothing!" Oliver begged. "So, we want you to get this warped notion out of your head; and please, for god's sake, don't mention this idiotic bull to mom and dad. Do you want to kill them?"

"I can't promise that," Juan said.

"Then man, I'm through," Andrew said, as he got up from the booth to leave.

"Juan, please don't do anything you'll regret. Once you accuse Sissy, once you put this nonsense out into the universe, you won't be able to take it back," Oliver said.

"Why don't you believe me?" Juan pleaded.

"It doesn't matter, Juan, whether we believe you, or not believe you. We're not going to do anything that would hurt Sissy, upset mom and dad, and disparage the Trumpleton name."

Oliver looked at his younger brother for a long time hoping Juan would relent. When Juan said nothing, he said, "Good bye, Juan."

Andrew said nothing.

Neither brother picked up the check.

CHAPTER 27

ABDUCTION OF BEN WRIGHT

The curtains were raised for intermission and Ben went to the cash bar. He was standing directly behind the stunning woman he had noticed earlier sitting a few seats down from him. As he placed his order for vodka and OJ, he gently bumped her.

"My apologies," he said, and flashed her a dazzling Biden smile. "Bartender, Grey Goose with that please."

"Sorry sir, no Grey Goose. I have Absolut."

He was disappointed and the smile disappeared.

"You can have a shot of my goose," the woman said, who turned to face him. She was holding an intricately designed flask.

The Biden smile reappeared.

She ordered a diet Coke.

"A woman after my own heart," he said, and changed his order to orange juice only.

"May I buy you a drink?" he asked.

She looked at the bartender. "Do you have G.H. Mumm?" she asked, giggling, knowing they didn't carry champagne.

"Sorry ma'am, we only have white wine."

"Well, I will have a glass of wine instead of the coke since he is buying," she pointed at the man. As she waited for the bartender to pour her wine, the stranger and she talked about how each other was enjoying the play, *Phantom of the Opera.*

"I have wanted to come to New York for years to see this on Broadway," she said. "Finally, my dream came true."

"And it has only been running twenty-five years. You almost missed it," he joked. "Did you come alone?"

"Yes. I came up on Amtrak this morning," she said. "I do not drive anywhere for four hours and then have to deal with those tolls too. No way."

"Up?" he said. He was hoping she lived near him.

"Yes. I have a home about twenty-seven miles outside of DC," she said.

"I live in DC," he said. "What a small world? When are you returning?"

"Tomorrow. How did you get here? Did you drive?" she asked.

They were interrupted by the chimes alerting patrons that intermission was over.

"Where are you seated?" he asked.

"In the orchestra section." She pulled the ticket from her gold, beaded evening clutch and said, "Seat 105."

He looked at his ticket. "Surprise, surprise, I am seated in 110." They walked back together to their seats and promised to meet at the entrance after the show.

She left as soon as the curtains dropped, before the cast did curtain call. She wanted to get to the restroom before the line became unbearable. *Only a man would design a woman's restroom in this manner—ten toilets for hundreds of women.* As she heard the roar of applause, she recalled that she told the gentleman she would meet him after the show, but neither stated specifically where, only at the entrance. As she exited the restroom, she looked around to see if she saw him in the crowd that was flooding out the doors. The commotion was excitable.

He was tall and distinguished looking, so she thought it would be easy to scout him out. Someone shoved into her and as she felt herself falling forward unable to regain her balance or grab on to anything, she felt a strong arm yank her back up. She was frightened; she hated crowds and this was the reason she rarely ventured out to public events. She was shaking uncontrollably and all she could think of was being in a stampede.

He could feel her trembling. "Are you okay?" he asked. Before she could utter a word, he said, "That's what happens when you try to dodge someone."

She tried to laugh but it came out as a nervous giggle. "I was looking for you," she said.

"Come on, let's get out of here," he said, and took her hand and pulled her behind him.

They were moving too fast and she stopped, stood still. He looked back, alarmed that something had happened.

"Where are you taking me?" she demanded to know.

He regrouped quickly. He realized he had lost all sense of decorum. Here he was a no-name stranger practically dragging her to god knows where. "I'm sorry," he said. "I don't know what got into me. Honest, this is not the way I behave when I meet a beautiful woman." He paused to gather propriety. "You just looked like a deer in head-lights and I was trying my best to get you to safer ground. I must have frightened the dickens out of you pulling you off like that. I am truly sorry." He finally let go of her hand. "Please forgive me and let me start over."

Her heart stopped palpitating against the walls of her chest. Her breathing returned to normal. She appreciated his empathy. "Apology accepted," was all she said.

He held out his hand. "I'm Benjamin Wright."

"Please to meet you, Ben." She shook his hand. "May I call you Ben?"

"Yes. What shall I call you?" he asked.

"Sissy," she blurted out, which felt like an ambush because she hadn't heard the sound of that name in years.

"Incognito?"

"For now."

He understood she was being cautious since they were strangers. He recalled her saying she travelled via Amtrak to New York. "What time does your train leave?" he asked, looking at his watch. "It's ten forty-five now."

"Two forty-five," she said.

"Tomorrow afternoon?"

"In four hours," she said, clicking off the hours with her fingers. "Eleven forty-five, twelve forty-five, one forty-five, two forty-five." She did this because she was still unsteady and needed a moment to steel her nerves.

"Are you hungry? Would you like to go to B. Smith's for a late dinner? It's not that far from here. We can catch a cab or the 'A' train," he said. "Or we could walk. It's less than a mile." He didn't dare mention his car was parked nearby and he could drive them there.

"I would love to walk, if you don't mind," she said. "It is such a beautiful night."

"I don't mind at all." They chatted about the play all the way there and lost track of the time. They couldn't believe it when they arrived at the entrance. The restaurant was crowded and after a thirty-five minute wait, they were seated near the door where they could look out the window and watch people stroll up and down forty-sixth. The street was so well-lit; it was difficult to believe it was almost midnight.

Without asking her, he ordered a bottle of Robert Mondavi Fume Blanc. She looked at the menu and was glad he selected B. Smith's. She was ravenous. She hadn't eaten since earlier in the day when a Greek salad and bottled water were all she consumed, which was included with the Doris Baxter Day Spa "pure indulgence package" where she had been pampered with a European facial, sea salt body scrub, manicure and pedicure, and a hot stone massage.

She ordered fried green tomatoes for her appetizer and he ordered corn flour crusted calamari. They shared. When their entrées appeared, they were envious of each other's dish. She had shrimp and grits and he had the Swamp Thang. They shared that too. After drinking an entire bottle of wine, he wanted to order another bottle, which she declined. They were too full for dessert so he ordered mocha mousse to take back to his hotel.

When the waiter brought the check, she reached for her clutch but he covered her hand and said, "I got this." He was touched that she was offering to pay. A woman hadn't offered to pay for anything when on a date with him in a very long time.

She, however, wanted to pay because she didn't want there to be any misinterpretation that this was a date and that his hotel room would be an automatic layover. "I want to pay at least my share," she said.

He understood immediately what she was really verbalizing and assured her that it was just a dinner between a man and a woman who were enjoying each other's company.

It was one-thirty in the morning as they walked toward Penn Station.

"I really don't want this night to end," he said. "I haven't had this much fun in more months than I care to remember. I promise, if you come back to my hotel," he threw his hands in the air, "I will sleep in the bed and you can take the sofa."

She looked up at him and rolled her eyes.

"I'm kidding," he said, "you can take the bed."

Bingo! So easy, yet again, she thought.

"That is very chivalrous of you. I tell you what," she said, "I really do not feel comfortable going back to a man's hotel room, one that I just met, at two o'clock in the morning. We could get your car and drive back to DC?"

"At this ungodly hour," he said. "I don't think so. I'm too exhausted to drive around the corner. I need at least a couple of hour's shut-eye."

"I will drive," she volunteered.

He stopped walking and turned toward her. "I thought you didn't like driving for hours and hours."

"I will drive as far as Philadelphia, allowing you to get some sleep and then you can take over and drive the rest of the way to DC." She looked at him with pleading eyes.

Oh god, those eyes will be the death of me. "Alright," he agreed. They turned about-face and headed toward his hotel to pick up his car.

She waited in the lobby while he went to pack his bags.

* * *

The evening backfired.

His plan had been to get her out of that theatre, up to his room and rip that little black dress off of her. He hadn't accidentally bumped into her at the bar. He spotted her the moment she was shown her seat by the yakking elderly attendant five seats down from him. The understated, refined dress she wore hugged her body like a glove. The dress wasn't low cut, there was no cleavage showing, but her back was bare with triple straps running across. She sat with her legs crossed and the top of her stocking was visible. He couldn't get the image out of his mind.

So when she started conversing about the play at the bar, he had to pretend he was enjoying it as much as she was. When he returned to his seat after intermission, he focused on the remainder of the play so that when they talked again, he would be able to articulate his review intelligently.

He was amazed that she did not fall for the ploy of him trying to extricate her from the crowd. He was a good-looking man and that maneuver had worked a number of times. When she demanded that he stop, it threw him off his game. She was different from all the broads he was accustom to dating. She was classy, so he reverted to the days when he was a gentleman, before he became an arrogant son-of-a-bitch.

"Bags all packed," he said, as he walked briskly into the lobby holding a toiletry travel kit and a suit bag slung over his shoulder. He noticed she had changed clothes, so he looked around the lobby to locate where, and noticed a ladies restroom off to the side.

She pointed to her oversized bag.

She had on a white Polo shirt tucked inside creased Khakis, and penny loafers adorned her small size-six feet.

How could I have missed that bag? She could have changed in my room. Damn! He wished he had thought to ask her if she needed to change clothes. She probably would have said no; but what if she had said yes. He had blown a perfect opportunity to get her upstairs. He wanted to kick himself.

* * *

"What is it with men," she wondered. "How can they be so darn gullible?"

Well, that fallible characteristic made her job all the easier. She didn't have to use the Scopolamine on this one. He had fallen asleep before they had gotten to the first toll. His seat was reclined all the way back, almost into a horizontal position and he was sleeping soundly. He never stirred, not even when she pulled off the highway at a truck stop in Delaware to go to the ladies room and grab a Three Musketeers candy bar. At six fifteen, she was pulling into her garage. The rolling up of the garage door woke him.

"Where are we?" he asked, sitting up and rubbing his eyes. "Have we gotten to Philly yet?"

"Two hours ago, sleepy head. We are at my house. Would you like some breakfast?"

He was wide awake now. He actually grinned. "Sounds great." He got out of the car and walked out of the garage. He was astonished at her home. The view was breathtaking.

He forgot his wicked intention of seducing her the moment they stepped inside the house. "May I take a walk down to the dock?" he asked.

"Be my guest. I will get breakfast started. Bring your bag when you come in."

This was getting better by the second, better than anything I had planned. He walked down to the dock and was already envisioning his boat in the slip. He stood there captivated, taking in the view and magnificence of this place. *Who was this woman? How could she afford a place in a location like this?* He was in awe. He was born, raised, and lived in DC all his life and had never seen anything like it. He looked around and noticed that other homes were not as large as hers, but nevertheless, still as grand. He loved the seclusion; it was as if her property was a tiny island.

He sensed her nearing him and looked up.

"I brought you a cup of coffee?" she said.

"This place is beautiful. How long have you lived here?"

"I just purchased it a few months ago."

He was bowled over. He had no words. He looked upward in prayer. *Thank you God for not letting me make a pure asshole of myself last night.*

After breakfast, she invited him into her bedroom. "I do not want you to go home," she said. "I would like you to stay a while."

"I have no plans today. I'd love to stay."

"That is not what I mean." She repeated the spiel she had with the other men. "I need you to stay two, maybe three weeks max."

"I probably could make arrangements to do that." He couldn't believe his ears. This woman he had wanted to devour from the moment he laid eyes on her was asking him to hang out with her for a few weeks in this fabulous house on this fabulous island. "What happens after the three weeks?" He didn't know why he asked.

"Then you leave," she said. "We part ways."

"Just like that." He was perplexed. Somehow the roles were reversed. In every relationship he had ever been in, once he had sex with the woman, all of a sudden they were *in* a relationship; she was in love. It didn't matter how many times he said he didn't want to be in a one-on-one relationship, she would do everything, anything in her power, to convince him to fall in love with her. Then, when the so-called relationship didn't work out according to plan—it inevitably ended on bad terms—he was always the one on the receiving end being called all kinds of no-good MF'ers. Now, this woman was giving him a taste of his own medicine. She presented him with the whole enchilada and asked if he would accept the deal.

"So, it's deal or no deal." He mused where she was going with this line of reasoning. He had miscalculated her. He thought he was the hunter and realized too late that he had been hunted from the very beginning. He could only hope that he would not be slaughtered. The rules of the game had swung to her side.

"No," she said, "you do not have a choice."

He did not have time to think of a rebuttal before he felt a mist on his face.

CHAPTER 28

MISSION ACCOMPLISHED

It was midnight and Jackie was sitting in her sun room admiring the scenery of the Occoquan River and the beauty of the night sky. The night was serene. This was the beginning of what she had envisioned all those years ago when her life first intersected with those pimps in the seventies. She wanted that kind of control and power. She wanted the ability to control men the way pimps controlled prostitutes. There was a significant difference, however. Unlike pimps, she didn't want ownership of their mind, soul, and earnings. She just wanted control of their body, their manhood. And she was amazed at how easy it was to obtain control.

Jackie couldn't understand how a woman, whether a prostitute or a lady, a professional or on public assistance, a religious woman or a deviant, relinquished that kind of power willingly. Yes, one could lose control in the heat of passion, but only that, a moment like she had with Joe. *I will not go there,* she thought. But, you quickly regain it. Once you have a taste of power, a mere sniff of it, you never, ever want to renounce it.

She was excited, thrilled, and could hardly believe that an embryonic thought had come full circle to maturity under her tutelage.

The whistle of the teapot brought her out of her reverie. She went to the kitchen to steep six cups of tea, but then thought better of that idea. She had thought of asking the gentlemen to join her in the family room but it would have been five against one. Even with the Scopolamine in hand, if they got enraged, it would be no way she would be able to control all of them from ganging her, and maybe even gang-banging her. One-on-one they had been well-behaved. *I shouldn't be taking any chances*, she thought. *Maybe a glass of champagne for me would be a better idea.* She went to the wine cellar and grabbed her favorite bottle, G.H. Mumm, and for the purpose of feeling ladylike, grabbed a flute.

She went to the top of the front winding staircase and stood on the landing. She looked down at two of the three hallways and was astonished at the work the contractors had completed. It was simply marvelous. That was the only word befitting to describe what was before her eyes. They finished ahead of schedule and she gave them a sizable bonus. And in gratitude, when she arrived home later in the day, her entire home, every room, was filled with roses, orchids, and carnations.

She went to her white-on-white bedroom and lounged on the chaise, which was partially covered by a handmade quilt bequeathed to her by Aunt Bessie. She hit the intercom button and activated one of the bedroom speakers. Since she had been conversing with the men regularly, they were on a first-name basis.

"Good evening Ian, are you awake?"

"Yes Jackie, I am."

"Do you need anything? Are you comfortable?"

"I'm fine, thank you." He was still trying to reconcile why he enjoyed being held here against his will. But, of course, he couldn't let Jackie know his true feelings.

"Ian, as we discussed earlier, tomorrow my associates are flying in."

Ian interrupted her. "Did you say associates?"

"I meant associate, Ian, slip of the tongue. Like I was saying, I want to thank you for agreeing to stay on for three weeks. Again, I am sorry for the inconvenience and the manner in which I got you here. I do not know what else to say."

"Jackie, let's get something straight. I didn't agree to stay on. I'm a hostage in your home or is this really your home. So, don't get it twisted. Are you really sorry or are you just trying to assuage your guilt? You said associates. Are you making me a male prostitute? Is that your angle?"

"Ian, first, would it make any difference whether I am sincere about my apology or not? And second, no, you are not and will not be a male prostitute, I promise. You can say 'no' and I swear I will honor your request."

"I don't know, Jackie. I guess I have to just wait and see. So, the bottom line is that I can say 'no' to anything sexual, but you won't let me out of here before three weeks have expired. Do I have that correct?"

Jackie neither agreed nor disagreed with his assessment. She knew unequivocally once the girls arrived and she got them on board, which she believed wouldn't be a problem, none of these men would be turning down any sexual favors. She would bet her life on it. She sighed and took a sip of Mumm.

"Ian, if you really do not want to participate, that is okay. But, do you really want to leave?" She thought she had been treating them well.

"Jackie, I will tell you this. This last week has been a lifesaver for me. I was seriously down in the dumps and I guess I can thank you for helping me through a rough patch. It has been a long time since I've been treated in this manner. The room, the meals, the clothes; everything was better than I would have expected under the circumstances. I really don't want to leave tonight, tomorrow, or maybe even the day after. I just don't like the idea that I have no power to leave when I choose."

"Understood," Jackie said, and she hit the disconnect button.

She made identical calls to Ron, Brian, and Ben, and the confab was basically the same. She made sure to say associate versus associates. That was the bombshell and she had let it slip accidentally when speaking to Ian. She probably should not have been drinking.

Jackie did not call Joe. She was not confident in her ability to control her emotions in his presence and she couldn't figure out why. *He is just a man, for heaven's sake.* But he was like a magnet; she was pulled toward him powerlessly, akin to a rag doll. Every time she spoke to him, she lost control of the one-to-one. So, she knew without a doubt she could not be alone with him to discuss anything.

CHAPTER 29

VISIT TO OCCOQUAN

The associates were filled with anticipation and couldn't wait to meet up with Jackie and each other at the airport. It had been eleven months since they last saw each other. This gift Jackie sprung on them, their own vacation Mecca, was a dream that none of them believed would actually materialize. It was just that, a dream, or so they thought.

In order for them all to arrive around the same time, they had to fly into Dulles International Airport. Jackie would rent a stretch Hummer H-2 limo. The luxury vehicle was larger than they needed, but she wanted everyone to have room to stretch out during the 35-mile drive to Occoquan.

The girls saw one another as they were retrieving their luggage from the baggage area, but waited until they saw Jackie to do their dance. Babbling away, they rode the escalator upstairs and there at the top stood Jackie beside the limo driver who was holding a sign that read Jackie's Associates. They squealed with delight and dropped their bags, one by one, as they stepped off the last step. Right there, as they waited for the last associate to step off, and without a care in the world, they commenced their ritual.

"We sing our song of freedom.

We got away from boredom.

Gracias, Gracias.

We all do the hug."

And the five women huddled, closed in together tighter than any other previous vacation, and did a group hug. This time was different, special, and they all felt it. This was a new beginning.

On the ride to Occoquan, Jackie asked the driver to close the partition. The girls spotted five buckets, each holding a bottle of their favorite champagne. Jackie had thought of everything. The vacation spot was more than an hour away in rush-hour traffic so this would be enough time to provide them the highlights of their vacation. She had already sent the associates pictures of the retreat. Everyone was excited and Jackie was exuberant to witness this. She was nervous about the news she was about to share and hoped they wouldn't find her idea of fun and relaxation as obscene and offensive.

She started with gifts that she had purchased for each associate. The packages were beautifully wrapped. The girls were touched at this gesture because they had never exchanged gifts before, not even on one another's birthday. Indeed, they didn't know what date each other's birthday fell on. She watched as each associate opened her present.

Jackie had handpicked wearable Masks by Dalili, a selection of leather, Venetian, and feather masks.

Ruby gasped. "This is so beautiful Jackie, thank you. Oh my god, I love it."

Nadine concurred. "Jackie, what can I say? You've already done so much, giving us a free vacation and all. I certainly wasn't expecting a gift."

Bernadette piped in. "Jackie, I'm speechless. Are we going to a costume party?"

"I know what's going on," Laura said. "Jackie's from New Orleans so the theme of the vacation must be Mardi Gras."

They all looked at Jackie for confirmation.

"I have a secret to tell you," Jackie said, "and I trust you will not judge me until you have heard the entire story."

The girls were on pins and needles because in the twenty-some odd years they'd known Jackie, they had never heard her exhibit such a serious tone. *What in the world had gotten into her?* She was kind of scaring them. Each woman looked at each other and then at Jackie.

"No, I am not dying," Jackie said, sensing their anxiety. They looked so fearful that she had to say something.

The women's relief was visibly evident.

Bernadette took a gulp of Henriot. "What's wrong, Jackie?" she asked. "Did you bite off financially more than you could chew, because pictures of that mini mansion blew my mind."

The girls nodded their heads in tacit agreement but remained silent. They realized that an invisible line had been crossed.

"Wait a minute," Nadine said, breaking the somber mood, "let's hear what Jackie has to say before we make any assumptions." She didn't want to have any discussions about money, just in case Bernadette was going to proffer up any. When the trip to South Africa had been called off, Nadine attended a Sunday morning church service and gave thanks to the Lord. She was finally caught up on her second, new payment arrangement for the trip last year to Greece and had gotten the collection goons off her back. She didn't want to go through that nightmarish, humiliating torment ever again. The one and only time she charged something, forgetting her parents' advice about saving, she was caught in this predicament.

"Is everyone okay with us asking questions?" Laura interrupted. She looked at Jackie for corroboration.

Jackie hit the intercom button and asked the limo driver to go through DC before heading to Occoquan. She needed much more than an hour to tell the girls what was in store for them. This was the only time she would thank God for rush hour traffic in DC.

"Absolutely. You can ask me anything you want," she said. She gave them a surreptitious glance. "Just do not execute me," she said jokingly.

Jackie reminded them of the story she told when they were together the year before. "You know I am a control freak especially where men are concerned. Ever since I was introduced to the decadent lifestyle of pimps, prostitutes, and drag queens, I have never been able to forget or relinquish that part of my life. I am sure you recognized that I enjoyed reliving the story and it was extremely beguiling for me. I have always wanted to be an intricate part of it and now I found a way."

"Huh," Laura said.

"Okay. You know I purchased this mini mansion; but what you are not aware of is that I transformed it into a place of erotica, for us, where we can explore our sexual desires, fantasies, and appetites with no guilt, no inhibitions, no rules, no strings attached."

The girls looked mesmerized and appeared to have a newfound something for Jackie. She wasn't sure if the visible emotions were awe, angst, shock, or what.

"If I wasn't hearing this firsthand," Bernadette said, "I would tell whoever was spreading the vicious gossip to go screw themselves. But, this is coming straight from your lips to our ears. Frankly, I don't know what to say or how to react."

"When you say no rules, just what are you suggesting?" Nadine asked. Now, she was down for anything outside of the box, but she wasn't going to be experimenting with lesbianism. She loved men and she loved a good hard cock. And she had no intention at this late stage in her life, forty-nine, to learn pearl diving. No way. No how.

Jackie leaned forward and looked at Nadine first, then the others. "There are five, handsome, virile men at the house right now, one for each of us."

The women gaped in disbelief.

"Wait a minute. You picked out men for us or you invited men over so we can choose whom we want?" Ruby asked, not comprehending what Jackie was verbalizing.

"Well, not exactly," Jackie said. "Have you all been watching the national news lately?"

The women nodded, wondering what Jackie was leading up to.

"Those five missing men ..." Jackie paused.

The girls waited for her to continue.

"They are at the Mecca."

They stared at her, trying to assimilate the information she had just delivered.

"What are you *not* saying, Jackie?" Bernadette asked.

"I abducted those five men for us to share," Jackie said nonchalantly and her eyes never diverted.

"Bitch, are you crazy!" Laura yelled. "Have you lost your everlasting mind?" She entertained what Jackie had just told them. Then, unexpectedly, she clapped her hands. She leaned back in the seat and kicked her legs to the roof of the Hummer, almost knocking over Nadine's bottle of Moët. When she glimpsed the girls staring at her private area, she looked down and noticed her dress had risen and bunched up around her waist. "Oh don't be priggish," she admonished, "I have on a thong," and pulled the thin band from her waist to prove it.

Jackie looked steely and avoided replying to Laura right away. She didn't see herself as having lost her mind—how had Laura described it—everlasting. Jackie always had a motto or some parable she relied on when she didn't have a readily available, applicable justification. *It is better to beg for forgiveness than to ask for permission.*

"O. M. G. You're serious," Laura said. "Only you would pull off something far-fetched like this. Nah, wait a sec. You're lying. You expect us to believe that the missing men that the FBI and cops are searching for, and that's all over the news, are at your house. Right now!" Laura continued laughing and then composed herself. "Are you pulling our legs, Jackie?" she said. Then, she thought about it. "I don't believe I'm about to make this outlandish, ludicrous statement considering that I'm floored by this. But, Jackie, please tell us you're *not* lying."

Nadine was doing the twist in her bucket seat. "This is unthinkable," she said, "I love it." She was eager. "When do we get to meet them?"

"Tomorrow night," Jackie said. She was pleased with their reactions. She had expected chaos.

Ruby was still trying to process this incredulous piece of news. She shook her head trying to silence the alarm that was going off. "How ... how did you pull this off, Jackie?" Ruby was flabbergasted, and quite frankly, blown away. *What could have been going through that thick skull of hers to think that we would be party to this illegal act? You think you know someone your entire adult life and wham, out of nowhere, you learn you don't really know one iota about them. Who would have thought Jackie was capable of such a brazen act.*

Ruby surmised that Bernadette, Laura, and Nadine didn't share her sentiment, from the way they were behaving.

Jackie observed Bernadette. It wasn't like her to not comment. *I wonder what she's thinking.*

"No comments, Bernadette," Jackie said.

Bernadette was looking through the CDs that were stacked fifty deep in the side cabinet of the Hummer. In response, she looked at Jackie, and said, "Let's find some Marvin Gaye, I'm ready to get it on."

"Girl, that's old school," Nadine said, "Look for, *I Want Your Sex,* by George Michael."

Jackie sat back in her seat and closed her eyes. She could feel four pair of eyes watching her.

It was done.

She had finally unveiled the secret that had burdened her for months.

The limo entered the circular driveway at the end of Poplar Lane. The girls were captivated by the splendid house before them. The pictures Jackie sent didn't do the resident justice. Their Mecca was simply breathtaking. The girls exited the limo excited to commence their new adventure.

No one mentioned or seemed to care about the legal implications.

* * *

Bernadette, Laura, Nadine, and Ruby were in the solarium looking out at the Occoquan River. They each had their own bottle of champagne and were giggling like a group of teenage school girls. They were beside themselves with exuberance and anticipation for the beginning of a one-of-a-kind, orgasmic, two-week vacation. They giggled incessantly.

"Okay, girls, what dream have you scratched off your bucket list?" Jackie asked, as she entered the sun-drenched room.

"Are you kidding? Laura said. I'm thinking that by the end of this vacation, all my dreams will be checked off."

"Forget that bucket list gibberish," Nadine said, "I'm ready to meet our prey."

They all looked at Nadine without mouthing a word. They realized that without really discussing the legality of what they were about to do, they would become an accessory to Jackie's transgression.

"There is only one thing I ask before you meet your mature Adonis," Jackie said. Everyone turned their attention to her. "That you wear and never remove your mask while you are in their company."

They were intelligent women and everyone understood the consequences of not abiding by that simple request.

Ruby repeated her question, deviating slightly, because Jackie had skirted explaining how she pulled this off. "Jackie, how were you able to abduct five men?" Ruby's tone turned serious.

All eyes were on Jackie. She knew she had to provide details. It was the right thing to do after her huge proclamation.

"Do we need more champagne," Jackie evaded the question momentarily. "Let us get a bottle and go down to the dock, sit under the stars, and we can continue this conversation there."

"Where is the fridge?" Bernadette asked. Jackie walked over to a hidden panel in the wall, pushed a switch and Bernadette heard the whisper of a door sliding open. The huge, double door Subzero refrigerator appeared. Bernadette was impressed. She opened the doors and saw five cases of their favorite spirit on the bottom two shelves. She grabbed a bottle out of each case, handed them to Jackie one-by-one, which was handed off to the girls, and they proceeded down to the dock.

It was a beautiful, clear night. A full moon was dazzling in the dark blue sky and every now and then there was a flicker of lights from an airplane flying overhead going to its final destination. It was a quiet night and since it was the Labor Day weekend, Jackie's neighbors, whom she had not met and knew nothing about and preferred it that way, had disappeared to locations unknown. The Occoquan River was unusually quiet, not a boat in sight, except for the ones in boat slips.

The girls got comfortable in their individual chaise lounge and Jackie chronicled how effortless it was to kidnap five men.

"Actually, it was six, almost seven," she revealed. "I still cannot believe how simple it was to hustle men and redirect their attention. Girls, when women with sex appeal enter a man's periphery, he loses his mind—young or old men, it does not matter. It never ceases to amaze me what a man is willing to do, or lose, for sex. The initial approach was straightforward. I would enter a public establishment, settle my periscope on the man that fits one of our criteria and put my ruse into play. I would be assertive and approach the man wearing a seductive, not provocative, outfit. Every single time I approached using this tactic, they literally became putty in my hands. They do not see or hear anything else around them. They are like a horse with blinders, focused on one thing—how to get my panties off. Of course, that is when I am wearing any." She shook her head. "Okay, that is a story for another day. Getting them to the house was easy. Keeping them here once they realized they were not getting any poon tang was another."

She paused.

"So, on several occasions I had to use Scopolamine."

"You used what?" Nadine asked. "What is that?" She frowned and looked at the other girls. They hunched their shoulders in a "don't look at me; I don't know" manner.

Jackie knew she had to tread lightly here or they would view her as a lunatic.

"Devil's Breath," she said. And before she could see their disdain, she rushed forward and described what it was and what it does. "It is derived from a tree with white and yellow flowers that grows wild in Bogota, Columbia," hoping to appeal to their love of foliage, and deliberately not using the word drug. "If blown into someone's face, it renders them incapable of freewill and they have no memory of what happened." She risked a peek at them and saw their bewilderment as they scrutinized her. She quickly amended her statement. "It is harmless, really. It has a variety of uses in medicine."

"Like what," Ruby interrupted, with no telltale sign of her impending censure.

"Motion sickness, sea sickness, and a little intestinal cramping," Jackie said.

"But in small doses, right?" Bernadette said.

"I am not crazy girls. I took precautions," Jackie said. "I only used it when I needed complete control of the situation."

"How did you even find out about this drug?" Laura asked. "It is a drug, right?"

"Quite by accident," Jackie said, without labeling it. "When I was twenty-nine, thirty, I thought I had been slipped some GHB at a private function I attended. While researching the information at the library, I came across Scopolamine. I guess I never forgot the flower and its subliminal power. Accessibility to it was easy."

"Yeah, right," Bernadette said. She had a mischievous look in her eyes. "I have a feeling you have been conjuring up this master plan for a long, long time."

Nadine returned to part of the conversation that took place more than an hour earlier. "Did you say you took a periscope into a restaurant?"

"Yes, two of them," Jackie said, and pointed to her eyes.

* * *

The men had to fit a certain mold, of course. The criteria, however, were flexible: tall, neither slender nor fat, between forty and sixty, well spoken, accomplished, have a sense of humor, love life, enjoy mental stimulation, and disease free. Looks were immaterial to Jackie because she understood that attractiveness was in the eyes of the beholder. As long as the men were appealing overall, they were a candidate.

When Jackie was on the prowl, she would trespass into their personal space when they were travelling alone. It could be in a bar, restaurant, pool hall, club, fitness center, or even the theater. The places men hung out were far too many to count. So it made her job easy to abduct them. She detested that word and would have preferred "persuade;" but of course, they didn't come on their own volition, didn't make a conscious decision to come to her domicile, especially since they didn't have all the facts beforehand. Jackie knew they would have come voluntarily if she teased them with the promise of sex. She wasn't about to entertain that scenario. It was no way she'd engage in sexual deeds with any of the men prior to one of her associates. *How would that be fair to them?* Well, that had been the original plan prior to Joe sabotaging her, she thought. She would either have to make known that indiscretion or on the first night of the sexual escapade choose Joe as her partner, something she really didn't want to do, but she accepted the fact that she had no choice.

Jackie hadn't contemplated unlawful activity, whether it was right or wrong, legal or illegal; all she had concentrated on was being in control of everything, not quite like a pimp, and not quite like a madam either. No money would exchange hands. That's not what she wanted from these men. She wanted four things: power, control, giving sexual pleasure, and receiving sexual pleasure.

* * *

"Okay girls, let us campout downstairs and have a pajama party. The fun starts tomorrow night. Did you all bring pajamas?" Jackie asked.

Laura quipped. "After tonight, we won't need any." She licked her lips.

"What are they like? Who are they?" Bernadette asked.

Jackie gave them newspaper articles and printouts that she had prepared beforehand. Sadly, all the men's personal and private lives were incorrectly documented in *The Washington Post,* and on *CNN* and the *Huffington Post.* It didn't matter which online article was read, all the men were described as being in dysfunctional marriages or relationships.

The associates toasted each other with empty champagne bottles and headed downstairs to the entertainment area.

* * *

The following evening Jackie pointed out everyone's suite.

The women excitedly, and with foreboding, prepared to meet the Adonis that had been held captive in the en suites Jackie had designed specifically for each of them.

The sexual escapades began without incident.

CHAPTER 30

IAN MEETS LAURA

Ian was sitting at the table looking through the latest copy of *GQ* when he heard a soft knock at the door. He still didn't know where he was nor did he care. He turned and said come in. A tall woman entered whom he assumed was gorgeous. He wasn't sure because of the exotic half mask she wore. She had an olive complexion, almost golden, and a voluptuous body that was visible through the flowing peignoir.

He blushed.

She rolled in a tray of food that smelled delicious and put it on the bedside table. He removed the lid but couldn't take his eyes off of this curvaceous specimen before him. This predicament he was in was a dream come true. "God, if I'm dreaming," he thought, "please don't let me wake up. This is better than any wet dream I've ever had."

"I hope you're hungry," Laura said, in a soft, sensuous voice. "There's filet mignon cooked medium rare, garlic red mashed potatoes, and a Caesar salad with anchovies."

Ian was hungry but not for any food.

She noticed the lust in his eyes and was taken aback because she had never witnessed this look in a man's eyes before. Sex had always been a "slam, bam, thank you ma'am" encounter. This man had yet to ask where he was or what he was doing here.

Laura walked over to the Bose and inserted a CD. When she turned, Ian was right there, real close, so close she was inhaling his exhaled air. Her breath caught. He went to touch the mask, but she caught his hand in time and shook her head. She moved his hand to one of her buxom breasts instead to let him know it was okay to touch her there.

His member sprang to attention. Instinct told him to slow down. This woman was meant to be devoured slowly. *If I Were Your Woman* by Gladys Knight began to fill the room. It was as if she knew what he needed, what he was missing at home. He pulled her to him and started slow dancing. He called god's name a second time. "Oh God, I needed this," he whispered in her ear.

Laura crooned, singing along with Gladys.

"I have to be dreaming," he said, as he was being guided to the bed. She laid down first and scooted up to the headboard with her arms stretched out to him. He crawled to her and laid down. She turned to him and he leaned in to kiss her and she accepted his tongue. She stared at this distinguished looking man with salt and pepper hair and thick eyebrows, and almost said aloud, "please, let this be for real." She made a decision at that moment to never dye her hair again to cover the few gray strands that had begun to appear.

Jackie hadn't provided the associates with any descriptions of the men or how they were specifically selected for each woman, only how she ingratiated herself into their surroundings; and like a spider, spun her web to entrap her prey. No photographs had been provided, not even pictures from newspaper articles.

Laura couldn't take her eyes off his face. He had long eyelashes, somewhat of a bulbous nose, and full, sensual lips. He was unshaven and she liked the look of his newly grown stubble.

His eyes said I want you. She allowed his hands to roam her body, which arched with delight. She couldn't believe her luck. She was there to talk to him, to explain in brief detail why he was here, and to give him pleasure, but the opposite happened. He wanted to pleasure her. He didn't remove her peignoir as his tongue traversed down the sheer fabric. She felt his hands, then his tongue rub her erect nipples against the fabric. By the time he reached her navel, her head was going from side-to-side with anticipation. He moved to her flower and it was more than moist. He wanted to mount and enter her but dared not. He needed to smell the fragrance, taste the nectar, and feel what it would be like to have her quiver against his lips. He reached there and wasn't disappointed. His tongue circled the insides of her flower deliberately and teasingly, and he held her close to his face because he felt her trying to move away. He heard her soft moans and groans.

When he found the spot, her secret place, she writhed and exploded in ecstasy, crying out, please god don't stop.

"Please, please don't stop," she begged. And he didn't stop until the center of her flower expelled all its sap. He laid there in the epicenter until the eruption subsided.

Neither said anything.

Gladys' song repeated the verses.

Laura began to think that this man, hands down, was the right selection for her.

For the second time that night she thanked her lucky stars.

And Ian thanked his.

CHAPTER 31

RON MEETS BERNADETTE

At the end of the long hallway, in another bedroom suite, Bernadette had entered cautiously, shrouded in her Venetian mask and wearing a silk camiknicker. She thought Jackie had lost her mind, but so what, she was game for this adventure. She would try anything once. The only difference in this vacation from the many others over the years, she convinced herself, was that their sexual excursions weren't prearranged for them. They chose whom, they chose when, and they chose where.

She thought about the many heart-to-heart the girls had and tried to remember whether there was ever a time that Jackie had hinted to doing anything so irrational. During their last vacation, Jackie had disclosed a lot of information about herself. *I wonder if that was the clue.* She viewed Jackie as eccentric at times but nothing over the top. Definitely nothing on this scale.

Bernadette thought Jackie was as pretentious as her name, Jacqueline Ophelia Antoinette Trumpleton. But then again, if Bernadette wanted to be honest with herself, she was envious, inspired, and in awe of Jackie. No matter what foolish, irresponsible idea popped into that head of hers, Jackie didn't give it a second thought. If the idea materialized, the plan was realized. *I wish I had the bravado to seize the bull by the horns and take those kinds of risks.* Bernadette recalled a tale during one of their very early vacations when Jackie informed them that she had quit her job on the same day she went to settlement on the purchase of her first home. *The woman had balls!* The closest Bernadette got to experiencing eccentric behaviors was when she lived through Jackie's adventures.

Bernadette stood at the far side of the room. Jackie didn't say how in depth she had gone to check out these men's backgrounds, only that she had tested them for sexually transmitted diseases and HIV. So, as far as anyone knew, and it was only the five women, she could be in this luxurious suite awaiting a murderer or rapist to lunge out of the bathroom, and here she was dressed like a hooker in a skimpy teddy hidden behind a mask asking to be sexually assaulted. *This is tempting fate,* she reasoned.

When Ron walked into the room sporting dreads almost to his shoulders, a goatee, and only a hand towel wrapped around his neck—his body still damp and glistening from a shower—all Bernadette's premonitions magically disintegrated. It took all the self-control she could unearth not to run toward this man and rape him. *Oh god, he's magnificent,* she thought. *Thank you, Jackie,* she whispered.

Ron looked up because he thought he heard something. He had been at the house a few days and still did not comprehend the purpose of his captivity. Although he was being held against his will, he was being fed well and treated cordially. He loved the attire afforded him and he actually enjoyed the few days of solitude after that debacle with Rhonda.

He turned to admire himself in the mirror when he thought he heard something again. He turned around quickly and saw a vision of beauty. A woman about five seven with luscious milk chocolate skin was standing there in this captivating mask, barely clothed. He could tell it wasn't the woman from the restaurant because this one was shapelier. She had perfect round breast with large nipples. He was already envisioning his tongue rolling over them. He was aroused as he approached her because he knew he wanted her and he wanted her right then and there.

Ron was pleasantly pleased when she moved toward him faster than he could get to her. Bernadette ripped the towel from his neck almost giving him carpet burn. He didn't protest. They both dropped to their knees simulta-neously to pleasure one another. They couldn't, so they held each other, kissed, and played tongue tag. He pulled back and sought out the eyes behind the mask. As he kissed her again, he pulled down the straps of her teddy and moved to those plump nipples that were begging to be nursed. He palmed her breasts and the nipples stood rigidly upright. Then, he felt her hands delicately massage his teabags. He laid back and pulled her atop of him. The glide was easy, as if they had done this a thousand times. He had his hands at her waist and her head was thrown back in ecstasy. The driver and passenger rode each other equally hard. The ride at times was plunging, submissive, demanding, and compliant. The passion didn't abate until both were spent. She collapsed on him exhausted with her mask askew. Before he could glimpse her face, she straightened it.

"May I see who you are," he asked.

"I'm sorry, I can't."

"Can you stay the night?" he begged.

"I'll be back tomorrow night, if you want," Bernadette said.

"I want," he said, and she stealthily left the room.

Ron slept peacefully for the first time since his wife left him that tacky voice message.

CHAPTER 32

BEN MEETS RUBY

When Ruby entered her suite, Ben was not prepared for the wild sight before him. He had been expecting Jackie. Ever since he met her in New York and they dined at B. Smiths, he was consumed with sexual fantasies that involved her. He was disappointed that he had been at her home almost a week and the closest he got to her was chitchat via a two-way intercom system. He couldn't complain though because everything, except his sexual needs, was being fulfilled. After the talk with Jackie last evening, he spent the remainder of the night into the wee hours of the morning fantasizing about her while pleasuring himself. *This will have to suffice until I can have my way with her.* And his plan was to turn her inside out, so to speak, after the scam she pulled on him, conveniently forgetting, or rather neglecting to remember, the scheme he had intended to pull on her in New York.

So, instead of Jackie, another woman appeared—this wild thing, Ben thought. She was quite tall and wearing an overly elaborate mask that had wiry hair extending from it in all directions. He took a step back. He thought the masked woman might be some sort of game—a reenactment of *Phantom of the Opera*. This scenario was an enigma, even surreal.

She was wrapped in a heavy, oversized white terry cloth robe that wasn't attractive on her at all. It was in direct contradiction to the ornate mask. The robe was the type found in an expensive hotel and the type a man would wear. She was barefoot and her toenails were painted French manicure to match her fingernails. She had a glass of champagne in her hand.

Ben didn't know what to say so he blurted the first thing that came to mind. "Do I get to wear a mask?"

Ruby shook her head. "But you can wear these." She pulled a pair of pressed, men boxer shorts out of the robe pocket. He stared at the boxers.

"You want me to undress?" he asked.

"What's your fantasy?"

"Excuse me."

"Do you have a fantasy that you would like me to fulfill?" She was pleased at how confident she sounded.

"Yes."

"What is it?" Her voice was sultry.

"I've always wanted to have sex with two women," he said.

Ruby rolled her eyes. *Jackie was right. Men are so unbelievably predictable.* "So, if you could have any sexual desire fulfilled," she asked, "that would be your wish."

"Yes." He was practically salivating.

"Okay then, I'll be back," she said.

"Wait, where are you going?"

"Your wish is my command, but it will have to wait until tomorrow, maybe the day after." Ruby's act was a diversion because she knew, without a doubt, that a threesome wasn't happening tomorrow, the next day, or in her lifetime where she would be a participant.

He couldn't let her leave. He was horny, although he didn't know why since she wasn't appealing in that robe. "I want you," Ben blurted out.

"Are you sure," Ruby said teasingly. "That's not what you said less than three minutes ago." She walked toward him and demanded he undress. "Put on these boxers," she ordered. *I'm loving this.*

Ben obliged.

"I'll be right back," she promised, and went into the bathroom. When she returned, the robe had disappeared; and, if it had not been for the mask and wiry hair, he would have sworn it was a different woman. All she was wearing was a pair of fitted men boxers that matched his, except hers was made of lace.

He was both confused and turned on. He couldn't believe the body before him. She was skinny but with an hourglass figure. She walked over to him. If it weren't for his hard on, he would have thought he was paralyzed. He couldn't move.

"Sit," she said. *Fifty-two years old and this is the first time I've spoken to a man in this manner. It's liberating.*

He backed up slowly to the bed and sat down.

She kneeled before him and rubbed her hands up and down his thighs, playfully scratching him with her nails.

He laid back with his hands behind his head.

Ruby rubbed and kneaded and kissed every inch of his body with the exception of his organ. All he wanted, at that moment, was to feel her hands on it. When she gently grabbed it and started moving her hand up and down the shaft, he wanted to feel her mouth on it, her lips around it, and told her so.

She pretended not to hear his pleas. Each time he was ready to let loose, she changed direction to lessen the sensation. She stroked the area between his gonads and orifice.

He couldn't take the fondling and teasing anymore, and started begging Ruby for release. She drew him in and started contracting her cheek muscles and lips to make a vacuum.

Finally, Ben got the powerful release he hungered.

CHAPTER 33

BRIAN MEETS NADINE

Brian was getting impatient with being locked up in a bedroom. There was no TV, only books to read or music to listen to. He had been secluded in this room for three days and three nights and it was beginning to feel oppressive. He was about to hit the intercom button to complain when he heard his name. "Brian, I have some news."

Jackie talked about an associate coming in and the adventures that he would encounter over the ensuing two weeks. Even though he was a whore at heart, it was always on his terms. This time it would be different. He wouldn't be calling the shots. He was excited about this new adventure though.

Then, his thoughts turned to Ian. He couldn't wait to tell his boy about this mind-boggling journey. Brian refused to accept that Ian was in harm's way. He believed in his heart that Ian just needed to get away from Evelyn. He probably just went off somewhere to be alone. He still wished Ian had called him. Brian looked at the bedside clock. It was five o'clock.

The adventure would start soon so he went to the bathroom to freshen up. After a long, hot steamy shower, he brushed his teeth and patted on some "1872." He dressed in the evening attire that was hanging in the closet, slid his feet into moccasins, and walked out of the bathroom brushing his hair. He could tell that someone had been in the room and immediately went to the door. Of course, it was locked. He really didn't care. Escape didn't cross his mind now because the promise of sexual adventures was really all the key and lock that were needed. Something told him that Jackie knew this too.

Brian walked over to the table and lifted the lid from the silver tray. On the dinner plate were broiled salmon with a scoop of crabmeat on top and lemon slice decorations with a vegetable medley and rice pilaf. Also on the table was an unopened bottle of Chivas Regal and a shot glass. Where ever he was, he had to admit, he was being treated royally. He could not have asked for better.

He sat down to eat and heard a knock at the door. Before he could say come in, a woman wearing only a decorative mask that he'd only seen during Mardi Gras, walked up to him with her hand extended.

"Good evening, I'm Nadine," she said. She was naked from chin to painted toenails with the exception of a neatly trimmed, upside-down triangle at her center. He had seen a lot of naked women in his day but nothing like this. Her body was turning him on. *She has to be at least forty-nine, fifty,* he thought. Tiny boobs that would fit in his mouth were placed perfectly on a petite body that could be lifted without straining. He didn't care what her features behind the mask bestowed, that body would make up for any flaws.

He stood up too fast and knocked over the entire tray of food.

"Oh God," he said. "I'm so sorry." He bent down to clean up the mess.

"It's not a problem," she said. "I'll get you another plate. Leave it."

He couldn't believe he was bumbling around, making a fool of himself. He shook her hand. "I'm Brian, but I'm sure you know that already."

Then, the unthinkable happened.

He screamed, "No! No! No!" He couldn't believe it.

"Brian, honestly, it's no problem," Nadine said.

He looked down at Willy who was forsaking him. "Why? Why? Why?" he scolded. He felt miserable. He looked back at Nadine, embarrassed, and said, "Do you mind coming back in about thirty minutes or so. I need to have a serious powwow with Willy."

"Not at all," she said, and left the room with a gloomy look on her face.

Brian had never used Viagra. *Thank God I saw some in the medicine cabinet.*

By the time Nadine reappeared, the little blue pill did its job. She came in the same manner as before, but this time with a plate of food in hand. "I've already eaten," she said, with a twinkle in her eyes, which moved from his face and down his body. "I see you won the battle with Willy. Do you mind if I take a shower while you finish your meal?"

"Not at all." He could barely get the words out of his mouth. *So now what, my voice is going to forsake me too?* All he could think of was a sexy, naked woman in his bedroom wanting to take a shower. He wasn't hungry anymore; food was the last thing on his mind.

Nadine went into the bathroom and left the door ajar. She stepped in the oversized shower and let the cool water run down her body. After a couple of minutes, she was amazed that Brian hadn't joined her. She opened the shower door and called out to him.

"Yes." He was still sitting at the table, unable to eat, still enraptured about what was going to happen soon.

"You can join me if you would like to."

By the time Brian got to the shower door, he had discarded his evening attire and slippers. He entered the shower and saw this exquisite woman wet from her shoulders to her toes. She was facing him and the mask she wore was dry. Something told him he wasn't allowed to touch it.

"You are so beautiful," he said.

"Brian," she said, ignoring his compliment, "please screw the living daylights out of me."

"Yes ma'am," he saluted, "as long as it's okay with Willy." He looked down and all his wariness disappeared. "But, it has to be my way, Nadine."

"Okay," she said.

He grabbed the tube of perfumed liquid gel and squirted a lot in his hands and rubbed them together. He turned Nadine around so that she was facing the wet wall of the stall and gently pushed her forward. She raised her arms as she laid flat against the cold marble. He started rubbing gel at the back of her neck. He spread the gel around to her throat and moved down to her breasts. He knead them with both hands until her nipples were hard as pebbles against his fingers. She moaned and pushed her buttocks into his groin. She was ready; he was not. He leaned into her so that his organ was sliding between her cheeks. He moved his hand down to the end of her torso and started soaping her there. He enjoyed the water pounding him and running down his back. He cupped her, fingered her, and circled her bulb. Her moans were getting louder and she kept pushing against him. He playfully pushed her back up against the wall and started gyrating against her. When she pushed back against him again, he accepted the invitation. He entered her and continued to rub her bulb. He started slamming into her. He was afraid he would hurt her so he tempered his tempo. He heard her whisper something and bent his head down toward her mouth.

"Oh god this feels good," she was saying.

He increased the tempo and enjoyed the pleasure that was building within him. She was rotating her hips and he was in ecstasy. Brian and Nadine screamed simultaneously as the passion expelled from them. She went limp and they both slid to the floor of the shower. They laid there while the water splashed their bodies.

After five minutes, he wanted more. The little blue pill turned Willy into a sex-crazed monster. He turned her over and noticed that her mask was soaking wet. He moved down the center of her wet body with his tongue and felt himself getting aroused. He licked her cleavage and moved slowly to her inverted navel and tongued the crevice before moving down slowly to her bulb. She pulled her legs up in preparation for his tongue. He obliged. Just as she was peaking, she had him in a head-lock. He teased her bulb until she couldn't take it anymore. She detonated and her legs shot straight up in the air and then went limp.

The shower still rained on them.

She laid there and was still thirsty with lust for this man whom she had just met and who had completely satisfied her sexual hunger. She looked down and saw he was ready to go again.

You go Willy.

It was his turn. She bathed him with the gel as he had done her, but she started at his center. She enjoyed rubbing the soap up and down Willy using both hands. She looked up at Brian and he was in pure ecstasy. She removed one hand to soap his family jewels. She heard him say "yes baby." When the water rinsed the lather away, her lips followed where her hands had been only seconds earlier.

He had nothing to grab onto because they were lying on the shower stall floor and the faucet handles were half way up the wall. He grabbed the back of her head and thrust.

"Oh baby," he yelled again and again until he was spent. He pulled her up on top of him and they laid that way while the shower water continued to rain down on them.

CHAPTER 34

THE LAST NIGHT

The two-week vacation had wound down and the only time the associates left the premises was to visit the Pentagon and Martin Luther King, Jr. Memorials on Thursday. No one, not even Jackie, watched the news, read a newspaper, or accessed the Internet during this time.

The girls couldn't believe they were at the finale of the best, extremely unusual, and most rewarding vacation they could have ever imagined. They were seriously contemplating early retirement; they did not want to return to the miserable existence that would from this day forward be branded their dull lives in purgatory. Surely, the nirvana they just experienced was heaven.

The vacation began with both excitement and trepidation, and ended with reckless sexual abandonment. All anyone cared about was getting their freak on and as often as possible. No one was selfish or held back emotions. Inhibitions were shed. Each girl thought Jackie had hit the ball out of the park with this vacation.

This *was* a house of pleasure, pure pleasure and nothing less.

Bernadette couldn't believe how fortunate they had been to experience this selfless gift from Jackie with no apprehension of risk to themselves.

"The words *thank you* can't adequately express my gratitude of what you've done for us Jackie," Bernadette said. "When you first told us that the house was a retirement gift—that, in itself, was extraordinary. But this, these two weeks of uninterrupted gratification, unadulterated passion, and like you said, no rules, no guilt, no strings attached, I can't think of a better gift than this to bestow on a girlfriend. Now, I know you don't think of us as girlfriends, but I don't care. You're the wildest and best girlfriend I've ever had."

"Here, here," Ruby said, raising her bottle of Gosset in the air. She started crying. The girls stayed put. "Jackie," she said, "we've spent, how many, around twelve or so vacations together; and yes, I've enjoyed every single one of them. But this one touched a place so deep in my being that I feel if I don't express it, my heart will suffocate under the pressure. When you first mentioned this idiotic hogwash, I was petrified that you would get us all locked away for life and the key thrown away. I seriously considered catching the next flight back home. I didn't know what to think about you, and all kinds of names came to mind. And I have to be candid, Jackie, they weren't very nice."

Laura started to interrupt Ruby but Jackie motioned with her hand to stop her. She wanted to hear what Ruby had to say.

"I thought you were only thinking of yourself with no conscionable concept whether we would be affected or legally implicated, our livelihoods damaged, and our reputations destroyed. I even pondered calling the authorities. Then, sitting on the dock surrounded by the calmness of the night with you all around me eased my nerves." She looked at Jackie with a tear-stained face. "I want to apologize for those thoughts, Jackie," Ruby said.

"No apologies necessary," Jackie said. "I understand how you feel, I do, and hope you all can forgive me for my arrogance in assuming that you would be party to, without reservation, this maniacal notion of mine." She looked around and kept her eyes locked on each of the girls for a few seconds. "I had no right to spring this on you in the manner I did. I wholeheartedly will accept any blame, because I have put you all in a situation that could have monumental consequences. Granted, I did not think that far ahead. You know I am impulsive, but here is my solemn oath to you. If anything untoward, whatsoever, transpires due to my transgression, I, and only I, will take the fall and full responsibility for the outcome. I will hold myself accountable and accept any punishment set forth. Omertà is our bond."

The girls understood without exception.

"Let me get my two cents in," Nadine said. "Occoquan is exactly where I want to vacation until we retire here. I love the idea of unleashing our inhibitions. I've never had so many big Os in my life and I'm forty-something years old. Yes, that's right, you bitches," she said good-humoredly, "I'm forty-something and dare any of you to dispute it."

She waited for a dispute she knew wasn't forthcoming.

"Hey, I'm with you," Laura said, tapping her bottle.

Nadine started again. "How does one man know all the right places a woman wants to be touched, fondled, and kissed without a woman having to pinpoint every damn spot to him every single time? How does he know when to just hold you and cherish you, or love you and screw you until you scream, please don't stop!"

The girls jumped because she literally screamed the words, "please don't stop."

"I know how," Laura said, "it's because they've been around the block. They have had years and countless experiences to get it right."

Jackie disagreed. "I think being here made the difference. Once they met you, there were no stress, no burdens, no fear of rejection. They encountered five women who wanted, needed, and savored wanton sex the same as them."

"I wish I could bottle up Brian and sell him," Nadine said, and sat back and thought about it. "Nah, that would be a bald-faced lie!" she said. "I'm selfish. I want to keep him all to myself."

"I know what you mean," Laura said. "I've fallen in love with Ian. He's the most sensitive man in the world."

"The world!" Nadine said. "Exactly how many men have you slept with?" she asked jokingly.

"None of your damn business," Laura retorted.

"Jackie, I can only speak for myself, but how did you know what type of man would be the right one for me. Was it luck?" Laura asked.

Jackie was touched at this admiration for her. "No, I am not that good," she chuckled. "Like I said, the men just fit a mold, a predictable pattern that I thought was suitable for strong black women like us. We *know* each other. We *feel* each other's pain and *rejoice* in each other's happiness. I do not know how else to explain it. We *are* indistinguishable when it comes to our emotions."

"Well, whatever it was," Laura said, "bless you and thank you from the bottom of my heart." Laura stood up and curtsied to Jackie. "I would kiss your feet if you hadn't been walking around barefooted all day," she said, giggling. "Ian was the best lover I've ever been in a twosome with. He's kind, accommodating, and umph umph," she said, thrusting her fists down at her side. "Wow, wow, wow, that's all I can say. May I move here, Jackie, please?"

"Are you serious, Laura?" Bernadette asked.

"Yes," Jackie said, "you can move here anytime you want. It is *our* Mecca."

"I'm serious," Laura said, "I've decided to give my two-week notice first thing Monday morning. Now that I've tasted the pleasure of happiness, there's no turning back. I'm accepting nothing less in my life from now on, and that starts today."

Bernadette halted Laura. She did not want her making hasty decisions based on an orgasm or even a hundred orgasms. "I think you should wait Laura before making such a drastic decision. Go home and digest what we've done, what you're feeling, and see what's going to come of all of this." She treaded softly here because she didn't want to offend anybody. "Sometimes, as women, we confuse climaxing with love. We have the best orgasms in our lives and we think we're in love."

Everyone looked at Bernadette and realized that she made an honest assessment.

They were older now, no longer in their twenties, and they knew better. They knew the difference between sex and love.

"You're right," Laura said. "I've gone mad and lost my head for a minute."

"It is alright," Jackie said. "We have all been there at one time or another in our lives." She looked at the girls. "Anyone of you can move here anytime you want. This is *our* oasis."

* * *

Bernadette didn't let slide that Jackie hadn't mentioned anything about her rendezvous with Joe. "Okay, girl, give it up," she said to Jackie. "Why are you keeping us in the dark about Joe? Was he any good?"

Jackie looked at them with a straight face. "Girls, he is the bomb diggity!" she said. "Oh my lord, that man can put a hurting on you!"

The girls leaned forward, attentive as ever. Jackie was in her own world. It was as if Joe had a key to the gate of her erogenous zone. "That dude can stick, lick, and hick me all night long."

Ruby was fit to be tied. "What in god's name does that mean?"

"Stick me with that hard-ass dick, lick me with that long-ass tongue. Put hickeys on every inch of this," she said, imitating a Reiki movement—hands-on, no touch technique—all over her body to describe the visual in detail so the girls got the complete picture.

"Ohhh, you experienced the three-in-one universal package," Laura said.

"Speak English please," Bernadette said.

"She's on a physical, emotional, and spiritual-level high," Laura said.

"Oh Laura, call it what it is," Nadine said, "the bitch came!"

The girls hooted.

"Well yeah, I can't argue with that," Laura said.

"Jackie," Bernadette shouted to get her out of this self-meditation she was glorifying in. "Jackie to earth, Jackie to earth," she called out, cupping the sides of her mouth. "Give us details and I don't want to hear this ray-key mumble jumble either."

Jackie covered her eyes and shook her head. "I think he cast a spell on me."

"Cast a spell on the Voodoo Queen?" Bernadette said. "I doubt that." She was making fun of the situation. "After these two weeks of sexual escapades and exploitations, and don't think I didn't love every second of it,"

Bernadette said, "not to mention the Devil's Breath, I think Marie Laveau has been raised from the grave."

"Oh that's not fair," Nadine said.

"No," Jackie said, "Bernadette may be on to something. You know, the Voodoo Queen was from Louisiana, like me. I did administer magical powers, if you want to call Scopolamine magic, and I granted sexual desires for everybody." She had a wicked grin.

"You know I'm only kidding, right, Jackie," Bernadette said.

"Of course you are," she said, and winked.

Jackie provided the girls with an overview of her sexual interlude with Joe but refused to give them blow-by-blow details.

* * *

In the privacy of her en suite, Jackie reminisced her last night with Joe.

She had donned the mask even though he knew who she was—she had fallen in love with the game, maybe Joe too, then shook that thought out of her head—and knocked on the bedroom door.

There was no sound from the opposite side.

She had dressed purposefully—not too sexy, not too casual, and definitely not bare-assed like the previous time.

She knocked again.

He must be in the shower, she thought.

She entered and before she was fully inside the room, he snatched her and pulled her all the way in. She was caught off guard. The Scopolamine was in one of her pockets, she couldn't recall whether it was the left one or right one, and she wasn't quick enough this time to retrieve it. He was behind her holding her in a playful bear hug and reached into both pockets simultaneously, pulled out the canister with his left hand, and asked, "Is this what you're looking for?"

He whipped her around to face him.

She was frightened. She hadn't felt this way in years.

When he saw the fear peer out from behind the mask, he shifted gears. He released her, took two steps back, put his hands on his head with fingers interlocked, and spread his feet apart. "I'm sorry Jackie," he said, "I didn't mean to scare you."

She gauged her next move.

He was standing too close to the door for her to run pass him. *And he smelled so good.* She could run into the bathroom; what was she going to do, stay in there all night. *I would go crazy thinking about him on the other side of the door.* She couldn't bear that he had the upper hand again. *Why am I so attracted to this man?*

"Do you want me, Jackie?" he asked.

She had not prepared for this. *Oh god yes!*

"Because I want you. All week I've hungered for you, I've dreamt about you, I've ached for you, and you never showed up. Why have you been avoiding me?"

She didn't answer.

"I want you. I long for you. Don't you know that?"

I do now. She didn't know how to respond to him. There was this six-pack abs, six-five dude, dark, and bald man pouring his heart out. *Please stop, okay. This is not the way it is supposed to be.*

"Are you mad at me?" he asked.

Her eyes remained averted to the floor. *No. I want you so bad, I ache too.*

"Jackie, you have to tell me what you want. It's obvious we want each other but I can't read your mind."

Just make love to me and don't stop until I tell you to.

"Okay," he said.

Her head jerked up and she looked at him.

He was looking at her.

"I did not say anything," she said.

"You don't have to," he said, as he moved toward her.

She took a step back.

He stopped and handed her the Scopolamine.

She stared at it.

He turned to walk away.

She said, "Please do not leave."

He stopped. She didn't see his smile. He was angst-ridden she would let him walk away. He wanted her to want him as much as he wanted her. He had laid all his cards in the deck on the table. The ball was in her court.

She wanted him in the worse kind of way. Jackie had never felt this way before. She was hot and feeling tingly all over. She walked to the bed and stood on it and asked him to come to the bed.

Standing on the bed would put them at eye-level.

He didn't turn immediately and she was fearful. *Maybe he did not mean everything he said.*

He turned.

Thank you, Jesus. She closed her eyes.

He walked over to her, and she held his face and kissed his eyes. Her arms embraced him and she snuggled up close. She loved the feel of his chest against her breast. Jackie moved back and started unbuttoning the pearl buttons on his PJs. She slipped the top off his shoulders and it slid to the floor. She leaned in to kiss him and he kissed her back. She realized that he was going to let her do all the work and that was okay. She would savor every second. Jackie kneeled down and untied the string at his waist, and the pants followed the shirt. He lifted her up and they kissed softly at first. Then, the kissing became demanding, almost savage. He lifted her, moved her to the head of the bed, and laid her down gently. He nibbled her earlobes and returned to her lips.

"I want you," she said.

He could hardly believe it. He didn't think he would ever hear those words from her lips. His heart softened.

"Please say it again," he begged.

"Joe, I want you, now."

He slid his hands underneath her dress and was delighted to find no panties, only flowing juices.

He entered her and she gasped. He asked if he was hurting her and she said no. Joe wanted to go slow and gentle, but she wanted to go fast and furious. She kept grinding against him and pulling his cheeks into her until the base of his pelvis was touching the base of her pelvis.

Her legs wrapped around him and she pumped passionately nonstop. That was the key for him. All hell broke loose. He rode her like a Stallion.

She cried out so many times that he lost count of the number of times she climaxed before he reveled in his own.

"Jackie!" he screamed out.

When her heart stopped pounding and the waves stopped splashing, she said ever so demurely, "I love you, Joe."

They both froze.

"Where did that come from?" she laughed nervously. "I do not love you," she announced quickly. "I am sorry."

So, he let it slide. He didn't say anything. He slid her rumpled dress up and over her head, moved his hands to her naked breast and his mouth to her nipples. He sucked them 'til she cried his name. He hoped to hear, "I love you" again. Then moving downward with his tongue, he bypassed her pierced bellybutton and went straight for her honey pot, the scent drew him in like a bee to a flower.

She wanted to open her legs but he held them flat in place.

He wanted to nibble her joy button his way.

She felt his lips, his tongue, his teeth and tried again to spread her legs but he wouldn't allow it.

He kept nibbling until she screamed out. When the spasms died down, he moved back up and entered her again. His movements were long strokes and gentle gyrations.

This time she didn't hump wildly against him. She went with the flow until her dam broke in concert with his.

Joe rolled over onto his side and Jackie spooned him. He reached around, grabbed her arm, and pulled it up around his chest. He held her hand and laid awake assessing her declaration of love, trying to make heads and tails of it, although she had retracted the words almost immediately, the moment they were emitted. She apologized for the endearment and he had remained reticent.

Her breathing was regulated; she had fallen asleep and he wasn't that far behind.

He stirred when she removed her arm and turned over. He turned with her and stayed in the spoon. She extracted herself and went to the bathroom and he watched the silhouette of her body. *She is so sexy,* he thought. *My wife, my ex-wives, my mistress, and all the sexual encounters in between—there's no comparison.*

There was no sound coming from the bathroom so he got up to make sure she was okay. She had not closed the door fully so he watched her through the gap. She was standing at the wash bowl, naked, with no mask. It was almost as if she was holding on to the sink for dear life. Then, she sat on the commode in "the thinker" position. She actually looked sad, as if some invisible boulder was bearing down on her shoulders. He knew she heard him approach but she wouldn't look up, didn't move. So he got down on his knees to her level.

"Is there anything I can do, Jackie," he said. He was surprised at this side of himself. It was the first time in his life that he cared about someone other than himself.

She shook her head.

"Talk to me."

"Please hold me," she said.

He stood and lifted her so she was standing on the stool; he hugged her and they stayed like that, without words, for five minutes.

"I've got to take a leak, Jackie," he said, disrupting the moment.

She stepped down and walked back into the bedroom. She heard the water running and then her name. She returned to the bathroom. He was sitting on the toilet and when she saw his body again in all its magnificence, her sadness melted away. She went to him and sat face forward on his lap. She felt his hands on her breasts and his mouth moved to each one. Her upper body arched back and her pelvis moved forward. He moved his hands to her lower back and pulled her in. They found one another and connected. They couldn't get enough of each other. This time he gave her reign to take control. She moved her body back and forth, up and down. Her breathing was spasmodic. Her fingernails dug into his shoulders and he didn't care. He loved the way this woman, this goddess, was making love to him, the way she was making him feel. Even the few times he took Viagra, his erection never felt this hard, this strong. He was pulsating. His heart rate, blood pressure, and respiration were at an all time high. He could no longer hold himself at bay. He was at a point of no return; the force was stronger than him. He reached the peak of the mountain and the sexual buildup was released. "I love you too, Jackie," he screamed unabated.

CHAPTER 35

THE FBI GETS A CLUE

The FBI's Major Case Contact Center included a website, an anonymous eight hundred number, and an electronic tip line. They were begging citizens to come forward with anything, anything at all, regarding the disappearances of five African-American men between the ages of forty and sixty from the Washington, DC, metropolitan area. "Please contact the FBI" was the phrase of the day.

Agents, police officers, and detectives were out in force, working around the clock bearing down on informants, setting up roadblocks, and distributing flyers to find any clues about these men, no matter how negligible.

The FBI was making some headway. There were numerous hits on the website, and several comments and many inquiries from the same IP address from a residence in New Orleans.

One night, unexpectedly, the FBI received a reputable tip from a muffled voice on the phone. The number was traced to a phone booth located in Metairie, Louisiana, a suburb located on the south shore of Lake Pontchartrain in Jefferson Parish, a parish that saw more than its share of hurricanes.

Metairie made history in 1990 when white supremacist David Duke was elected to the Louisiana state legislature. Then in 2005, fifteen years later, Metairie was in the news again televising and reporting Hurricane Katrina. This catastrophic disaster caused residents from the Orleans Parrish to migrate to Jefferson Parrish, which ironically, created a racially neutral migration in the search for housing.

This was where the anonymous call had originated.

The caller, believed to be a man, said he thought he knew the identity of the kidnapper, which at best, was only a guess because it was based on circumstantial evidence. "I think the kidnapper is my sister," said the unknown caller. Before the agent could delve further, the caller hung up.

Juan made the call. He accused his sister of this vile act that was all over the national news. After the meeting with his brothers, he fought the temptation to call the authorities. He re-read Sissy's journal for a third time just in case he *was* making a mountain out of a molehill as Olli had censured him.

Juan hadn't conveyed to his brothers that he had re-produced the entire journal. He had implied that he copied only the pages he presented to them. After reading the journal again for a fourth time, he stood by his choice to contact the FBI. *I made the right decision,* he reasoned. *It's too late to turn back now.*

He was all alone. The call was made and there wasn't a single comrade he could turn to for support or comfort. Once the call was connected to him, which he knew it would be with all the FBI's sophisticated equipment, all hell would break loose in Metairie, west of New Orleans.

This was the break the BAU was hoping for—the missing link. "Everyone to the hole immediately," Supervisory Special Agent Madison announced over the paging system. After everyone was seated around the conference room table, Madison informed his agents that they had a break in the case. "We received an anonymous tip and the man claims the kidnapper is his sister. We need to talk to Clyde Hariston again. Apparently, he was telling the truth when he made his original report about being abducted by a woman." He looked at Agent Kelly. "Good foresight, Kelly, on figuring that out earlier," Madison said. He recalled she brought that possibility to their attention a week ago, which had been casually dismissed after learning nothing concrete from Clyde Hariston.

"Thanks," Kelly said, beaming at the rare acknowledgement.

"We need to rearrange our evidence. Hariston probably was the first victim. And because he was HIV positive, he was discarded. It makes sense that it's a woman. Has anyone heard about a brothel being operated here in the metropolitan area?" Madison asked. As soon as the words were out of his mouth, he knew it was idiotic. If that had been the case, it would have been shut down and the madam, prostitutes, and customers arrested.

"Agents Kelly and Coffy, I want you two to coordinate efforts with the chiefs of police in Arlington, Bowie, Alexandria, and DC, to investigate massage parlors in their jurisdictions. We need to make sure a bordello is not being operated right here under our noses. How can one woman abduct and hide five men? Are there other women involved? Are the men willing participants?" Madison started throwing out ideas left and right. We need to know what this woman is doing with them.

He pointed at another agent. "After we're done here, you come with me," he said, "I have an assignment for you. Find the name of the person who was on the other end of that anonymous call. We need to interview him, find out who his sister is, where she lives, and hopefully, collect any information that will lead to finding these missing men."

Madison pointed at Kelly and Coffy. "I want you two to pay Hariston another visit. Kelly, let Coffy question him this time around."

Kelly frowned. "Sir, we can't do both. Can you assign that task to another agent? ASA Gonzales is available."

Madison stared at Gonzales. "Do you think you can take this assignment seriously?" he asked her.

"Yes, sir, and again I apologize for my insolence," she said. "Thank ..."

Madison dismissed her. "Then, that's fine with me but I want a tenured agent to go with Gonzales," Madison said.

"Yes sir," Kelly said.

CHAPTER 36

ARREST OF JACKIE TRUMPLETON

It was three o'clock in the morning when Jackie was snatched out of a sound sleep by thunderous pounding at the front door. She was fearful that someone was trying to break into her home, which was dispelled as soon as the notion appeared, when she saw flashing blue and red lights streaming through the bedroom windows. She threw a silk robe on over her peignoir and peered out, and noticed what appeared to be a hundred police vehicles. The number was magnified because the revolving lights were being reflected off of the Occoquan River. The Town of Occoquan was under siege and lit up like Las Vegas.

The banging got louder.

She had reached the foyer when the special-ordered security double doors that cost over three thousand dollars splintered and came crashing down, almost landing on top of her. She jumped back, stunned at the manpower standing before her. She had only seen a S.W.A.T. team, Special Weapons and Tactics, on television shows like *Criminal Minds* or at the premier of *Ocean's*

Eleven, not up close and in person, so this picture was surreal.

* * *

The words still rang in her ears. "Jacqueline Ophelia Antoinette Trumpleton, you are under arrest ...," *Jesus, did the agent have to bellow her full name*, "for the stalking, abduction, and holding five men hostage." *That alone brought forward extinguished memories.*

Before the police had a chance to read her the Miranda rights, Jackie requested an attorney. She was immediately handcuffed, led to a police vehicle, and transported to Arlington County Detention Facility, a high-rise smack in the middle of Arlington that attracts correction officials from around the world because of its non-jail like appearance, which camouflages its high-tech security system.

Jackie was placed in a holding area to keep her separate from the population. There had been many arrests that night, but none as high-profiled as hers.

Afterward, she was duly processed.

She had never been arrested before so the process was daunting. All Jackie wanted at that moment was to be left alone. That wasn't happening! Again, she had to recite her full name. She was asked about her psychological and medical history.

"No, I am not crazy or psychotic," she yelled.

"Please don't yell at me, Ms. Trumpleton," the female deputy sheriff said politely.

Jackie was humiliated by this civil reprimand because normally she herself was well-behaved. She calmed down, looked at the deputy's badge, and expressed regret for her errant behavior. "I apologize, Deputy Campbell. It will not happen again," she said.

Since she was in sleeping attire when arrested, she had no property that needed to be confiscated. She was fingerprinted and issued a jail uniform, a god-awful bright, neon orange jumpsuit that hung off of her like a burlap potato sack. She laughed at her incongruous situation as a vision of Ruby's sexless clothing materialized.

Jackie was offered the opportunity to make a phone call. She decided to spend the night in jail. It was only a few more hours before Nate's office opened, and she didn't want to wake him in the middle of the night with business that was not real estate-related. She would wait until nine o'clock to call him for the name of a criminal defense attorney.

It never occurred to her to call one of the girls.

Sitting in jail gave Jackie an opportunity to profile herself. She had come to terms with and accepted the underlying reason she found herself behind bars, regardless of the criminal wrongdoings and impending legal issues. It wasn't just about controlling a man and his sexuality. It was about being in control of her life, her destiny. Over the last forty years, she had been stripped of any kind of power, which began with her mother. When she finally escaped the imprisonment of East New Orleans and relocated to DC, she was still stripped of empowerment.

Pimps *wanted* to control her, lovers *tried* to control her, three husbands-to-be *struggled* unsuccessfully to control her, and employers *did* control her, until one day, she snapped; she had had enough.

She was tired of running away. When the opportunity presented itself to make her dream come true, she took full advantage of it. She masterminded a way to have the power. If it meant controlling a man sexually, so be it.

CHAPTER 37

RELEASE OF THE MISSING FIVE

The commotion outside and downstairs was unsettling to the abducted men who for the last three weeks had been sequestered upstairs in separate bedrooms.

Police were trampling all through the home, going from room to room in search of the missing men. Once a man was found, he was asked to put on some clothes if he was naked, and was then shuffled down to the family room where there were paramedics, FBI agents, and more police officers.

As each man entered the room, he was confounded that another victim was being brought forward too. In all, there were five men; and each had thought he was alone in his captivity. It never occurred to any of them that they were part of a serial kidnapping.

Brian was talking to one of the paramedics when he heard someone call his name. When he turned around, he saw Ian coming through the door. Brian was flabbergasted. He stopped talking to the medic, jumped up, and walked toward Ian.

"Ian!" he said, not believing his eyes. He was confused and didn't know what to say first. "We've been looking all over for you. What are you doing here? Man, this is wild. I'm dumbfounded."

Before either could say anything or do a man hug—right arm diagonally across the chest, hand balled in a fist, and a lean forward, avoiding torso contact—Agent Kelly stepped between them with her arms stretched out.

"Sorry guys," she said, "we need to speak to each of you individually first." She motioned for another agent to come over and assist.

Brian ignored the agent and yelled as Ian was being led away. "Man, you were here this whole time too?"

Ian was stunned. *How in the world could both of us be entrapped like this?*

They were carted off in different directions before either could say another word.

* * *

The media was all over the Town of Occoquan. With a population of less than a thousand residents, this was big news.

An anonymous caller from the Arlington PD tipped off NBCNews4, the local television station, early in the day of a break in the case and an impending arrest after midnight. They set up on the grounds of the old Lorton Prison Reformatory, now the transformed Workhouse Arts Center, waiting for the call to travel to the property and have unencumbered access to the scene. The news station was promised full coverage once the arrest or arrests began.

Other TV stations had a difficult time getting close to the scene, even though they were located in the middle of it, due to the small town's makeup of one way, narrow streets that also allowed resident and visitor parking.

Occoquan covered only 128 acres and bordered the Occoquan River. A town government, fine restaurants, boutiques, coffee houses, bakeries, craft stores, and a variety of upscale salons dotted the landscape. Its inhabitants lived, worked, and played in a quaint community, rich in history with well to-do residents with median household incomes around ninety thousand dollars. The median age was forty-two; and at the last census, the racial makeup was eighty-six percent white, eight percent black, and six percent everything else, housed in a mixture of detached single family homes, townhomes, and condominiums.

Since these TV stations weren't making any headway, they started accosting residents in the historic town.

"This is Channel5 News," the reporter spoke into the microphone. "I'm here with a longtime resident who has lived in Occoquan for more than thirty years."

The elderly woman tried to grab the microphone, but the reporter wouldn't let go, so they both held the microphone close to the woman's mouth.

"I can't believe it," the elderly resident said. "I've lived here thirty-nine years, raised my children and grandchildren in my house right down the road there on Union Street, and nothing like this has ever happened."

The reporter brought the microphone back up to her mouth and announced that she had another resident of

Occoquan who was also stunned by the unusual events unfolding here in his town.

"This is uncivilized behavior," the middle-aged white man said. "The wife and I just moved here a year ago from Fredericksburg, Virginia. We love this town. Now, look at the elements that have moved in. Unbelievable!"

Over on Washington Street, Channel 7 was stationed. The television crew walked over to Commerce Street.

"What in God's name is happening at the end of the river?" asked an older black gentleman who was sitting out on his front porch with a large German Shepherd mix, maybe with Rottweiler—the dog was huge—sleeping at his feet. "My family has lived here for generations, since slavery, and hasn't seen anything like this mess down here. See right there across the street," he pointed at Ebenezer Baptist Church, "that's where we went to church. It looks like that ... what's that woman's name?" he asked.

"Jackie Trumpleton," the reporter said.

"It looks like Ms. Trumpleton wasn't brought up a Christian woman. My pappy would be rolling over in his grave if he saw what was happening right here in front of this house." He shook his head and mumbled, "would be rolling over in his grave."

NBCNews4 broke the story first, which went viral via the Associated Press.

"Jackie Trumpleton, a real estate agent and new resident of Occoquan, Virginia, has just been arrested," the reporter announced. "I'm standing here with Arling-

ton Chief of Police Maurice Johnston." She faced him.
"What can you tell us?"

"All we can make public at this time is that we're still
processing the crime scene. As you noted, we have taken
Jackie Trumpleton into custody and she has requested an
attorney. The FBI, my officers, PG County, Alexandria,
and DC, are still conducting interviews with the five men
held hostage."

"Why do you think Ms. Trumpleton asked for an
attorney so quickly?" the reporter asked.

"It's her right to do so and I will neither speculate nor
comment on that," the chief said.

"What charges will be filed against her?"

"Until we talk to all the hostages and ensure that a
crime was committed, it's difficult to provide answers
right now. We're looking at a multitude of charges and
until we are finished with the crime scene and interview
process, we will not comment on that part of the investigation."

"What do you mean by ensuring a crime was committed? Are you saying the men were complicit in their
abductions?" she asked.

"Let me repeat, we will not comment until the investigation is completed," the chief said.

"Thank you Chief Johnston."

The reporter turned back toward the camera. "Well,
you heard it at the same time I did. According to Chief
Johnston, there is a possibility that the hostages may have
been involved in their own abduction. Information is

continuously rolling in and we'll keep you updated as we learn more."

She jerked her hand across her throat in a sharp, short motion for the cameraman to stop rolling the tape.

The cameraman shook his head. "You're going to get in trouble again with the editor," he said.

"What?" the reporter pretended she didn't know what he was talking about.

"You know what I'm getting at. The chief of police did *not* say that the men were somehow involved in their own abductions. You twisted his words."

She hunched her shoulders and said, "Well, that's what I heard."

* * *

The interviews with the men lasted a few hours before they were transferred to the Arlington PD for processing. The police station in Occoquan was too small to handle a case of this magnitude and since the majority of the missing men were residents of Arlington, the FBI deferred to Chief Johnston.

After the men were processed, they hung around to talk to one another. They exchanged cell phone numbers and agreed to meet in a week or two to share their experiences. Then they proceeded to leave the police station.

As they exited the station, the media pounced all over them. Reporters were rushing them, pushing mikes into their faces, and sputtering a multitude of questions, all at once.

Ben stepped forward.

"I'm Ben Wright. As you can see, we've been through a harrowing night and would appreciate some privacy and space at this time."

A question was hurled at him even as he was speaking.

"Don't you mean a harrowing month?" the reporter asked. The tone of the question insulted Ben.

He didn't acknowledge the reporter. "I can't speak for the other guys, but I'm willing to speak to any reporter after I've had time to assimilate what I've gone through, and not a minute before."

Ben turned his back and walked down the side steps.

"Which one of you is Joe Bradford?" a reporter asked.

"I am," Joe said, stepping forward.

"Did you know that both your wife and mistress were here earlier tonight?" Even though Joe heard the reporter say, "earlier," he still looked around and searched the crowd for either one of them. He was visibly shaken.

"Oh, they were arrested and carted off," the reporter said. "It was a bloody mess though. Tore at each other like mountain cats. Neither thought the other had a right to be here tonight. Do you have anything to say Mr. Bradford?" the reporter asked.

"No comment," Joe said, and walked away.

Ian started talking to the reporter to take the attention off of Joe. "I'm Ian Ferguson and until tonight, I thought I was alone. When I learned that my best friend, Brian Taylor, was also here, I was shocked."

The reporters kept bombarding the men with questions. "How were you treated? Is it true that this was a sex resort? Are you a victim or part of the sham? How were you abducted? Did you know or have a relationship with Jackie Trumpleton prior to being abducted?"

The men did not take any of the questions. They furnished individual spiels.

"I'm Ron Brown, and honestly, I can't think straight right now. I really don't know what to think. I didn't realize until tonight that I was party to five missing men."

Six men, he heard someone from the back of the crowd yell out.

Ron searched for the broadcaster and saw a hand raised.

"It was six men, Mr. Brown," he heard the words repeated.

Ron was speechless and before he could respond, another reporter sprung the details.

"A Clyde Hariston from Arlington was also abducted, then released, once the madam found out he was HIV positive."

A commotion ensued. The reporters turned their attention away from the missing men and pounced on this new piece of information they had not been privy to.

The reporters' extrication was agreeable to Brian because he had no intention of speaking to any reporters—not now, and maybe never.

* * *

Evelyn was standing outside of the station when Brian and Ian exited. Brian nudged Ian and looked toward Evelyn. He told Ian he would catch up with him later. Brian ignored Evelyn as he passed her on the stairs. Now that Ian was safe, he and Evelyn could return to their stoic positions of despising one another.

Ian looked at Evelyn. Any other time he would have been excited to see her standing there to greet him. Now, he loathed her. He had many days and nights during the last three weeks to mull over their toxic marriage and he had reached a decision, especially since the abduction turned out to be a blessing in disguise.

He had plenty of time on his hands to think about the ways some of his friends and coworkers mistreated their wives. They cheated on them, argued constantly about taking separate vacations, and some even provoked arguments on Friday nights as an excuse to stay away from home all weekend. He, on the other hand, treated his wife and women the way his mother taught him to, with respect.

Ian had loved his wife unconditionally—that emotion had deteriorated with no chance of reconciliation. He would never again allow any woman to regard him as a weakling, or mistreat him and take advantage of his kindness.

He descended the steps and faced her.

She was happy to see him and looked apologetic.

"Ian, I've missed you and I'm so sorry," she said. "Can you ever forgive me?" and held out her arms.

Prior to being kidnapped, Ian would have run into her open arms and accepted her apology.

"Hi Evelyn," he said. "I'd prefer to discuss this later at home." He walked passed her toward the car and sat in the passenger seat.

She shouldn't have been caught unaware by his reaction, but she was. She walked to the driver side, plunked down in the seat, and drove home.

The silence was excruciating.

When they arrived home, he went out to the patio and turned on the gas grill. "Do we have any steaks?"

"Yes. I'm not hungry." She was miffed. She couldn't believe that he didn't also offer an apology for his dreadful behavior on that awful night.

He went into the house, grabbed one steak, seasoned it, returned, and threw it on the grill without so much as a glance toward Evelyn.

She waited until he flipped the steak. "Are we going to talk about what happened?"

He didn't know whether she was referring to their calamitous blowup or the kidnapping, nor did he care.

"No," he said.

That was a strange response, she thought. "What do you mean by no, Ian?" she asked.

He hadn't realized until that moment how much he despised her. He couldn't breathe. He had to escape. He watched the one T-bone steak sizzle on the oversized grill until it was charcoal black. It was synonymous with his life—alone and dark in a big ass condo.

"Evelyn, I want a divorce," he said indifferently and walked out of the room, out of her life, without uttering another word.

* * *

No one had been at the police station to meet Joe, Ron, or Ben, so they left together and went to a nearby bar. Once they retrieved their drinks and gulped it down right at the bar, everyone had gotten a double shot of something—gin straight up for Joe, whiskey on the rocks for Ron, and tequila with a slice of lime for Ben—they ordered another round and told the barmaid they would run a tab.

"This round is on the house," the bartender said, recognizing them from the breaking news alert.

They spotted an empty lounge area and took refuge where they could kick back and be themselves.

Joe spoke first, not about the catfight between his wife and mistress, but about the last three weeks. "Man, I don't know about you but I still cannot believe what happened to me. I'm a married man with a mistress, as you heard, and this is my third marriage. I've never had as much sex, as much variety, as much fun that I've had since being abducted. It's unreal. If this had not happened to me personally, I wouldn't believe it."

"I'm with you man," Ron said. "This was unbelievably awesome. I learned a thing or two about myself. Those romps in the hay made me realize all I wanted to do was reciprocate. I wanted to take Bernadette to heights she had never been and let her experience the limits of her pleasure too. I've never experienced that before. As long as I got a nut, that's all I cared about. If the woman got her rocks off, that was great. If she didn't, 'oh well.' I would just have to do better the next time. But here, it was different. I made sure she had as many orgasms as she could tolerate and I didn't care if I had to hump all night in order to make it happen."

"Man, I'm still reeling. It's surreal," Joe said. "Did the cops or FBI ask you about testifying against Jackie or any of the other women?"

"Yeah, they tried pressuring me into signing some statement," Ron said. "I told them I wanted an attorney before discussing or signing anything. That riled them up; tried to accuse me of being in on it."

Joe signaled the waitress for another round of drinks, then said, "Get an attorney. They had the insolence to tell me and my attorney that if I didn't give a statement against Jackie that they would charge the five of us with impeding an investigation. When that tactic didn't produce the results they were expecting, they told me that they would charge us with accessory after the fact and go after us for reimbursement of all the monies that were spent on the search and rescue operation. Man, we're the victims here, *the missing five*, and they're haranguing us. It's not our responsibility to make their case for them. If they have evidence against Jackie like they swear they do, I say leave us alone and go press charges then."

Joe and Ron high-fived each other.

The waitress returned with their shots and asked if she should start a tab. "We already started one," Joe said.

"They finally got the picture that I wasn't going to say a word without an attorney present, even with their good cop, bad cop ploy," Ron said.

"She would be the last person I'd turn in to the cops," Joe said. "I'm sorry about their search and rescue, but they did the job our taxpayer dollars pay them to do, which I make a contribution. Personally, I don't care that she abducted me against my will. She didn't abuse me, she didn't terrorize me, and look here," he thumped his chest, "she didn't kill me. I'd gladly allow her to do it again. Really, I want more of her."

Ben wasn't participating in their discussion and the guys noticed. He was sitting slouched in the chair, legs crossed at the feet, and turning his drink in his hand.

"Are you okay?" Joe asked. "You haven't said much of anything since we sat down."

Ben uncrossed his legs and sat up straight. "I don't know guys. It's obvious nothing like this has happened to any of us before but suppose this had been the other way around—one of us had abducted, held hostage, and raped five women."

"Rape!" Joe said. "Is that the way you picture it?"

"Let him talk," Ron said.

Ben spoke. "I met a stranger at a play. She tricked me into coming to her residence. She informed me that I did not have a choice to leave. And, her girlfriend seduced me into having sexual relations with her repeatedly without my permission over the last two weeks. Yes, that's exactly how I see it," Ben said.

"And you didn't enjoy it," Joe said.

"Be truthful," Ron said.

"Well...yes, I did, but that's not the point."

"So, you're righteous and want to correct a wrong, is that it?" Joe asked. "And, what is the point?"

"I'm saying what Jackie did was illegal and she should be held accountable for her actions," Ben said.

Joe understood Jackie broke some laws but would not commiserate with Ben on this. "Well man, only you can make the decision regarding what you will do. But I won't stand with you. No way!"

"The paramedics said they found some type of drug that she sprayed on us," Ben said.

"Yeah, apparently Jackie used something called Scopolamine—this reminded Joe how he got the canister from her and then gave it back—which rendered us incapable of exercising freewill. This is how she got us under her control and into her home," Joe said. *Dear God, I want more of her.*

"Well, that Scopo-shit, whatever it's called, could have killed us!" Ben said.

"But it didn't," Joe said, "and we all checked out okay."

"Well, I won't make any hasty decision today about my subsequent steps. I have a lot to think about," Ben said.

"Do you feel the same way, Ron?" Joe asked.

"Hell no!"

Joe put it straight to him. "Ben, while you're making that decision, I want you to think about something. You're about the same age as Ron and me, mid-forties to late fifties, right?"

He didn't wait for an answer. "This is a once in a lifetime experience. This is the stuff men our age dream of. Hell, this is the stuff any man dream of happening to him. And, it happened to us, man, to us!" he poked his chest. "Did you enjoy it, Ben? Did you have the best three weeks of your life?"

"Ditto that," Ron said.

Ben looked down into his drink, stirred it with a finger, and took a swig. He thought about what Joe said. "Yeah, I'll think about that. Yes, I'll give that some serious consideration," Ben said. "I need to get home. I am mentally exhausted."

Ron said, "Well, I'm sexually exhausted, believe it or not."

"Oh, I believe it," Ben said.

They traded numbers, knocked fists, and agreed to touch base in a week or so.

Joe and Ron stayed behind and got comfortable. They stretched out and relaxed in the worn-out, somewhat cushiony chairs. Neither said anything for a long time.

Then Ron broke the silence. "Joe, I bet some of those cops were just upset that they weren't one of us," he said, setting his drink down so hard it splashed. *Oops, no more liquor for me*, he thought.

"Man, I'm going to let you in on a secret. I think I'm in love with Jackie," Joe said. "All my life I've been a womanizer, a cheater, ever since my first sexual encounter as a teenager. I've never been monogamous. I've always believed being anti-monogamous was in my genes. Now, I know that's not true and I appreciate why. I just had never found one woman who could fulfill all my needs. Ron, she fulfilled every single one of my needs—intellectually, physically, and sexually. I could not have created this woman if I had the tools."

They left the bar hours later when the bartender told them he had to close down.

Joe neither called nor went to either Dolores or his mistress, that's if they had been released from jail. He didn't know and he didn't care.

Ron didn't have a home to go to.

So they went to the Embassy Suite and checked into separate rooms.

* * *

Brian called Ian on his cell and they met at Hooters.

"Man, I want to apologize for all the times I ragged on you about Evelyn," Brian said. "I let you down. I should have been there for you."

"I'm okay Brian, seriously man," Ian said. "Being kidnapped probably saved my life. My wife was slowly killing me. It took something this drastic to happen for me to realize what you've always known about her. Evelyn *is* a cold-hearted bitch. She never loved me. She belittled me every chance she got. I can't believe how long I stayed in this marriage. Then something like this happens and I meet Laura who knows how to treat a man. Brian, from the moment I met her, I wanted to give all the love I had stored up for Evelyn to Laura."

"I understand, man," Brian said. "You know I'm a whore at heart but I finally found a woman that was more than I could handle. Can you believe it?"

Ian shook his head. "No, I can't."

"Honestly, I didn't realize there were women out there who enjoyed sex just as much as men did, and with no game plan. Nadine wore me out and taught me things about women that I've never read in any book. And the lingerie! Each and every time she entered my room, she looked sexy and treated me like I was a king, you know, the way I was meant to be treated."

They exhaled a long laugh. They missed each other and it was good hanging out again.

"I tell you man," Ian said, "if I ever get a chance to thank Jackie Trumpleton, I'll do so from the depths of my soul. I will, no kidding. She gave me my life back, bro. And the district attorney actually thinks I would testify against her or anyone else. Yeah right, keep dreaming mister D.A."

"I know," Brian said. "They kept badgering me about testifying against Jackie. I acted as if I didn't know what they were talking about." Brian started thinking about his immediate future. "I don't know where I go from here. I don't want to be married anymore either. I can't believe I married my ex's best girlfriend. You know, Ian, it was raunchy how I treated Trish. She didn't deserve that."

"No she didn't, but it's water under the bridge now," Ian said.

"You think?"

"Brian, you don't have a shot in hell with your ex. Just leave her alone. You know she's better off without you. You'll only throw her out with the garbage again."

"Wow man! Are you trying to get back at me for calling you pussy-whipped?"

"A little, but you know I'm right," Ian said.

"Yeah, yeah. What are we going to do now that we're single again?" Brian asked.

"Well, we roomed together in college. Let's do it again until we can make heads or tails of our lives."

"That's a deal," Brian said.

"And for at least a few days, we should probably check into a hotel until this craziness blows over," Ian said.

CHAPTER 38

DISTRICT ATTORNEY'S OFFICE

District Attorney Eric Calhoun and the Arlington Chief of Police were deep in a heated debate, while Lieutenant Neathers looked on.

"You have nothing," DA Calhoun said to Chief Johnston. "We cannot charge Jackie Trumpleton with one thing: not kidnapping, not transporting victims across state lines, not running a bordello, not the use of illegal narcotics, not sexual battery, not stalking. There is nothing here."

"Why?" Johnston asked. This didn't add up. He had a difficult time believing they could not charge her with a single crime.

"First, not one of those men will press charges. Second, we have no proof of a crime being committed. As far as we know—what the evidence shows—five men walked away from their lives of their own free will to explore their sexual fantasies. Third, without their testimonies, there is no proof that anybody was transported across state lines. Fourth, not a single one of her girl-friends will come forward and testify against her. And five, Ms. Trumpleton did not charge any of the men for sexual services so we cannot charge her for running a brothel. Look," the DA said, "my office is as sick about this as your department. But, we cannot prosecute a case if we don't have witnesses who will testify."

The chief was upset and in denial. After all the detective work and man hours that his department—along with Alexandria, PG County, DC, and the FBI—put into this case, it would all be for naught. "But her brother alerted us that she was the abductor. If it had not been for him, we would be in the blind. We would still be running around with our heads stuck in our asses. Mr. Trumpleton told us his sister had been planning this for years. He will testify against her. He gave us the journal to prove it."

"He gave you a *copy* of an *alleged* journal," the DA corrected him. "Where is the original? What is Mr. Trumpleton's motivation? That is what concerns me."

He looked at Lieutenant Neathers point blank, man-to-man. "And, what did you all do when Clyde Hariston first notified you about being abducted. Remember him? You all were condescending toward both him and his wife. You cackled about them like hyenas. The only thing you guys were concerned about was how one woman could immobilize grown men. Do you recall that?"

"Yes I do," Neathers said. He felt chastised.

"We have her brother's written statement? Can't you use that?" The chief had an axe to grind. He wanted Ms. Trumpleton charged, at a minimum, with serial kidnapping.

"Maurice," the DA said, calling the chief by his first name because he empathized with him. "Her brother was suspicious based on copies he made of what can best be described as a teenager's diary. This was after she graduated high school and moved here. She had to be, what, eighteen at most. A first year defense attorney will look at how long ago it was written and tear Mr. Trumpleton a new asshole. His testimony would be useless! I can already hear the questions. Was it a novel she was writing? Do you and your sister get along? Why didn't you bring this to the FBI's attention before now if you were concerned she was doing something illegal? There are a million and one questions that the defense can ask that could put Mr. Trumpleton in a strait jacket."

Neathers took over the conversation because the chief was seething. "Well, what about the other brothers?" he asked. "She has two more."

"What about them?" the DA asked.

"Do you think they'd make good witnesses?"

The DA looked at Neathers as if he had just landed in a spaceship. "Where have you been, lieutenant, under a rock? Have you been listening to the news? Both of the brothers came forward and said they thought their younger brother was doing drugs, and that he fabricated the entire story. They swear he's angry at their baby sister for abandoning the family and not telling anybody about that mansion she bought over there in Occoquan."

Neathers felt like he had been hit with a ton of bricks. This was news to him.

Chief Johnston wouldn't let it go and did not address the DA by his first name. "Can we press charges against any of the men then? We have expended hundreds of man hours on this case, which is going to cost our citizens tens of thousands of dollars. Is there a way we can require them to make restitution?" Johnston asked.

The DA stifled a snort. "We threatened Joe Bradford with reimbursing PG County for knowingly participating in a crime and his attorney informed us in no uncertain terms that if we tried that ploy, that all the men would claim Stockholm syndrome."

"You've got to be kidding," Neathers said. He was now as indignant as the chief.

"We won't find a jury that will convict five hostages who display empathy toward their captor," the DA said.

"What is the FBI's position?" Johnston asked.

"SSA Madison informed us that their Hostage Barricade Database System shows that twenty-five percent of hostages show evidence of Stockholm."

"So we got nothing, squat, not a damn thing we can charge Ms. Trumpleton with. Unbelievable." Neathers slammed his fist down on the desk.

"That is what I have been trying to get through to you since you walked in here. Get me something to corroborate Mr. Trumpleton's allegations. This office needs witnesses! Try putting pressure on her girlfriends. See if you can get a statement from the men without their attorneys in tow, and you didn't hear that from me. If you want me to prosecute this case, give me ammunition to win."

CHAPTER 39

An Unexpected Visitor

"Ms. Trumpleton, you have a visitor," the guard said. The steel door was unlocked. "Please follow me."

She thought she was being led to a room of booths where phones would be affixed on each side of clear, heavy duty, probably bulletproof partitions. Instead, she was led into a room with a table and four metal chairs. She assumed it was Juan come to apologize. When she was told that her brother, Juan, had turned her in, she broke down and cried like a baby, something she rarely did. That had been only the second time she shed a tear since leaving East New Orleans. Juan was the only one of the whole Trumpleton clan she trusted and he was the only one who had betrayed her. He had broken her heart.

The man on the other side of the door, seated at the table, was not Juan. She saw the man who had left her stranded, without so much as a goodbye, in a hotel room a couple of months ago. It never occurred to her that she would ever see him again—not in person anyway.

He stood and extended his hand.

She shook it and a lopsided smile appeared.

He nodded for her to sit and he sat opposite her.

A million snapshots flew through her mind as she was being led to this room, but not the words she heard him express.

"Thank you," he said.

* * *

Alec Strauss was a man that couldn't be manipulated by the allure or promise of sex. He had been taught at an early age by the community of men who raised him that if you think with your head and not your dick, you'd be forever a happy man. "Women hold you hostage with their pussy," he was told. His father also repeated this declaration many times over the years. Since his father was a man of integrity, and one he revered and trusted implicitly, his father's words were akin to God.

His four uncles would snicker though when his father made these admonitions. They knew what went on behind the closed doors of Alec's parents. They'd enlighten Alec, although he hadn't inquired, "don't believe everything your old man tells you."

That's okay, he thought. He'd take his father's words to his grave. His father had to be right. Look at all the powerful men who lost everything because of a piece of ass: Dominque Strauss-Kahn, former leader of the International Monetary Fund; Elliot Spitzer, former Governor of New York; and John Edwards, candidate for President of the United States. King Edward VIII even abdicated the British throne for sex. *Well, history says it was for love but I don't believe it.*

Alec had been playing a game of eight-ball with coworkers, and winning too, when the stunning black woman whom he now knows as Jackie Trumpleton stood on the sidelines watching him play. He was prepared to pocket the eight ball, but upon seeing her, stood up straight, and deliberately walked around the table to chalk his cue stick that was not needed, then returned to make the shot. He wanted to get a close-up look of her. When the ball was pocketed, he looked up to see her reaction. She had turned and walked away.

He was beguiled because this was the opposite effect he had on women. The guys wanted to play another round but he declined. He needed to locate that woman and was hoping she hadn't left the pool hall. He walked through the hall to the front entrance and she was nowhere in sight. He ran out to the parking lot and saw no movement whatsoever. He walked back into the pool hall and went over to the bar and ordered a draft light beer. This was not his usual drink, but since he had to work the following day, he decided to take it easy.

He asked the bartender about an attractive black woman who had been there earlier. "She's about five feet, dark complexion like a semisweet Hersey bar, one twenty, shapely, with very short, curly hair."

The bartender whistled. "Wow, Alec, you noticed all that! Well, I saw quite a few gorgeous women tonight, black and white."

The bartender was no help at all.

All the way home, he beat himself up mentally. That's what he got for trying to play it cool. His father had also told him all women weren't alike—most were easy and few were not. She had fit in the latter category.

* * *

Jackie had not left the pool hall. She suspected he was full of himself and this was a test. She had gone out to the parking lot and stood at the side of the building. When she saw him run out and look up and down the street, she knew he was just like all the rest. *Black or white, men are all alike. I wish just one time it was not so darn easy.*

When he went back inside, she went to her car and drove home. She decided she would return another night. She had spoken to the bartender earlier inquiring about the good-looking white man in the back playing pool and found out he was no Minnesota Fats but he was better than good and he enjoyed the game.

There was no rush, she decided. She'd get him on her return. She would bet money on it.

Two weeks later she returned to an empty pool hall. He wasn't there so she played one game with another guy who was playing by himself. It was a slow night.

She returned the next night, and still he wasn't there. Since the hall was packed, she decided to play. This night, however, a few of the guys had quite a bit to drink and were placing wagers on the games. The bet was thirty dollars. Since she considered it a meager bet, she decided to gamble. She wasn't a sharpshooter—no Kelly Fisher from Great Britain—but she could definitely hold her own, for a non-pro woman anyway. Placing her bet got the men who were standing around riled up; they sounded like a pack of wolves howling at the moon. She looked around the room and noticed that she was the only woman present, which was disconcerting. Her internal radar sent out alarms. She instantly recalled that movie, *The Accused,* where Jodie Foster played a woman being raped by several men in a pool hall, and decided not to play after all. She said, "sorry guys, I changed my mind, but keep the bet," and proceeded to exit the room when she heard him.

"Scared," he said.

She knew it was him and she thought he was referring to her being around all those rowdy men. Without turning around, she said, "yes."

And he thought her answer was in reference to losing the game.

"Can we go somewhere not quite so bustling?" he asked.

"Absolutely," she said. "We can sit at the bar."

He groaned.

"Well, it *is* less commotion," she said.

The bartender quipped. "So, I see you two found each other."

They both gave him a knowing nod.

He waited until they were seated and had ordered drinks. "I'm Alec Strauss, Assistant DA. Why did you run out the other night?"

"Nice to meet you, Alec. I am Jackie. What are you talking about?" She ignored that he espoused his title.

"I don't play head games." He ignored that she didn't offer anything about herself, not even her last name. She was different. "Are you any good?"

"Depends." she said. She had a smirk on her face. She didn't really care what he was thinking—whether she played head games or was good at shooting pool.

"On what?"

"You asked if I am any good. Am I any good at what?"

Okay, so she wants to play head games. "Shooting pool."

"Hmm." She didn't react, just smiled.

"So, is that what brought you in tonight," he said.

"Actually, I came in looking for you."

He was caught off guard by her sincere, unencumbered response.

"Really!" he said.

"Really. I knew you were showing off the other night. You were so cocky."

"Are you always this brutally honest and straightforward with men you just meet?"

"How else should I be?"

"Well, you've got a point there. I'm still gobsmacked."

"Okay, Susan Boyle, why are you speechless?"

It was obvious he wasn't going to pull anything over on her. He wanted her to ask him the definition of the word. "Women I meet are ...," he searched for the right word, "acquiescent."

"Are you sure about your word choice," she said, a glint was in her eyes.

"Yes." He was amused.

"Then, you must be meeting some really young girls," she said, with an emphasis on girls, "because *women* in my age group are straightforward with everyone they meet."

He thought about her answer. She was right-on. He was forty-seven and always gravitated toward neophytes, women young enough to be his daughters. He considered for a few seconds why that was the case because this woman before him was built like a brick house, impeccably dressed, and articulate, with piercing brown eyes that bored through him. She was the exception. She had to be at least ..., he was pondering this.

"I am fifty," Jackie lied, as if reading his mind.

"No way!" he said. "I don't believe you." He looked her up and down. He was about to ask to see her driver's license for proof when she leaned into him.

"Your place or mine?" she said.

Once she had them ensnarled, the rest involved reeling them in.

* * *

His father's voice was booming in his ears.

Jackie was in the bathroom, she wanted to freshen up, and he ordered room service—club sandwiches, their cheapest bottle of wine, and a dozen strawberries. They didn't go to either his or her place. He didn't know anything about this woman, so he suggested the Marriott, which was only a few miles away from the pool hall.

He undressed and put his iPhone in the dock station on the bedside table. He pulled up the Pandora App and chose a jazz station. He couldn't believe his good luck. This attractive black woman had been looking for him and she was fifty years old. Who would believe it? *If that's the way older women are looking these days, I have to reconsider my weakness for younger women.*

He heard the shower going and decided to join her. Huey, his egotistical man part, was standing at full attention and raring to get started. But, he kept hearing his father's voice, his uncles' voices, and all the men in that community voices. He didn't have a handle on what was happening. The warning wouldn't subside. This had never happened before. He sat on the bed trying to figure it out. *I'm in control of this situation. She's not. I am!*

He felt foolish. He could get a woman out of her clothes and into the sack in ten minutes flat without a second thought. No amount of pussy in the world could trap him. Yet, this time felt different; he felt it was some kind of trap—not a booty trap, but a mental trap. He actually wanted to get to know this woman. Maybe even have a relationship. He didn't want this to be a one night stand like all the others.

He got dressed, put on his slacks, but couldn't zip his fly. Huey was mad at this turn of events and wouldn't cooperate. Alec threatened him with ice from the champagne bucket.

When Jackie came out of the bathroom fully clothed to announce her change of mind—that she didn't want to go through with this—Alec was gone. She looked around the room and saw a note in the middle of the bed. *Jackie, please accept my sincerest apology. I had to leave. Duty calls. Alec.*

She was pleasantly relieved. They had both come to the same conclusion but for different reasons. Hers was more of a reincarnation. She couldn't quiet the screams of the drag queens. "He's a cop, honey. Run!"

For Pete's sake, not only is he white but he's also the assistant district attorney! she reminded herself.

* * *

Jackie stared at Alec with apprehension.

"I want to thank you," he said again.

"For what? I do not play head games."

I like her. "For not making me a victim."

She didn't know what to say, so she said nothing; but her uncomprehending eyes stayed locked with his.

"You could have easily suckered me in," he said.

"Are you recording this, Alec?" She looked around the small room for a hidden camera. The dots weren't connecting.

"What? No, I'm not."

"Then, why are you here?"

"I was enthralled by you."

She leaned across the table and spoke in an octave above a whisper. "Oh, is that why you ran away and left me stranded, butt-naked, alone in a hotel room." She chuckled.

They both knew that was a tall tale.

"You're a good liar, Jackie, but I know you never removed one stitch of your clothes. The shower was running but you were figuring a way out of that room. If there had been a window, you would have climbed through it. Now tell me I'm wrong."

She kept a straight face. "What is going on Alec? Why are you here?"

He became serious. "The police have nothing to charge you on. The DA, my boss, is not prosecuting you because the missing men are not testifying and your friends refuse to talk. You are free to go."

She assessed what he had said. "What is going on Alec? Why are you here?" she repeated.

"When the noise dies down, in about a year I suppose, I would like to take you to dinner and maybe shoot a game of pool. I have to know how good you really are. Are you game, Jackie?"

She understood the subtle inquiry. She stood up, turned, and walked toward the door; her hand was on the doorknob. She didn't turn around. "Oh, I am damn good, Alec. And I am game. But are you?"

His father's screams were so loud, he was afraid she could hear them too.

She turned to face him.

"Until we meet again. Good bye, Alec," she said.

CHAPTER 40

THE END

The District Attorney, Eric Calhoun, could not prosecute Jacqueline Ophelia Antoinette Trumpleton.

Not one of *the missing five* would press charges against her. Not one of her associates would provide any information whatsoever. Everybody, without reservation or a second thought, remained silent, which was in line with the girls' Omertà. Therefore, there was nothing that could be used against them in a court of law.

EPILOGUE

Jackie Trumpleton always had a mind of her own, ever since she could remember, probably since she started talking. She was never the "follow the leader" type. She *was* the leader.

She believed in her dream and believed it was meant to be acted on and carried out. Consequences was a flickering omen, more or less, nonexistent.

Jackie dared to be different. She was a maverick. Bernadette understood her better than anyone else and her analysis of Jackie was right on target. "If an idea materialized, her plan was realized." And a decision to go forward didn't take years, months, days, or even hours to decide that she *was* going to do it, the decision was instantaneous. Jackie's single-minded focus, her purpose, was to make her dream a reality. When it finally came to fruition, and she could share it with her four long-time associates, she was exuberant and content.

To control men, and as an added bonus be completely sexually satisfied and satiated, was a powerful aphrodisiac.

Jackie had no fear or foreboding, only exhilaration for the freedom she experienced when she did things her way.

"Free at last. I am free at last," she whispered, and popped the cork off a chilled bottle of G.H. Mumm, and this time she drank the bubbly from a flute.

Acknowledgments

I never believed in "trying" to do anything. Whatever I set out to do I found I had already accomplished.

~ Johann Wolfgang von Goethe

Over the years, many people have entered and exited my life. But those who remain a constant through good times and bad, thick and thin, bring great joy, stability, intellect, humor, growth, and fortitude to what could have been an otherwise static existence.

They are the special ones who fulfill my life with unequivocal peace and happiness. I give thanks everyday for my family and friends who have always believed in me, have unquestionable conviction in my abilities, and assert that if anyone could or would make the leap of faith and do it, it would be me.

Immeasurable thanks to Debra Wilson and Denise Wilson, who have undying faith in me. They are my Rock of Gibraltar.

Enormous thanks to my long-time confidants, James Pegram and Miriam Rudder, who also keep me grounded. They committed unselfishly their time and advice to provide honest feedback and critique on my debut novel, *The Missing Five.*

Special thanks to family and friends, Diane Wilson, Blanchie Kelley, and Lisa Chick, who believe in me without reservation, and know if I say I'm going to do something, it's a done deal.

And last, but certainly not least, thanks to Burnetta Ballinger, who is my forever personal cheerleader. I can already hear her exclaiming excitedly to anyone in hearing range, "this is *my* sister's book!"

Please turn the page for a special preview of

Gwen Pegram's

New Novel

Dubbed The Masked Kidnapper

To be published in paperback

October 2014

CHAPTER 1

DUBBED THE MASKED KIDNAPPER

Jackie Trumpleton had slept eighteen hours straight when she was snatched out of a restless sleep. She didn't know if it was the thud of the newspaper hitting the damaged double doors caused by the SWAT team or the yelling of the neighborhood newspaper boy's scandalous broadcast. "Extra, extra, read all about it. There's a masked serial kidnapper living amongst us." The words tore through her ears. Even though she knew the bicyclist was farther down the street, she still heard him pedaling through the early morning darkness and pitching papers at her neighbors' doors. Jackie turned and pulled the covers over her head.

Swallowed in the comfort of Aunt Bessie's bequeathed quilt, Jackie couldn't, for the life of her, grasp the purpose of Alec Strauss, the Assistant District Attorney's unexpected visit. There was no reason for him to come to the jail to tell her in person that she would not be prosecuted. Deputy Campbell could have relayed the message. The ADA's actions didn't comport. Jackie would have to keep an eye on him. Shooting a game of pool may be the best bet after all.

Jackie didn't retrieve the newspaper from the front porch, which required opening her damaged doors. Doing so would have allowed the nosy neighbors to witness her debacle. Thank God she had just moved to the neighborhood and her neighbors knew nothing about her. She trudged downstairs, made herself a large Americano, and turned on her laptop. She typed WashingtonPost.com and right there on the screen for the world to see was her full name emblazoned across the top. JACQUELINE OPHELIA ANTOINETTE TRUMPLETON DUBBED THE MASKED KID-NAPPER! She forced herself to read the article.

Police Chief Maurice Johnston of the Arlington PD spearheaded the search and rescue of five middle-age African-American men who vanished throughout the Washington, DC, metro area. Just after midnight, the police and FBI closed off the quaint Town of Occoquan, 25 miles south of DC, and staked out the newly renovated assistant living building turned into a residential property owned by real estate broker Jackie Trumpleton of JOAT Realty. Only the media and residents were allowed to enter the town.

Over the span of a month, DC was in a panic. There was not a single clue to the men's whereabouts or the reason for their disappearance. We now know the names of the abducted victims: Ian Ferguson and Brian Taylor of Arlington, Virginia; Ron Brown of Alexandria, Virginia; Joe Bradford of Bowie in

Prince George's County, Maryland; and Ben Wright of Washington, DC. They had disappeared without a trace. Although there were similarities, there was no evidence to call the disappearances a serial kidnapping. Local police departments joined forces with the FBI's Behavioral Analysis Unit (the BAU) in order to combine resources. Once the FBI set up its contact control center, they got a clue via its anonymous tip line, which came from the kidnapper's brother, Juan Trumpleton, who resides in New Orleans and where the call originated.

NBCNews4 Reporter Linda Stephenson spoke to Chief Johnston who called the residence the Occoquan Whore House of Erotica. "I have never seen such debauchery in our county or our state," he said. "I hate to sound sexist but kidnapping an unknown male purely for sex is unheard of."

Jackie groaned out loud. She searched other online newspapers and found two more with similar degrading headings. "A Masked Female Serial Kidnapper Resides in the Nation's Capital Backyard," noted *The Huffington Post* and "Five African-American Men Held as Sex Slaves at the Hands of Jackie Trumpleton," stated *The NYTimes.*

Jackie did not read the comments. She glanced at them though and the number of comments kept ticking upward. She imagined they would be atrocious.

She was correct.